LIV HAD BEEN DREAMING AGAIN

In the dream the bride sat in her snug house deep in the woods, fearfully watching out the window at the encroaching night.

Her hands twitched as the moon rose, and she gripped the armrests of her chair desperately, before reaching down and yanking off her boots with a sob of defeat. Immediately the delicate youthful skin of those shaking anxious hands changed, growing a thick fur pelt. The bride's jaw cracked audibly, shifting outward, her teeth sharpening. As the full moon lit up the small room, she fell out of the chair onto the floor and all fours, her body morphing into that of an animal . . . a wolf.

They hadn't eaten the bride.

They had made her one of them.

A werewolf.

from **"The Howling"**

BOOK YOUR PLACE ON OUR WEBSITE AND MAKE THE READING CONNECTION!

We've created a customized website just for our very special readers, where you can get the inside scoop on everything that's going on with Zebra, Pinnacle and Kensington books.

When you come online, you'll have the exciting opportunity to:

- View covers of upcoming books
- Read sample chapters
- Learn about our future publishing schedule (listed by publication month *and author*)
- Find out when your favorite authors will be visiting a city near you
- Search for and order backlist books from our online catalog
- Check out author bios and background information
- Send e-mail to your favorite authors
- Meet the Kensington staff online
- Join us in weekly chats with authors, readers and other guests
- Get writing guidelines
- AND MUCH MORE!

**Visit our website at
http://www.kensingtonbooks.com**

THE BEAST WITHIN

ERIN MCCARTHY
BIANCA D'ARC
JENNIFER LYON

BRAVA

KENSINGTON PUBLISHING CORP.

http://www.kensingtonbooks.com

BRAVA BOOKS are published by

Kensington Publishing Corp.
119 West 40th Street
New York, NY 10018

All Kensington titles, imprints and distributed lines are available at special quantity discounts for bulk purchases for sales promotion, premiums, fund-raising, educational or institutional use.

Special book excerpts or customized printings can also be created to fit specific needs. For details, write or phone the office of the Kensington Special Sales Manager: Attn. Special Sales Department. Kensington Publishing Corp., 119 West 40th Street, New York, NY 10018. Phone: 1-800-221-2647.

Brava and the B logo Reg. U.S. Pat. & TM Off.

ISBN-13: 978-0-7582-4736-0
ISBN-10: 0-7582-4736-2

First Brava Books Trade Paperback Printing: September 2010
First Brava Books Mass-Market Paperback Printing: September 2011

10 9 8 7 6 5 4 3 2 1

Printed in the United States of America

CONTENTS

The Howling

ERIN McCARTHY

CHAPTER ONE

The first howl off in the distance barely registered to the bride, since she was so filled with joy and flushed anticipation as the sleigh sailed forth over the light dusting of snow.

The second mournful cry was closer, causing a small pause in the laughter of the six people crammed in together among the furs and robes.

The third voice, a response to the first two, was more feral than sorrowful, more aggressive than beautiful, and the bride reached for the arm of her new husband as the horses threw back their heads nervously and pranced, disrupting the sleigh's rhythm.

Uneasiness crept over the party as the driver whipped the horses, and the sleigh leapt forward, the crisp wind tossing the ribbons in the bride's hair and sending an unpleasant shiver through her. The groom squeezed her hand in reassurance, but the group had quieted as the sound reached all of their ears, the unmistakable bounding footsteps of the wolves falling into line behind them in pursuit.

Her fingers dug into the lace of her wedding dress beneath the fur laid so tenderly across her lap by the groom, as the faces in front of her reflected unease, fear. They all knew how fierce the wolves were, they all knew the stories of those who traveled these woods and disappeared, their sleighs overturned, bodies mutilated beyond recognition. She pressed her eyes closed and swallowed hard, trying to gauge how far the pack was from them.

Close. So close that she could hear the snarls and snaps of at least three wolves, maybe more, and she opened her eyes again in panic, head whirling around.

She wished she hadn't.

Under the harvest moon, the same lustrous white orb she had just been dancing beneath an hour earlier, giddy with love and happiness and the well-wishes of all those around her, she saw them.

Great beasts, wild wolves, snow flying behind them as their paws ate up the ground, narrowing the distance between them and the sleigh. They were enormous, snouts long, eyes pale and intelligent, teeth gleaming in the moonlight, fur thick and rich. There were six of them, the number of the devil, all running together as one, working in tandem to capture their prey.

Her groom let go of her hand and ducked down, then sprang back up. Startled, she watched him hurl the stones overboard from the bottom of the sleigh, stones that earlier had been heated and placed at their feet to warm them for the ride home. The first two thrown missed their mark, and a third barely clipped one wolf on the shoulder. The animal growled and snapped angrily, his eyes locking onto the bride's as she gripped her lace dress tighter.

The wedding party was all yelling now, moving around, dumping the stones, the furs, unceremoniously ripping the one the bride was wrapped in off her shoulders and lap and tossing it over the side as they tried to lighten the load. The horses snorted, the driver cracked his whip and yelled for them to go faster, and the sleigh jostled unsteadily as they picked up speed.

And still the wolves came.

She couldn't look away, mesmerized by their terrifying beauty, by their rhythm and speed and determination. There were better creatures, meatier, to feast on than humans, yet for survival the wolves would take down what they could. And maybe, just maybe, they did it for the challenge, for the right to know they had bested another animal of intelligence. The pack was so close now that the angry snapping of their jaws was like gunfire in the quiet night, their fur so near she could stretch down and slide her fingers through its soft thickness.

When rough hands grabbed her shoulders and her legs, she didn't realize what was happening. She turned and saw a fist plow into her husband's face, saw him struggling, a body pinning him down, and then she knew.

There was barely time for a kick, a shove, a scream, before they had her petite body up and in the air, their panicked eyes looking not at her, but behind the sleigh.

And as the bride grabbed desperately onto their

fancy dress jackets, the moon casting a perfect shadow over the sleigh on her wedding night, they threw her to the wolves.

Liv Lugaru sat up in bed, sucking in on a silent scream as she tore herself out of the nightmare. As she clutched the thousand-thread-count sheet, her eyes raced around the dark room, reassuring her she was in her bedroom, not in the cold sleigh in the ominous forest.

Wiping the sweat off her upper lip, she swallowed hard and waited for her heart rate to slow down. That was the fourth time in as many nights she'd dreamt of wolves, a nocturnal theme that had first appeared six months ago very sporadically, and now seemed to have taken over her sleeping thoughts completely. The dancing glow from the doorway and the mumbled voices told her the TV was still on in the living room. She knew Scarborough would be up working, doing mysterious things on his computer that somehow turned his vast amounts of money into more money. He was a financial genius and, unlike her, he only needed four hours of sleep a night.

He appeared in the doorway, still wearing his blue shirt and black dress pants. "You okay?" he asked, his face in shadow. "I heard you call out again."

"Just a nightmare," she said, voice scratchy, lips dry. "Sorry to disturb you."

Moving forward, he brushed the damp hair off her forehead. "You've had a lot of bad dreams lately."

Fighting the urge to pull away from his touch, she shrugged. "I'm fine."

Grateful the room was dark, she stared at him, dredging up a reassuring smile. She owed so much to him, she didn't want him to know that the thought of marrying him was terrifying her.

"Are they about him?" he asked, his voice even, curious, but with an underlying edge to it.

Liv didn't pretend not to know who he was referring to. He meant Sebastian, his brother, her former lover. "No," she told him honestly. Nothing in her recurring nightmare reminded her of the man she'd loved so deeply, so wholly, the man who had refused to marry her, the man who had disappeared six months ago, leaving her destitute and heartbroken. "They're running dreams. You know, where you run and don't go anywhere."

A lie, but she didn't want to describe the wolves, the chase, the fear out loud to him, and she didn't want him to think she was hiding something about Sebastian. She didn't want to hurt Scarborough.

Plus the nightmares were so intense, raw, disturbing.

So real.

To describe them out loud would only remind her of their intensity.

"Do you want me to come to bed?" he asked, dropping a light kiss on the top of her forehead.

Shaking her head, she touched his chest briefly. "No, I'm fine. I know you have work to do." She gave a small smile. "Besides, you'll just wind up sitting here wide awake and I'll be out in five minutes."

"That's true. And then my tossing and turning

will wake you up." The corner of his mouth went up. "We're not exactly perfect bed partners, are we?"

She wasn't sure if he meant that to sound as loaded as it did, considering they'd yet to have sex. She just hadn't been able to let go, to relax, to feel passion again, and he had been very understanding of that.

It was wrong and she knew it, but she had agreed to marry him out of devastation and gratitude. He'd picked up the shattered pieces of her heart and life, offered her a real future, and she'd said yes.

Now she knew he fully expected they would finally have sex on their wedding night, that their marriage would be real.

And she did care about him. Loved him.

Just not quite in the way she was supposed to, and God help her, their wedding was only ten days away.

"We muddle through," she told him, hoping it would sound lighthearted, afraid it was their truth for the foreseeable future.

They were supposed to exchange vows in a week and a half and she was dreaming she was a bride who had literally been thrown to the wolves.

"Remember I'm leaving tomorrow for a business trip. Four days in New York."

"Oh, I forgot." But it was the best news she'd had in days. "Make sure you wake me up when you leave so I can say goodbye."

And maybe when he walked out the door she'd finally feel like she could breathe again.

CHAPTER TWO

"**D**o you believe in past lives?" Liv asked Mary Fran as she shoved lettuce around on her plate at lunch the next day. The cafeteria at the University of Wisconsin wasn't the reason for her lack of appetite. Nursing school and the food they served were both fine. It was everything else in her life that made her stomach churn.

"Excuse me?" Mary Fran raised an eyebrow, her glass of iced tea on pause halfway to her lips. "What is going on with you?"

Liv didn't know. That was the frightening problem. "It's just a question. I keep having these dreams . . . they're very realistic. The clothing everyone is wearing looks nineteenth century and they're not here in Madison. The setting seems . . . European to me for some reason." She shrugged. "I don't know, I just thought maybe there is such a thing as past lives."

Plunking her iced tea glass down, amber droplets splashing onto the pristine tablecloth,

Mary Fran eyed her. "Why are they different than any other dreams? What happens in them?"

"The woman falls off a sleigh and, well, gets eaten by wolves." Liv jabbed a cherry tomato and studied it. "It's her wedding night."

"Oh, my God."

When Liv glanced up at her best friend, she saw the concern she could already hear in her voice.

"Liv. You've got to call this wedding off."

She sat silent, unable to tell even her best friend that she wanted to do just that. But she couldn't. How could she? Scarborough had been there for her. Been there in that terrible dark hysterical time when she had learned that Sebastian had betrayed her, disappearing with the little money she had accumulated. Gone. All their nights together, all those words of love, nothing.

"I know you feel grateful to him, but you can't build a marriage on gratitude. He can't possibly want that. Won't want that if you're honest with him."

The little food she'd eaten burned in her stomach. "I care about him."

"And you're dreaming about being eaten by wolves on your wedding night. Look, if you can't call it off altogether, just postpone it. Indefinitely. Tell him you're not ready. Just go on dating or whatever and give yourself time to figure it out."

"Do you think he'll be okay with that?" Liv asked, grasping on to hope. That seemed possible. Workable. It would buy her a reprieve.

But not from sex.

She should want to have sex. It had been six months since she had, and her body should be eager, primed, on fire, yet she chilled out and dried up every time she contemplated it.

"I honestly don't know. Scarborough doesn't exactly seem like a patient kind of guy to me. He's . . . brisk." Mary Fran made a face, her hand checking the back of her gold hoop earring. "But it's worth a shot when the alternative is a marriage you don't want."

Liv wanted to protest, but she couldn't even dredge up a convincing enough voice, so she let her silence speak for her.

Then Mary Fran spoke the words she couldn't stand to hear. "Just because you don't have family doesn't mean you're alone. Remember that. You have friends who love you. You're not alone."

Yes, she was. She knew Mary Fran meant well, and she knew her friends cared about her. But it wasn't the same. Since that horrible night twenty years ago when her parents had been murdered, she was alone. Growing up, some of her teachers, one couple out of the many foster parents, and a few close friends had all cared about her, but she didn't have family. Someone who was biologically or legally tied to her.

"Orphan" was a word she'd hated growing up, and Sebastian and Scarborough understood that, owning the lonely label themselves.

"Are you sleeping with him yet? How is that going?"

Looking uneasily around the crowded room, Liv pulled her dove-gray crew sweater closer around her. "No, we haven't."

"Why does he even *want* to marry you?"

The words were like a slap. "Probably guilt because his brother not only wouldn't commit to me, he stole what little money I had and left without a word. I mean, why else would anyone marry me? I don't bring a lot to the table, dead broke and emotionally stunted. It's pity, that's why he proposed. Hello." Saying it out loud was like taking a bullet, even as she hid behind sarcasm, but it was the truth. It wasn't like Scarborough was marrying her for true love either.

God, what a mess.

Mary Fran's voice softened. "That's not what I meant. Of course you bring a lot to the table. You're generous and smart and compassionate, and you're beautiful. Any man would be lucky to have you. But with everything that's happened, I don't understand the push for marriage . . . if Scar has feelings for you it would make more sense for the two of you to explore that slowly."

"I think we both want security."

For that reason, maybe more than any other, Liv would marry him.

He was giving her a home, a family, the possibility of children, a life she craved to the very marrow of her bones, and had since she was eight years old and had lost her parents in one swift brutal act of violence.

Scarborough was loyal and stable and motivated.

And he was the one man alive she trusted to keep her safe during her frightening all-night blackouts.

The October night was crisp and quiet as Sebastian raced through the woods, enjoying the freedom of his wolf form as he approached his brother's house from the south side, downwind. He had followed Scarborough to the airport that morning to be sure he really was flying to New York on business and not retreating into the woods north of his house to join the pack. Having been reassured his brother really was en route to the Big Apple, Sebastian couldn't resist the opportunity to check on Liv, to peer through the windows and engage in the sadistic self-torture of seeing the woman he loved, alive and well, yet living in his brother's house as his brother's girlfriend.

As he reached the property, he slowed down, cautiously picking his way over the perfectly manicured front lawn, listening, smelling, for any signs of the others or of danger. Sebastian couldn't chance being spotted by any of the four remaining werewolves of the pack, even with his brother gone.

He wasn't ready to fight, not yet, not until he knew Liv was safe.

And there would be a fight if he encountered Scarborough or the others, a fight to the death. They thought he was already dead, having left him bleeding out and caught in the rushing downstream river on the edge of their territory. But Sebastian had lived and had spent the last six months recovering from his wounds, struggling to survive and not be discovered, the whole time planning his return, his takeover.

He had never cared about being pack leader, had never appreciated his heritage as werewolf, had never wanted to make decisions and guide the others, or mate for the health of the pack. His leadership had been errant, his attitude nonchalant, his relationship with Liv solely for selfish reasons, because he loved her and wanted to be with her. He had wanted to protect her and shield her from the truth about who they both were. She'd known nothing of werewolves, and he'd wanted to keep it that way, knowing that for whatever reason, Liv had never shifted, despite the heritage Sebastian knew she possessed. It had been selfish, and naïve, but he had just wanted to live in quiet normalcy in love with a sweet beautiful woman.

It was different now. It was time to take his place, be the leader he should have been, but it would take careful planning and patience.

The house was a mini-mansion, a great, hulking, contemporary glass structure of concrete and steel, on the cusp of the thick forest behind it. There had been changes since he had last risked cruising by the house to check on Liv. Now there were giant pots filled with yellow and purple flowers and four pumpkins resting on the stoop in front of a bale of straw. A cheerful scarecrow sat on the straw, holding up a sign that read TRICK OR TREAT STOP. If Sebastian could have laughed in wolf form he would have.

There had been nothing funny at all about the fact that his brother had tried to kill him, then had stolen his girlfriend, yet seeing that goofy grinning scarecrow in front of his brother's expensive, architecturally award-winning contemporary house struck him as hilarious. Big bad wolf goes suburban. For a man as determined to control everything and everyone as Scarborough was, it was good to see he'd let Liv express her own decorative opinion.

Then the amusement was gone as quickly as it had arrived.

The thought of his brother with the woman he loved was infuriating, sickening.

It dredged up a jealousy so ugly, so black, that he sometimes felt like it had eaten him alive, consuming all the good parts of him and leaving nothing but the anger, the pain, the frustration, the burning, agonizing loneliness. It had only been two weeks since he had realized Liv was living with Scarborough, but in those fourteen days, Sebastian had changed. He had gone into the very bowels of emotional hell, had known an anger so sharp it dripped blood, a pain so severe it took his legs out from under him.

And with it had come the ability to shift into wolf at will. His entire life he had fought the shift, which had only come for him at the full moon, unlike his brother, who had been able to shift whenever he chose since his teen years.

Now Sebastian could do the same.

Which meant it was almost time to confront his brother and take back his life, his place in the pack.

And the woman he loved.

Sebastian padded around the back of the house and up the steps that led to the second-story deck off the master suite. The metal was cool beneath his paws, the three-quarter moon casting a pale glow across the floor. The exterior bedroom wall was all glass, the windows pushed open and unencumbered by screens. Scarborough and his architect had thought screens interfered with the view of the woods and disrupted the clean lines of the house.

Sebastian had thought it made for a hell of a lot of flies and mosquitoes in your bedroom, but he never claimed to be classy, just practical.

Yet no matter how stupid he'd thought it was two years ago when the house was built, it now allowed him to put his head through the window and watch Liv sleeping.

She was sprawled nearly sideways on the bed, the covers half off and bunched up, damp tendrils of her rich auburn hair stuck to her forehead and cheek. It was clearly a restless sleep, her breathing labored, hand twitching, the scent of her sweat and body lotion intermingling in his sensitive nostrils. There was another scent too, a subtle undertone to the first two, the sweet tangy allure of arousal.

Whatever dreams she was having, they were clearly sexual to coax that kind of response from her body, and Sebastian leaned forward and breathed deeply. He had missed her, longed for the touch and taste of her soft skin, the look of love in her eyes as he had moved over her, buried deep inside her.

Sebastian moved restlessly back and forth, the animal and the man in him overwhelmed by her presence, her femininity, her obvious need and desire for a mating.

Unable to stop himself, Sebastian backed up and soared through the open window.

CHAPTER THREE

Liv had been dreaming again.

In the dream the bride sat in her snug house deep in the woods, fearfully watching out the window at the encroaching night.

Her hands twitched as the moon rose, and she gripped the armrests of her chair desperately, before reaching down and yanking off her boots with a sob of defeat. Immediately the delicate youthful skin of those shaking anxious hands changed, growing a thick fur pelt. The bride's jaw cracked audibly, shifting outward, her teeth sharpening. As the full moon lit up the small room, she fell out of the chair onto the floor and all fours, her body morphing into that of an animal . . . a wolf.

They hadn't eaten the bride.

They had made her one of them.

A werewolf.

Liv tore her eyes open to escape the image of the gray wolf howling in despair.

Only to find herself face-to-face with a wolf in her room, pacing in front of her window.

She wanted to scream, but no sound came out of her mouth, only a frantic exhalation of air, like a strangled gasp. She hated these stupid windows without screens. She had told Scarborough that something was going to climb in, but she'd been thinking about serial killers and raccoons, not wolves.

Only there it was, a pacing wolf in her bedroom, and she had no idea what to do other than watch it, frozen in fear.

It cocked its head at her, and she realized it had one blue eye, and one green.

Like Sebastian.

God, she was still dreaming . . . though she didn't understand why it was always wolves. Every night, wolves . . .

No wolf in real life was that big, so she was definitely still asleep, but it didn't make her fear quiet at all. Staring down the length of her body at it, fingers clutching the top of her sheet, she waited for something, anything.

It backed up, its back legs crouching down, and she realized that it was going to spring right onto her bed and rip her heart out and her face off. The scream she'd been struggling to unleash finally hurtled out as she closed her eyes and waited for the impact of its heavy, lithe body, the pain of its teeth in her flesh.

"Shh, Liv, it's okay."

Her eyes flew open.

Now she knew she was dreaming. There was no longer a wolf in her room.

The form on the bottom of her bed, moving up toward her on all fours, was Sebastian. His mismatched eyes were filled with tenderness, compassion, lust. His shoulders were muscular and tanned, drawing closer to her, one side bearing a scar she knew her former lover didn't have.

And he was naked.

Fully, one hundred percent, gloriously naked.

The hard planes of his chest flexed as he slowly crawled up the length of her body, his thighs settling firmly on either side of her.

His thick impressive erection hovered over the apex of her legs.

Liv lost her ability to speak again, and for an entirely different reason this time. She hadn't forgotten how gorgeous Sebastian was, not really, but she had shoved aside the memories of what it felt like to have him invading her space, moving his body, his smell, his deep expressive gaze into her presence.

Desire kicked at her from the inside out, knocking against her womb, firming her nipples, flooding her inner thighs with a rush of warm lubrication. She could hear the sound of her own short, excited, and frightened pants of breath, feel the heat of his body over her, smell the earthy musk of his skin that was foreign and familiar all at once. It was Sebastian's scent, with an overlay of something new . . . something woodsy and primal.

A dull throb between her legs began as he stared down at her silently, her body so long unsatisfied, and so very aware of how close his erection was to her, nothing but a thin sheet and a couple of inches between them. She'd gone to sleep with a shirt on, but this was a dream, and it was bunched at her waist already.

All he needed to do was yank the sheet down and slide into her. . . .

He reached out with a finger and drew it across her bottom lip, slowly, painstakingly, from one corner to the other.

The soft whisper of a touch was maddening and Liv whispered, "Please."

"Please what?" His voice was gruff, his face so close to hers she could see the shadow of a beard on his chin. His finger continued to move, over her jaw, her cheek, her nose, cascading down over her neck, pausing at the edge of the sheet before heading north again.

Under different circumstances she would have appreciated the tender touch, the study of her features, the careful exploration of her, the woman, not just her, a female body. But now it was only stirring that deep ache into a painful swollen throb, a frustrating reminder of how passionate sex with him had been and how empty her life felt now.

"Please what?" he repeated.

She didn't know how to say what she wanted, how to tell him to make love to her, to fill her body and her soul in a way only he had been able to.

If she were awake, she'd have to slap him, throw him out, tell him precisely what she thought of him in cold and calm terms.

But she wasn't, and she was so lonely, so starved for touch. His touch. So that when words failed she simply shoved the sheet to the side, exposing her body, breasts still covered by her shirt, but her bottom half blissfully bare.

His eyes darkened. "You want me to make love to you? You want me inside you?"

"Yes," she said, then gasped when immediately his mouth dropped onto her nipple and lathered it with his tongue.

He moved in tight little circles around her nipple, over and over, then flicking the bud, then enclosing his mouth over it and sucking hard. The tingling and the tugging spiraled throughout her body, echoing between her legs.

Six months was too long. She moved restlessly, grabbing onto those hard, powerful shoulders, and trying to urge his head away from her breast.

Lifting his head, he said, "Patience." But it wasn't a gentle reassuring voice. It was edgy and gravelly, darker in tone than anything she'd ever known from Sebastian, and she knew it was her misery, her frustration, her anger and bitterness spawning a darker tone in him in her dream.

The last six months had been hell in real life, and he was responsible for that agony, but here, in the misty fog of sleep, she could forget and just remember the pleasure.

Sebastian sucked her other nipple at great length, before blowing gently on the moist, firm peak, causing her to shiver. She was on the verge of asking again, demanding more, but before the mumbled words could leave her lips his head shifted, his thumbs skimming over her tummy and her thighs as he settled between her legs.

Every muscle in her body tensed in anticipation, knowing that he could do amazing things with his tongue, knowing that in seconds she would probably orgasm from both the length of her celibacy and the skill of his touch.

He hovered over her, his nose tickling her, his warm breath teasing her clitoris. A hot desperate rush of fluid greeted him, so much that in reality she might have been embarrassed, but here, now, it didn't matter. In fact, it empowered her. She wanted sex, hard and pounding sex, and he was going to give it to her.

"Lick me," she demanded, lifting her hips slightly to bump her clitoris against his mouth.

Giving a tiny little flick over her clitoris, he breathed deeply, his eyes drifting closed. "I can smell you, smell how much you want me. That's what brought me in. It's a delicious scent."

His tongue moved then, sliding up and down between her folds, swirling around her clitoris, with just the right speed, just the right pressure. Liv moaned, eyes fluttering closed, the pleasure acute and tense. Her legs moved apart, wanting to be as open for him as possible, her fingers sliding into his short dark hair.

She came as predicted, fast and tight and immediately, her throat shutting off, forgetting to breathe for that sharp, quick release of her body at his touch. When she sucked back in a lungful of air, he was already flicking his tongue over her again, setting off an uncomfortable jolt from the oversensitive bud.

"It's too much," she told him, trying to push his head away.

It had been too tight, too swollen.

But he ignored her and continued to lick and suck at her, the pleasure mixing with an odd sharp pain.

"I can't, don't. It's too sensitive." Liv shifted, trying to get away from him.

"I haven't had enough," he said, the words mumbled against her folds as he pulled them apart. First his tongue plunged in, then he replaced it with his finger.

"Sebastian," Liv moaned. This was a different,

more demanding man than she remembered, and the paradox struck her even in her hazy, endorphin-filled sleep state.

Now he groaned and raised his head, his lips shiny from her dampness, his jaw set, eyes dark, finger pumping in and out of her as he stared at her. "Say it again."

"What?" she asked, bewildered, ankles shifting on the bed, hips rising without thought to meet the thrust of his finger. Oh, that felt so good, and even her swollen clitoris had relaxed. She was going to come again, soon, very soon. . . .

"My name. Say my name again."

"Sebastian," she murmured, distracted by the feel of him, willing to say anything he wanted as long as he continued.

His response was to dip a second finger inside her, then slide it down lower, between her cheeks, and slip it into her backside. Liv jerked a little, startled, fairly certain he'd never done that when they were together, but intrigued, shocked at how it felt, the two fingers moving in harmony, in and out, filling her everywhere. The tightness increased, spiraling up and out of control, and she cried out, the orgasm slamming into her. The feel of her muscles contracting around both his fingers had her bucking up off the mattress, but Sebastian held her steady, his stroking never slowing or altering.

As her body settled back down, she shook her head, cloudy, unsure of what to say or do, waiting, knowing that it wasn't for her to dictate anyway. Here it was all him, in charge, pleasuring her.

When he slowly withdrew his fingers, her body gave a spasm against the loss. The fullness had been so wonderful, and then it was gone. Her disappointment was so profound, she was going to beg to have them back, but instead, Sebastian settled between her thighs and pushed his thick erection into her wet, aching body.

"Oh!" she cried, opening her legs as far apart as they would go, back arching and hands reaching for him. Yes. This was what she wanted.

As she gripped his biceps, he thrust deeper inside her, as far as he could, then pulling out to the very tip, before plunging deep.

"Oh, God," she said, amazed at how good it felt, how much she had missed this, him.

"You like it, don't you?" he demanded, pausing half in, half out.

"Yes, yes." She moved beneath him, lifting her hips to force action.

He didn't disappoint. He started a pounding rhythm that had her insensible in seconds, the thick fullness of him deep inside so satisfying she wanted to scream in relief.

"He doesn't make you feel this way, does he?"

"Who?" she asked, struggling to focus, her breath coming in short, urgent pants, her thighs clenching around his cock. She was going to come a third time.

"Scarborough. He can't do this to you."

So lost to the pleasure, she didn't even pause, but answered truthfully, "No, no, he can't."

Sebastian grunted, and she felt the hot pulse of his orgasm, tripping off her own. They gritted their teeth and groaned in unison, memories of all their nights together mixing a desperate melancholy into the magic of the moment.

How could he have done this to her? How could he have left?

But there were no answers in the illusion of his eyes, and even as the last shudders wracked her body, Liv found herself drifting, limp on her bed.

As she lost the clarity of the dream, as the images grew shrouded and shifted, Liv's last thought was a cold one, one she needed to hold and own more so than any pleasure he had brought to her asleep.

Sebastian had not kissed her.

Not even once.

CHAPTER FOUR

Sebastian watched Liv fall asleep, her eyelashes fluttering as she settled back into slumber, nightshirt still bunched up over her breasts.

He shouldn't have come here.

Shouldn't have made love to her.

She didn't think he was real.

She was living with his brother.

And now he had the taste and touch and smell of her all over his skin, on his tongue, embedded in his brain, his heart, his soul. The memory of Liv had helped him stay alive, the reality seemed like it might kill him.

He couldn't have her. She was no longer his. And she had betrayed him as surely as his brother had.

Yet he lingered before he pulled the sheet up over her, allowing himself one last touch of his fingers over her full lips. Then he moved off the bed, unable to stay another minute. God, she had felt so good, and he could stay inside her forever.

But she was no longer his, and his brother had

seen and touched and tasted the same places on her body that he had and it made him sick, disgust and anguish overwhelming in their intensity.

Sebastian shifted and leapt out of the bedroom window. He padded carefully down the metal stairs, then when he hit the ground, he ran. Away from Liv, away from the past, away from the uncertainty of the future, and the temptation to claim her body with his yet again.

He ran hard, as fast as his four legs would carry him, into the thick lustrous forest behind Scarborough's house. Once under the cover of the trees, he dodged and weaved, sailing over fallen limbs and hurtling himself through brush. The crisp air felt good on his hot fur and the night around him whistled with an autumn wind and hummed with the presence of insects and nocturnal creatures.

Such as the wolf.

He heard the high keening howl immediately to his right and he drew up short, not wanting an encounter.

But it was too late. He smelled the scent of the other werewolf, and he knew it was doing the same. Before he could make the decision to retreat or confront, there was a werewolf with mottled gray-and-white fur in front of him.

Nick. His cousin, younger than him by two years.

Their eyes locked, and Sebastian bared his teeth, ready to battle.

Yet Nick did the unthinkable and shifted back to man, the expression on his face, as he crouched naked, incredulous. "Sebastian?" he murmured. "You're alive?"

It was that incredulity and the trust it took for

Nick to risk being human with Sebastian still as wolf, that led him to make his own shift.

"Obviously, yes, I'm alive. No thanks to you or any of the James clan."

While Sebastian was wary, Nick was jubilant. A grin split his face. "Man, I'm so glad to see you!" He clapped Sebastian on the shoulder. "I thought for sure you were a goner, but no worse for the wear, huh?"

Actually, he felt like a pickup truck with three hundred thousand miles on it, but there was no point in going into all of that. "Yeah, I'm alright. So when you run to Scar and tell him I'm back in town, you make sure he understands I know who put the knife in my shoulder."

Nick's smile fell off his face. "About that . . . we didn't know. The rest of us had no idea that's what Scar was planning, I swear to you. I never would have agreed to that kind of bullshit."

Sebastian wanted to believe him. Nick had always been a happy-go-lucky guy and a fairly docile werewolf. He was a follower, not a leader, and had no head for elaborate political scheming. Much like Sebastian had been. "You're trying to tell me that none of the four of you in the pack knew Scar was going to kill me?"

"Hell, no, we didn't know that. We've always known Scar was ambitious, but in human form. I never thought that he took the clan so serious. I never thought we were anything more than six guys who got extremely hairy and grew an overbite once a month. A family quirk, nothing more."

Studying Nick, Sebastian turned his words around in his head. Damn, he did want to believe him, but he didn't know who to trust anymore.

"And by the way, can I just point out that this is more than a little awkward standing here bare-assed in the woods with you? I hope we don't run into any campers . . . that's how rumors get started. And that could seriously affect my ability to pick up women."

The way Nick was looking around them uneasily made Sebastian laugh, no easy feat these days. "I probably shouldn't hang around too long anyway."

"Scar's out of town."

"I know." Sebastian felt his face fix into a hard frown, the way it always did when he thought about his brother now. "Why'd he do it? He could have talked to me about taking over the pack, he didn't have to kill me." He had turned that one around and around and while he thought he understood that Scar was motivated by power and control, it still seemed excessive to Sebastian.

But then again, he wasn't entirely lacking in human emotion.

"Because if you believe the legends, even if you had given the pack leadership over to Scar, you still had Liv."

"The sole survivor of the French clan of were-wolves." Sebastian ran his hand through his hair.

"Mated to her, it doubles his power."

Which was why Sebastian had never married Liv. He wanted no part of anything that smacked of ulterior motives when it came to her. He had loved her for her, not for what she could bring him.

"Liv has no idea who and what she is."

Nick nodded. "Just so you know, she's started shifting at the full moon. But Scar says she doesn't have any memory of it."

Sebastian's eyebrows shot up. "Liv is shifting? But she never did before."

"Extreme emotion triggers the first shift, you know that. It started almost immediately after you disappeared."

Yeah, he did know emotion could initiate the change. At sixteen, Sebastian and Scarborough had both shifted for the first time after their parents died in a car accident. Scar had internalized enough of his anger that he had learned to shift at will almost immediately, a dark talent Sebastian now possessed himself.

Sorrow for the pain Liv had suffered enveloped him. "What does Liv think happened to me?"

Nick cleared his throat like he was uncomfortable, but he didn't evade the question or Sebastian's stare. "He told Liv that you disappeared without a trace, no sign of foul play. She thinks you walked out on her and emptied her bank account right before you did."

"What?" Sebastian felt the anger rising inside of him, from his gut, feathering out to all his limbs in a hot rush. His hands twitched. "You're telling me she thinks I stole her money and skipped out?"

Nick shot him a look of sympathy. "She had no reason to think otherwise, especially since you would never marry her. I thought about telling her the truth, but why would she believe my crazy-ass story over Scar's? His was a hell of a lot more believable, and the money being gone just cemented what he told her. And then he would have just killed me too and he'd still be with Liv, so there was no point. But it was rough on her, Sebastian. . . . I've never seen her look like that. For weeks she was just . . ." He cleared his throat. "Anyway. I'm glad you're back, man. Your brother is a little out of control."

Sebastian couldn't believe it. No wonder Liv was living with Scarborough. The guy had attempted to kill Sebastian in cold blood, then had lied to Liv about it, claiming he had walked out on her without a backward glance, with all her cash. Then clearly Scarborough had been there as a shoulder to cry on.

The fucking bastard. It was so devious and cold and calculating.

It made Sebastian want to throw back his head and howl in disgust and frustration.

It made him want to go back and make love to Liv again, with more tenderness, with the truth between them.

And it made him want to rip his brother apart, piece by miserable piece.

"Oh, don't worry," he told Nick. "I have plans for Scarborough."

The alarm shattered Liv's sleep and had her reaching over to smack the quiet button on her cell phone to stop the squawking. Peeling her eyes open, she swallowed, her mouth dry, and clutched the sheet a little closer to her. She was freezing. She shouldn't have left the windows open, it was too late in the year for that. Plus she realized that somehow her nightshirt had worked its way all the way up to her neck so the majority of her body was exposed, nothing but the thin sheet covering her.

The dream came back to her then.

The bride, morphing into a wolf, then the bride's room morphing to her room, then the wolf in her room morphing into Sebastian.

It had been intense and so very real, like all the bride dreams were. Yet in this one, Sebastian had been there and he had touched and licked her, brought her to orgasm, and buried his erection in her.

Her cheeks heated and her inner thighs throbbed at the memory. It had felt so good, so powerful, so satisfying.

Clearly her body was hinting to her that she needed release. She refused to admit that it meant she missed Sebastian. She couldn't possibly still crave a man who had done what he had to her.

But there was no denying what the Sebastian in her dream had said when he was thrusting in her. He had demanded she tell him that Scarborough couldn't make her feel that way, and she had admitted it. It didn't take a psychologist or a professional dream interpreter to figure out what that meant.

She couldn't bring herself to make love to Scarborough, and that was a serious problem.

It meant she needed to be slapped for still wanting the touch of Sebastian when it was his brother who had treated her with kindness and respect.

Yanking her nightshirt back into place, she tried to ignore the tightening of her nipples and the tingle between her thighs at the lingering memory of the dream.

Maybe she should do dream analysis. The wolves were a curious repetitive theme of the last few months, one she really didn't understand. And not just wolves—these were werewolves, shape-shifting humans.

Liv forced herself out of bed. She didn't want to be late for class. She only had half a semester to go until she had her degree, then she could finally have a decent-paying job to both support herself and replace some of the money she had lost. The money Sebastian had stolen.

Maybe she should start taking a sleeping aid. Something to knock her out so that she didn't dream for a few nights. Because dreams weren't re-ality and she needed to put aside the false sense that Sebastian had come back to her, had touched her like he still loved her.

As she padded across the floor to the bathroom, Liv suddenly froze. It wasn't possible. It was just a dream. . . .

Yet she lifted her nightshirt, and in the early morning light streaming from the open windows, saw the distinct and telltale sign of semen trickling down her inner thigh.

CHAPTER FIVE

Liv spent the day in an anxious fog, worrying about her sanity. She sat through her classes, the professors' words white noise humming in the background of her rapid and frightened thoughts.

There had been semen on her leg. There was nothing else that it could have been.

So how did it get there? She had thought she was dreaming that she had made love to her ex-boyfriend, who was missing. She supposed it was possible that he could have returned, but it wasn't possible that he could have changed from a wolf to a naked man in front of her eyes.

Maybe she had still been dreaming at that point, but afterwards . . . maybe that had been real?

But he hadn't been there when she woke up.

And she didn't know what was real anymore.

Just that as she sat through endless lecture after lecture on hard chair after hard chair, she was in fact post-sex sore between her legs, a maddening reminder that something had happened, though she wasn't sure what.

Mary Fran called her as she was driving home, grateful it wasn't her day for clinicals. In no way should she be responsible for the care of patients when she was feeling as anxious as she was. Gripping the wheel tightly with her left hand, she answered the phone with her right.

"Hey, want to meet me for a drink? It's Friday night, and I for one am thrilled. My classes were endless this week."

Liv blinked hard in the dark, her headlights splayed out over a black road that seemed to be undulating in front of her. She normally loved fall, but it got dark early now and she was suddenly having trouble focusing on the road. "I can't. I'm not feeling good."

"Oh, I'm sorry, what's wrong?"

"I think . . . I think I'm having a panic attack."

"What! Where are you?"

"Driving home."

"Pull over. Put your head between your legs."

Hearing Mary Fran take charge, not freaking out or judging her, somehow calmed her down. "No, it's okay, I'm pulling in Scarborough's driveway. I'll be fine. I just need to lie down."

There was a gigantic pause, where they both knew what Mary Fran was dying to say.

Cancel the wedding.

Liv knew she had to. Something was not right in her head, in her heart. She had to at least postpone it until she got a grip.

"I will," she told her friend.

"I didn't say anything."

"I know what you were thinking. Don't worry. As soon as Scarborough gets back, I'll talk to him."

"I think that's a good idea."

"Yeah." Liv swallowed the bile that was crawling up her throat as she hit the door opener and pulled into the garage.

"Are you home yet?"

"Yeah. I'll talk to you later."

"Call me if you want to chat. I'll be around."

"Thanks."

When she went in the house, Liv stood in the middle of its quiet elegance, a house she had wanted to make her home. But it wasn't her home. There was still no real place for Liv to call her own. No home, no family, no happiness.

After three glasses of wine, she fell into a restless sleep in bed in front of the TV, wearing a soft T-shirt and PJ pants. When she saw the bride in her dreams, she almost sighed at the inevitability of her presence.

But the bride only briefly appeared before the scene shifted to the woods. Sebastian and Scarborough and their cousins were drinking beers and fishing on the edge of the river. The serenity of the scene, the good-natured joking dissolved almost immediately. There was a sharp movement, Scar over Sebastian, a knife in his shoulder, a shove into the river—the cousins shouting and waving arms and a general hysteria.

While Scarborough stood calm on the riverbank, his face a cool mask of satisfaction as he leaned down and wiped the blood off the blade in the grass.

The bride shifted back to human, and suddenly, Liv realized she was in the woods herself, in the body of a wolf.

*   *   *

Sebastian had been prepared for Liv to shift on the full moon a week later given what Nick had told him, but he hadn't really expected she would shift earlier. Yet he still found himself poised outside Scar's house in human form, watching, waiting. He told himself it was to ensure her safety, and that was true, but it was also the undeniable urge to be near her. He was here as a man so that he wouldn't smell her, so that he could resist the urge to enter the room and touch her the way he had the night before.

Now that he knew the whole truth, he was torn over how to handle it. He needed to deal with his brother, and he would as soon as Scar came back to Wisconsin. That wasn't worrying him. What was causing him to pace the edge of the woods behind the house as he watched the bedroom window was how to explain everything to Liv. She deserved to know the full truth, but he wasn't sure how to deliver that, knowing that her trust had been compromised.

He didn't know how to convince her that what they had shared was real, and that he wanted nothing more than to be with her.

Forever.

As her husband.

Preoccupied with his thoughts, he was unprepared for Liv to leap out of the open window and race down the stairs, so fast she actually stumbled on the bottom few steps before recovering her balance.

She was in wolf form.

Sebastian stared, astonished. She was beautiful. Petite and long-legged, her fur a soft auburn, snout small and delicate. It was exactly what he would have imagined she would look like, and the wolf in him growled low in his throat in appreciation.

This was his mate.

He knew that as both man and wolf.

Her hesitation as she moved across the grass gave him a clear view of her crystalline green eyes, and he sensed the uncertainty, the anxiety there. After shedding his clothes, he shifted, his plan to follow her.

But she had heard his movement and from ten feet away, paused in her intention to enter the woods, staring at him, and snarling a warning.

It was fear, not menace he heard and he stood still, hoping she would take off running.

She did, and he followed, allowing distance between them so she wouldn't feel threatened, but wanting to make sure she was safe. Only she realized he was in pursuit and she ran faster, forcing him to keep pace. Her maneuvers became a clear effort to confuse him, as she dodged in multiple directions, leaping over logs, her behavior frantic and frightened.

Sebastian wasn't about to let her out of his sight though, whether he was scaring her or not. Liv didn't even remember her nights in wolf form, and he couldn't have her out there alone. Eventually she would get tired from her efforts and either return to the safety of the house or approach him.

Finally, after an extended chase that had them circling back around closer to the house, she drew up short, panting, and turned to confront him. Her teeth snapped and she growled in warning.

Clearly she didn't understand who he was. Or

hell, maybe she did, given what Scarborough had told her.

He remained loose, nonthreatening, even resting on his haunches to show her he had no interest in fighting.

She eyed him for a second, wary, then she launched herself at him, baring her teeth. Sebastian stood his ground. He wasn't going to leave, but neither was he going to fight back if she chose to attack him. This was Liv, and he would defend himself only as necessary, but he wouldn't harm her. In a wild lunge, she snapped at his neck. He dodged her, but she managed to clip his shoulder, digging into the flesh beneath the fur.

The pain was minimal, but an involuntary growl came out on instinct.

Liv yelped, backed up, and shifted.

Astonished, Sebastian realized she had frightened herself right back into human form, and she was crumpled on a pile of leaves, naked, eyes glassy and confused.

She spotted him and opened her mouth to scream.

Sebastian shifted too, and the scream he expected never arrived. Her eyes widened in astonishment and she lifted her head slightly for a better view.

"I'm dreaming again," she murmured. "Dreaming, nothing more. Crazy, crazy dreaming."

"You're not dreaming. This is real," he told her, moving carefully toward her, wanting to offer some kind of comfort. "It's okay."

"It can't be real. You were a werewolf a second ago. I think I was a werewolf . . . none of that makes any sense. Those things aren't real."

"Do you feel awake?" he asked her, squatting down to the ground so he wasn't towering over her.

She hesitated, but then she nodded as she sat up. "I feel awake. I'm cold and damp and my nose is running. It feels sharp, like reality. But it can't be. I'm naked in the woods with you. This can't be real."

"I promise you it's real," he said softly. "And I promise you that I didn't leave you." Maybe he should explain other things first, like her shape-shifting heritage, but he couldn't help himself, and he didn't want her to stand up and bolt either. He reached out and brushed her hair off her forehead. "God, I've missed you, Liv."

"Now I know I'm dreaming." She swallowed visibly and shivered.

"Come on, let's go back to the house. It's cold out."

But Liv was staring at his shoulder. "You're bleeding."

He glanced down. The wound wasn't deep, but without a shirt on, there was blood chugging slowly down his arm. "It's not bad. Don't worry about it."

"I did that, didn't I?" she asked in a whisper, her green eyes enormous. Her finger came out to point at it, then quickly she drew it back, crossing her arms over her chest with a shiver.

"Yes. But it's not a big deal. I startled you."

"I bit you," she said, hand flying up to her mouth and scrubbing at her lips and chin. When it came away with a thin smear of blood on her flesh, her eyes rolled back in her head.

"Liv!"

Sebastian reached out and caught her as she slumped into a dead faint.

Gathering her in his arms, he headed for the house, scooping up his clothes on the way. Ten minutes later he had her tucked into bed, wearing a T-shirt he'd dug out of the dresser, the covers pulled up over her. She had woken up in his arms as he was carrying her back to the house, but she hadn't spoken. She had just looked up at him, then screwed her eyes shut again, her fingers squeezing his arms tightly.

Even when he had pulled the shirt on over her head after laying her down on the bed she hadn't spoken. She just stared up at him, eyes glassy, unblinking.

Unsure of what to do or say, Sebastian brushed his lips across her forehead. "It's okay. Do you need a glass of water or anything?"

Finally she spoke. "Did we have sex last night?"

Sebastian hesitated for a split second, then nodded. "Yes. I couldn't resist when I saw you. . . . I missed you so much, sweetheart."

"I thought I was dreaming."

Stupidly that hurt him. He'd thought she was groggy, but he had still thought she'd known what she was doing. That she was well aware it was him in the flesh she was being intimate with.

He dropped his gaze to the bed so she wouldn't see the pain there.

"No," he said, his tone harsher than he intended it to be. "Sorry. No dream. This is real and last night was real."

Her eyes darkened and her tone was suddenly feisty. "I want my money back."

"What money?"

"The money you stole."

"I didn't steal your money!" He was going to kill his goddamn brother for putting that expression on Liv's face. "Do you want to know what happened? Six months ago I went on a fishing trip with my brother and my cousins . . . you remember that, right?"

"Yes, I remember." She sat up and held the sheet in front of her. "You decided not to come back, leaving me with no explanation other than you're an asshole and a user."

"I didn't come back because my brother, my dear, loving brother, stabbed me in the fucking shoulder then tossed my body into the river to drown."

Expecting Liv to scoff or argue or roll her eyes, Sebastian was surprised when she went very still, her fingers relaxing their hold on the sheet.

"Ohmigod. That's what the bride wanted me to see."

CHAPTER SIX

Liv took deep breaths, afraid she was going to faint again. She couldn't believe Sebastian was standing in front of her, wearing nothing but a pair of low-slung jeans. He was as gorgeous as she remembered, as gorgeous as he'd been in the middle of the night when she'd been so certain she'd been dreaming.

And he had a wicked scar on his shoulder, one she had noted when he'd been poised above her, his body pushing into hers, but that she had dismissed as a quirk of her sleeping mind.

"What do you mean?" he asked, standing next to the bed. "Who is the bride?"

"I don't know who she is," Liv said, squeezing her eyes shut, trying to recreate the dream. "But she appears over and over in my dreams, dreams I've been having since you left. She was a bride, tossed from a carriage on her wedding night as they were being chased by giant wolves. The wedding party wanted to lighten the load so they could go faster, and she was the easiest to toss because she was petite. But she didn't die . . . they turned her into a werewolf."

The faint images of Scarborough stabbing Sebastian hovered behind her eyelids. "She showed me what you described. I dreamt it tonight. You and Scarborough at the river, him stabbing you, you going into the water . . ."

Liv snapped her eyes open. "I thought I just had a crazy, wild, active imagination, but . . ." She couldn't even articulate where her thoughts were going.

When Sebastian had first said that Scarborough had stabbed him on that fishing trip, it had suddenly all seemed to make sense. The dreams had been reality, or showing her reality, and she had felt like she'd stumbled on an answer.

Now it seemed like sheer lunacy again.

Liv rubbed her temples and tried to clear her head.

"It's not your imagination." Sebastian sat down on the bed next to her. "Here is the truth, Liv, the whole truth, as unbelievable as it seems. The bride in your dreams is your great-grandmother. She was the first of the Lugaru line of werewolves, turned the way you saw it in your dream. She and the pack migrated to Canada from France and moved down into Wisconsin with my ancestors, the James clan."

Liv knew her great-grandmother had been French, but she had known little other than that given that her own parents had died before she'd had much chance to ask them anything.

"Werewolves are real. I am one. You are one. Scarborough is one. As far as I know you never shifted before I was stabbed, but an emotional upheaval can cause the first shift."

It had definitely been an emotional six months, there was no denying that.

But werewolves? It was impossible. They were the stuff of horror movies and medieval legends.

Yet she had seen Sebastian shift with her own eyes. She had felt herself shift in what she thought was a dream.

Sebastian was confirming the scene between him and Scarborough was real, and he had the scar on his shoulder to prove it.

"I . . . I don't know what to say. This is . . ."

"Crazy. I know. But at least Scar and I had our parents to explain. Yours died before they could reveal the truth to you."

Sebastian reached out and took her hand in his, and Liv stared down at his callused fingers covering hers, the touch warm and familiar. It brought a melancholy ache to her heart and she felt the tears pricking at her eyes.

If she believed in the impossible, in the insane story he was telling her, then she was a werewolf, a hairy, snarling beast.

But it also meant that Sebastian hadn't left her willingly.

And God help her, she was actually thinking that was more appealing than shape-shifters not existing and Sebastian breaking her heart on purpose.

"I want you to understand something." His expression was earnest, open. "The reason I never asked you to marry me was not because I didn't want to be your husband. It was because I didn't want you to ever feel that I had chosen you even in part for the purpose of an alliance, for the strength you would bring to our pack. I was pack leader, and you're the sole survivor of our allies, a pack that has psychic abilities. Together, you and I would have given an edge to our pack, but I wanted no part of that."

Sebastian's finger trailed across her lip again, as it had the night before, and this time it was tender and soul shattering. "I just wanted you," he said. "I wanted to be with you, for no other reason than for the fact that I love you."

Liv felt her throat closing with emotion. The words he was saying were bizarre, convoluted, a description of a world she hadn't known existed and didn't understand, but when she stripped that away, what she heard was the truth in his voice that he did love her.

That the nightmare she'd been living in for the six months, the reality that had devastated her, was in fact fiction, and the dreams that had plagued her sleep were actually reality.

Nothing mattered but those last three words he'd just spoken. He loved her.

"Sebastian," she said, nearly choking on his name.

He hadn't betrayed her or used her. And now he was here, with her, and her emotions were sharp and too overwhelming for words. She could only stare at him, throat tight, eyes filling with tears, wanting to tell him she loved him, but unable to squeeze the words out.

But she didn't have time to wonder or worry why she was speechless, because he closed the distance between them and brushed his mouth over hers, a soft sigh of a kiss, a gentle worship of her lips. Liv closed her eyes on a deep exhalation of air, her shoulders relaxing, fingers losing their grip on the sheet as he hovered over her mouth, in her space but not touching, his fingers traipsing across her forehead, down her cheek. This is what she wanted. Tenderness. The night before had been raw, exciting, a fantasy, now she wanted real, intimate, loving.

"I missed you," he breathed, forehead resting lightly on hers. "The thought of you kept me alive when I was bleeding in that river."

"I wish I had known." Liv slid her hands down his shoulders, pausing to trace the mottled and angry outline of his scar. He had suffered as much as she had. More even, and her heart broke all over again for the pain he had endured, for how they had both needlessly suffered. There was dried blood on the laceration she had given him, and she shuddered as her fingers hovered over it.

Turning his head slightly, he brushed his lips over her fingers. "It doesn't matter. What is important is we're here, together, now. And that we'll be together tomorrow."

She sensed the question in that and she never hesitated. Sebastian's eyes had always been oddly fascinating, one a pale sky blue, the other a mossy green, so different that she'd often thought they worked independently of each other, conveying their own distinct thoughts and emotions. An illusion, no doubt, based on the fact that the light hit them differently, but now as he looked up at her, there was no disparity, no variance.

Having experienced such little deep and unwavering love in her lonely life, she knew it when she saw it, and it was there in Sebastian's unusual eyes.

"Yes, we'll be together. Today, tomorrow, always." Despite the last six months, despite realities that would have to be faced, it had always been, and always would be Sebastian for her.

Wanting to feel her skin against his skin, Liv pulled off the T-shirt he had just put on her and tossed it to the floor.

He kissed her then, a deep possessive kiss that swelled her heart and stirred her desire. As the touch lingered, as his hands moved to grip her shoulders, Liv became very aware of the fact that she was naked, he was naked. The sheet scraped against her tight nipples and rustled between her legs as she shifted to be closer to him. God, she had missed his touch, and as his kisses grew more urgent, hungrier, Liv dropped her mouth open and let him plunge his tongue inside her.

Tenderness had disappeared. His fingers were digging into her flesh and he was dominating her mouth, a hot skilled assault that left her limp and breathing hard, clinging to his arms for support. The fierceness of his possession both startled and excited her, and she suddenly realized there was one important piece of information Sebastian didn't have.

"I have to tell you something," she murmured between kisses, gasping when he nipped her bottom lip.

"Later." Sebastian yanked the sheet down and eyed her breasts with blatant longing.

"No, it's important." She swallowed hard and tried to ignore the response of her body to his piercing gaze. "I never . . . we never . . ." She took a deep breath and forced the awkward words out. "We never had sex. Scarborough and I." Her voice dropped down to a whisper on his brother's name, and she felt her face heating up. This was a conversation she had never expected to have with him.

Sebastian's eyes moved from her chest to hers and his eyebrows lifted. "Are you kidding me?"

She shook her head. "No. I just couldn't."

His hand came up and rubbed his jaw and he shook his head a little as he gave a small laugh. "That's very good to hear. But what the fuck is the matter with my brother? Why the hell would he agree to live with you platonically?"

"I thought he was respecting my feelings, that he was giving me space until I was ready." Now she wasn't sure what any of Scar's motivations had been. Not that it mattered. She was just glad she hadn't shared anything more intimate with Scar than sleeping alongside him.

"I would have never agreed to that," Sebastian said, his hand rising so that his fingers played with the very tip of her nipple.

The unexpected touch sent a jolt through Liv, and she sucked in her breath. "No?"

"No. I wouldn't have been able to survive being so close to you and not touching you. I would have had you."

"Very arrogant." Not that she minded. To hear his possessiveness was sexy, flattering, arousing. "What if I had said no?" Liv realized she was leaning into his touch, and she tried to move back to put force behind her question, but he pinched her nipple between his thumb and forefinger, holding her in place with the desire his touch tripped off.

"I would talk you into it," he said, his other index finger trailing down between her breasts to her belly button and dipping inside briefly before heading farther south. "And you wouldn't regret it."

Right as he reached the top of her pubic bone, he pulled his hand back and rested it on the linens pooling between her thighs. Liv gave a gasp of disappointment. In return, Sebastian gave her a small smile of satisfaction. "You wouldn't regret it, would you, baby?"

She shook her head, her tongue suddenly feeling too thick to speak.

Sebastian yanked the sheet away from her body so that she was completely exposed to him, his palm pushing her knee so that her legs opened. His fingers fluttered over the small strip of hair there, tickling and teasing her. "Would you?"

Finding her voice, she said, "No. I wouldn't regret it."

Her reward was his finger smoothly sliding inside her. Liv gave a tiny moan. It was an unusual angle, with her sitting up, legs out, and the angle of his touch had him stroking her G-spot with unerring accuracy. "Oh, damn," she breathed, her instinct to move backwards, away from the intensity of the pleasure.

But his hand on her thigh held her in place. "Stay."

It was the simplicity of that command that had her going still, her thighs tensing as she tucked her feet behind them for a more comfortable position, her back arching as her hands came down on either side of his arm.

"You are so beautiful," he said, his head dipping so that his lips were on her neck, kissing and sucking lightly.

His shoulder brushed against her chest and Liv shivered, every nerve alive and excited, every inch of her body aware of his. She had refused to think about this for six months, and only in her dreams had she indulged the idea that her sexuality still existed, buried under heavy emotion. But a few skillful kisses, a finger inside her, and a look of lust interlaced with love on Sebastian's face brought all of her desire rushing to the forefront.

She loved sex with him, hot and wet and hard sex, and she rocked her hips into his touch with a total lack of self-consciousness. He made her feel beautiful, sexy, and she wanted to perform for him at the same time that she wanted to please herself. The way his eyes darkened indicated he liked what she was doing and she moved a little faster, pushing him a little deeper inside her.

"That's it," Sebastian breathed.

Liv leaned forward for more leverage and let the sensations sweep her away. The intense pleasure was like a whip, spurring her on to a quick, sharp rhythm, her eyes locked on his.

"Damn, that's sexy," he said. "Did you do this to yourself while I was gone? Did you use a vibrator?"

It hadn't been often, but she had, so she nodded.

"Maybe you don't even need me," he said, his voice teasing.

It hadn't even come close to satisfying her the way he did. "I do need you." She panted, her muscles tightening around his finger, her hips slowing down. "I'm going to come."

"Not yet." He pulled his finger out.

Liv's eyes flew open. "What the hell?" She had been right there, two seconds from completion.

"Shhh," he said, his fingers brushing across her nipples as his lips teased her mouth. "We'll get there. We have all night. I want to take it slow."

Slow could happen later. Now she wanted to feel him inside her, full and throbbing and taking her, while she was one hundred percent awake and aware of what she was doing.

Sebastian was leaning over, his intention clearly to pull her nipple into his mouth, and she knew he wasn't going to enter her yet.

Liv grabbed his head and stopped him. It was her turn to torture.

He looked at her in question.

She gave him a sly smile and moved down over him, gripping his erection firmly with her hand and flicking her tongue across the tip.

The moan he gave was almost as satisfying to her as his touch had been.

CHAPTER SEVEN

Sebastian closed his eyes and gritted his teeth against the onslaught of pleasure. Liv's tongue was tracing slick lines up and down his cock, teasing him, her hand rising and falling slowly on his flesh.

To say he had missed her touch was the understatement of the millennium, and this was different, better, than any time before. There was an edginess to both of them, a need to dive in and take everything, to grab and hold on to their ecstasy. She had always been an enthusiastic lover, but she had never been aggressive, never had that kind of smirk on her face that she was wearing now. Everything seemed sharper, more intense between them.

Her hair slid over her shoulders, a soft auburn wave tumbling down on her creamy flesh as she bent over him. Sebastian had always loved a woman's mouth on him, hell, he couldn't imagine a guy who didn't love this. But now, after nearly losing her entirely, Sebastian was overwhelmed as he watched Liv moving over him.

Sensations both physical and emotional were assaulting him, the beauty of her body arching, the unleashing of all his love for her, the spike of desire with each stroke of her hand, all mixing together in a delicious slow motion. Each touch, each lick, each second, mattered, an intense appreciation for everything that he had just found again after suffering the agony of loneliness for the last six months.

"You're amazing," he told her, resting his hands on her head, the silken tresses of her soft hair surrounding his fingers. He meant the words to encapsulate everything, the way she was caring and giving, the way she loved him, the way she made him laugh, her beauty, the way she was taking him deep inside her mouth right at that very moment.

It was all amazing.

She was amazing.

The strokes got a little faster, his cock slick from her tongue and her mouth, her hand gripping him tightly, each squeeze, each slide, driving him further into ecstasy.

He fought the urge to close his eyes. He wanted to watch her, wanted to see himself disappearing between her lips over and over, wanted to see the curve of her ass moving forward and back with each suck, wanted to admire her hourglass shape.

His body was tight and throbbing and he knew he would come if he waited much longer. But it felt so good, so hot and right, and he pushed it, one more slide of her tongue, one more deep pull where nearly every inch of his cock was covered by her slick warm mouth.

Then grabbing every ounce of willpower he possessed, Sebastian pulled back, pushing Liv's head away from him, shuddering at the pleasure and the loss. He had been right there, and he needed a second to get it under control. Liv was breathing hard, her lips swollen and shiny with moisture, her breasts tempting little mounds right in front of him. He palmed both of them, squeezing her firm smooth flesh, skimming his thumbs across her nipples.

She sighed, eyes half closed in a sexy slumberous look that nearly undid him.

He swung his legs over the side of the bed and told her, "Come here."

"Where?" She didn't look like she had a clue what he was suggesting, but she also looked perfectly open to anything he might suggest.

"On my lap."

"Ooohh." Her eyes darkened and she shifted one leg over his thighs.

Sebastian held her waist as she settled against him, her breasts brushing his chest, her lips hovering in front of his, her damp inner thighs making a teasing light contact with his very hard erection.

"Hi," she said, in a soft flirty voice.

A grin split his face. "Hey. Funny meeting you here."

Her expression went from amused to serious, and Sebastian immediately regretted his words. He hadn't meant to imply anything. It was just a standard expression, a response meant to be funny, not in any way suggestive of where they were, in his brother's house.

God, in his brother's bed.

He was about to open his mouth and apologize,

reassure her, but Liv lifted her hips and with a single motion impaled herself on him. The hot enclosure surrounded him immediately and unexpectedly and Sebastian groaned, gripping her hips tightly. "Oh, damn," he murmured.

"I'll meet you anywhere," she said, her green eyes piercing him. "Remember that."

He needed to hear that, needed to know that she would always be with him, at his side. He could see the love, the loyalty, the devotion in her eyes and he was flooded with gratitude, love, pleasure.

"And I'll love you everywhere. Always."

Sebastian thrust up into her, setting a slow, even rhythm, watching her mouth drift open on her ecstasy, her legs locked around his, her fingers light on his shoulders. She gave the most delightful little hitch of breath every time he pushed up into her, and he kissed her, wanting to catch that breath, wanting to take her inside him, wanting to touch and feel every inch of her.

When the kiss broke, her arms moved down and around, to his knees, and she arched her body, hair cascading back. Sebastian gave a low moan at how sexy she looked, how erotic and free, and he maneuvered one hand between them and stroked her clit.

She came with a cry, the pulses of her orgasm squeezing him and nearly taking him with her. But he wanted this one solo for her, so he gritted his teeth and controlled it, slowing down and just watching her beautifully undulate in her passion.

When she slowed down, Sebastian lifted her off him and onto the bed, needing a position that would let him pound into her, to have total control.

She gave a sigh of disappointment and started to lie down, but he tapped her backside. "Up on all fours, babe."

He needed to take this home.

Liv heard the tightness in Sebastian's voice and immediately obeyed. She knew that sound. He was close to coming, so despite the fact that she felt like she'd lost all control of her muscles from that amazing orgasm, she crawled into position on the middle of the bed. She barely had time to grip the duvet for stability when he pushed inside her.

God, she had missed him, this. He filled her fully, perfectly, deliciously.

He knew just how to stroke to please them both, knew the angle that made her crazy with desire. The thrusts were hard and fast, his hands holding on to her waist with a steel grip. The soft grunts of appreciation that came from him pleased her, had her inner muscles contracting again around him in a satisfying mini-orgasm.

That quivering sent Sebastian over the edge, his grip on her tightening. He exploded and Liv held on to the bed with white knuckles, and on to him with her warm and wet body.

He gave a final shudder, then a short laugh.

"Damn, that was amazing. You're amazing."

What she was, was in love. Liv collapsed on the bed in satisfaction, wanting to turn so she could see him, touch him.

Sebastian fell facedown next to her, falling so completely that Liv bounced up a little off the mattress from the impact. "Don't wake me up for three days," he said.

Liv laughed. "I doubt you'll sleep for seventy-two hours straight."

She expected him to make a crack in return, but he just rolled onto his side next to her and cupped her cheek.

"It feels like I've been running in my sleep for six months," he whispered. "Now that I'm back with the woman I love, I can finally rest."

Liv's heart swelled and she looked deep into his mismatched eyes as she shifted in closer to him. "Then close your eyes and sleep. I love you."

They could both rest now, back in each other's arms.

The black wolf stared at her in the woods, his dark eyes filled with hatred and disdain. He was bigger than the others, stronger, quicker. He led with cunning and an unspoken threat. They were afraid of him, standing behind him uneasily shifting on their paws, one padding back and forth in nervous agitation.

She was alone, the lone human.

And he was going to kill her.

Liv fought the instinctive urge to run, knowing it would make no difference. He would catch her, and then he would have the satisfaction of knowing he'd sent her scrambling in fear.

She swallowed hard, staring him down so he wouldn't hear her panicked and ragged breathing. This wasn't how she wanted it to end, but if she was going to die, she wanted him to have to see her eyes locked on his until the very end.

Then he could take the image of her hurt and disgust through eternity with him.

Fisting her hands, she shifted her feet slightly apart, bracing for the impact.

With a growl, he sprang. . . .

Liv sat straight up in bed, sucking in a lungful of air in panic, eyes darting around the room. It was still dark, Sebastian snug against her under the sheet, sound asleep.

The room was empty, silent, except for the soft snore from Sebastian and the tick of the clock in the hallway. The windows were closed and the room was warm from the heat she'd finally turned on for the fall and upcoming winter.

Nothing was wrong or out of the ordinary, yet her heart was racing, and she had the urgent and persistent feeling that they were in danger.

"Sebastian, wake up." She shook him, feeling guilty about interrupting his sleep, but unable to stop herself.

"What?" he murmured, eyes still closed. His hands snaked out for her. "Climb on up and ride me again, baby."

Normally she would have found his scratchy sleep-voice endearing, but she felt the anxiety creeping across her skin like a spider, covering every inch of her. "We have to go," she told him without preamble.

His eyes shot open. "What? Why? What's the matter?"

Now that she could see he was fully awake, Liv got out of bed and went to the dresser to pull out some clothes to throw on. "We need to get out of here. We're in danger."

Sebastian sat up, on alert, looking around. "I don't see or hear anything."

Pulling on her panties, she told him, "I don't have a solid reason. It's just a feeling. A strong feeling. I dreamt a black wolf came to kill me."

There was a pause, then Sebastian climbed out of bed. "Okay, we'll go to my place. We need to talk about all of this anyway. I'm sure you have questions, and we're going to have to deal with my brother."

Obviously that was the danger she felt . . . they were sleeping in Scarborough's house, and though he was still in New York, there was nothing to prevent him from coming home early.

The full truth of what had happened and who she was hit Liv hard, and she paused in the act of pulling on her jeans. She couldn't wrap her mind around all of this, and she sucked in deep breaths to try to calm herself down, the peace of lying side by side with Sebastian again shattered by reality.

"Hey," he said, coming in front of her, his expression concerned. "It's okay, we'll work it all out. You have a lot to adjust to, but I'm here. It's all okay, Liv, I swear."

She nodded, wanting to believe that, and yanked her pants the rest of the way up. "You've been staying at your place?" Guilt crashed into her. She hadn't even asked where he'd been the last six months once she'd known he hadn't left her. There was a lot they needed to catch up on.

"Yeah. I wasn't planning to stay there long since I thought my brother might figure it out, but I had cash hidden in my bedroom, which I desperately needed and I had to get it. Access to all my accounts has been cut off."

"Your condo is in foreclosure," Liv told him, a lump in her throat as she stepped into sneakers. "Scarborough said he wasn't going to pay your mortgage while you betrayed everyone who loved you, so the bank is in the process of taking it back."

The guilt took an even stronger hold. "I'm sorry. I should have stopped him. I shouldn't have believed him in the first place."

"Liv." Sebastian squeezed her hand. "It's okay. With all the facts in front of you as they were, of course you believed him. There was no evidence of anything else. I'm not upset with you at all. I just wish you hadn't suffered. That hurts me, that you hurt."

She nodded. Now wasn't the time to wallow in damaging emotions. They would need time to heal and process and let go, and they would over the next few months as they started a new life together. Right now they needed to get the hell out.

Five minutes later they were in Liv's car and driving to his place when her cell phone rang in her purse.

"It's four in the morning. Who's calling you?" Sebastian asked, glancing over at her from the driver's seat.

Liv pulled her phone out to check the screen, but the iron grip of fear had already settled around her heart. There was only one person it could be.

The lit-up screen mocked her, the ring loud and jarring in the quiet of the night.

"It's Scarborough."

"Does he usually call you in the middle of the night?"

Liv shook her head and dropped the phone in her lap. "No."

Chapter Eight

"You'd better answer it," Sebastian told Liv, uneasy as he drove, the phone resting in Liv's lap like she was afraid it would bite if she got too close to it.

"No! I can't talk to him."

"But won't he think it's weird that you're not answering?"

She shook her head. "Why would I answer? As far as he knows, I'm sleeping. I have my phone on vibrate at night normally."

Sebastian didn't like the sound of that. He stared at the yellow lines of the road in the dark. "So then why would he call you? It must be important."

The ringing had stopped. "If it's important, he'll leave a voice mail."

As they pulled into Sebastian's condo complex, the phone chimed, indicating that Scar had left a message.

"Shit," Liv whispered.

She looked scared, and that pissed Sebastian off. He hadn't intended to deal with his brother immediately, but it seemed imminent. He wasn't going to have Liv living in fear, nor was he going to have Liv staying in his brother's house any longer.

"It's okay, babe. Can I listen to the voice mail?"

Instead of handing him the phone, she put it to her own ear, punching buttons as he pulled into a free parking spot. She stared through the windshield as she listened. Sebastian turned off the car, feeling impatient.

Finally she hung up the phone and turned to him, her face pale in the beam from the overhead parking lot light. "He wasn't expecting me to answer. He just wanted me to know there is a problem with the venue for the wedding and he's coming home on a five A.M. flight to deal with it."

Sebastian's heart dropped into his gut. "What wedding?" he asked tightly.

Her eyes went wide. "My . . . mine and his. We're supposed to get married next Saturday," she whispered. "I thought you knew."

A roaring flooded his ears and Sebastian's vision blurred from an anger so intense he could taste it on his tongue. "You're marrying him?" he asked, a little growl slipping out before he could control it.

"I thought you knew," she said, her hands fluttering nervously in her lap. "It was a mistake, obviously. . . . I was already having serious doubts before I even knew the truth about you."

Sebastian gritted his teeth. He could feel the change starting, his red-hot anger triggering a shift. He slowed his breathing, fighting it back.

It wasn't anger against Liv, but against Scarborough, against the whole situation.

"I didn't mean to let it get this far. . . . When you disappeared and I thought you stole my money, I was so devastated. He was there for me, a shoulder to cry on, offering me the one thing I've always wanted—a home, children, a family. . . ."

She stopped speaking, her words trailing off, but they rang in Sebastian's ears.

A home.

Children.

A family.

She had contemplated all of that with his brother.

She had intended to marry Scarborough, to have sex with him, to bear his children.

Now he was angry at Liv too, even as he knew it wasn't totally rational.

His jaw throbbed, his fingers twitched, his legs moving restlessly.

Without a word, he got out of the car and stepped out of the streetlight, behind a row of bushes. Kicking off his shoes and tearing off his shirt, he felt the fur sprouting, his knuckles cracking, body arching.

He closed his eyes and gave in to the change.

If Liv had doubted the veracity of any of what Sebastian told her, or what she had seen, and felt in her dreamlike states, she could no longer doubt it.

When Sebastian had stepped out of the car without a word to her, she had followed him, knowing from the look on his face that he wasn't taking the news of her impending marriage well. Wanting a chance to explain, wanting reassurance that he forgave her, she stepped behind the bushes.

And witnessed his shift right in front of her eyes. It was the most fascinating and appalling thing she'd ever seen. It looked painful, with his bones crackling and snapping, and his face contorting, yet she knew it had happened to her, and she didn't remember it. Sebastian had fallen down onto all fours, and in less than thirty seconds, he was fully wolf, shifting restlessly on his paws.

Unsure what to do, Liv just stared, realizing that it was her confession about her wedding that had caused him to shift. Intense emotion. That's what he had told her.

But she had shifted involuntarily, and she didn't know how to force the shift intentionally, so she had no clue what to do now other than to wait for him to return to human form.

Sebastian moved purposefully around his discarded clothes, then looked pointedly at her. She figured he must want her to collect them for him, so she quickly scooped them up.

There was no fear that he would harm her as she moved closer to him, their faces mere inches apart. What she feared was that he wouldn't understand, wouldn't forgive her for intending to marry his brother. "I'm sorry," she whispered, giving in to her urge and pushing her fingers into the thick fur of his neck and rubbing it.

He was warm, inherently masculine even in wolf form, and she suddenly felt very cold and alone when he moved away from her touch. His head turned to the building and then he nuzzled his jeans in her arms with his snout.

She realized he wanted her to go inside his condo. His keys must be in the denim pocket. When she pulled them out and said, "You want me to wait inside?" there was nothing she could consider a confirmation from him.

He simply took off running.

Gone. And she had no way to know where he was going, when he would come back, or if he was willing to discuss any of this with her.

Fingers shaking slightly, Liv readjusted her purse strap, held his clothes against her chest, and went into his condo. There was a staleness in the air, but nothing had changed. Scarborough hadn't disturbed any of Sebastian's possessions. He had clearly intended to let the bank have them, which sickened Liv.

It was hard to believe that the man she'd been living with for the past three months was capable of such callousness. Part of her wanted to think that there was another explanation, because Scarborough had never shown her anything other than kindness and compassion. But it had to have been an act, and that was scary, that she had never picked up on it, that she had been so desperate for companionship, she hadn't noticed anything was off.

Wandering aimlessly around Sebastian's musty and cold condo, she knew she couldn't just sit there, worrying. He had clearly been hurt, and she understood that. She only hoped he would give her the opportunity to have a rational discussion about it.

In the meantime, she needed to cancel her wedding to his brother. Both for herself and her own peace of mind, and for Sebastian's reassurance.

Leaving a note for Sebastian right inside the front door taped to the back of a kitchen stool she had dragged over, Liv put his house key on the stool and left.

* * *

Sebastian paced in front of Nick, who was sitting in his easy chair looking distinctly uneasy, his hair standing on end.

"Why didn't you tell me?" Sebastian was wearing a pair of Nick's sweatpants. Despite the cold, he hadn't bothered asking for a shirt. He actually felt like his anger was generating a heat from his insides out.

"Tell you what?" Nick yawned. "Dude, I need some coffee."

"That Liv is marrying him next Saturday!"

Nick's eyebrows went up. "I don't know," he said. "I guess I figured if you knew about them being together, you knew that too. And I didn't think I should be bringing it up . . . thought it might be a sore subject for you, ya know?"

That it most definitely was. "Well, what the fuck! Why would she do that?"

"I'm guessing you need to talk to her about that, not me." Nick shrugged. "And maybe it was just because he asked and you never did."

That was exactly what he didn't need to hear.

"Thanks a lot."

"Sorry, but what do you want me to say? Bad shit has gone down, man, and I think it's more important that you figure out what you're going to do about it from here."

"I'm going to stop him. I'm going to take over the pack again." Sebastian knew Scarborough would be back at his house around eight. He would deal with him, then go back to his condo and get Liv. The whole thing could be handled in the next two hours.

Nick leaned forward, hands on his knees. "I support you wanting to take leadership again. I'm there with you. What your brother did was beyond wrong. But I can't be a part of murder."

"I'm not going to kill him unless I have to."

That was the difference between him and his brother.

He still had a conscience and moral boundaries.

"Can you get the others and meet me in the woods beyond Scarborough's in about an hour?"

Nick still looked reluctant, but he stood up. "Yeah. What are you going to do?"

"I'm going to Denny's for a steak and egg breakfast."

His cousin gave a snort of laughter. "Nice."

"What?" Sebastian touched his bare stomach, the pit there driving him to distraction. "I need protein."

"We are one wacky family, man."

"Tell me about it."

Liv tried to watch TV, glancing at the time on her cell phone every five minutes. Seven-thirty. Scarborough should be there soon. She was a bundle of nerves, alternating between staring blankly at the TV and checking her phone for both the time and to see if either Sebastian or Scarborough had called her. Neither had, and she was about to crawl out of her own skin if she were left alone any longer.

She jumped when she heard the *whirr* of the garage door going up.

When Scarborough came into the family room, rolling his suitcase behind him, dressed to the nines and looking alert and fresh despite the fact that he couldn't have slept more than a couple of hours, Liv swallowed hard and tried to force a smile.

"Hey," he said, looking surprised. "I didn't think you'd be awake so early. It's Saturday. You usually sleep in."

"I couldn't sleep. How was your flight?" Liv hugged her knees to her chest and mentally rolled her eyes at herself for making such an inane comment.

"Fine. My call didn't wake you up, did it?" He left his suitcase by the kitchen door and came over to her, dropping onto the couch next to her and squeezing her knee.

Shaking her head, she said, "No." Liv searched his eyes for any sort of anger, animosity, evil, but she couldn't see anything. They were just . . . eyes. Maybe a little empty, but that wasn't a crime, was it?

"I missed you." He smiled and leaned forward.

He wanted to kiss her, obviously. Like normal. Like anything was normal anymore.

"We need to talk," she blurted out, unable to fake her way through even a simple kiss. She just couldn't do it.

He sat back, his face calm, a smile still playing across his lips despite the fact that she knew she must look slightly crazy. Liv could feel her fingers shaking on her legs.

"Okay. What about?"

"I . . . we . . . I think we should really think about postponing the wedding."

His smile disappeared. "Why would we do that?"

Liv told herself not to give in to fear. Just be honest, explain how she felt. He would understand. "Because I have all these feelings, all these questions and concerns, and I think the thing is that maybe we rushed this."

"I don't think we rushed it at all. I've cared about you for years, we know each other backwards and forwards. You're just feeling pre-wedding jitters. I think everyone has those."

Damn. He wasn't going to make this easy. "Do you have them?"

"No. But then I never doubt any decision I make."

That was definitely true about him. "See, I doubt every decision I make. I just feel like something is off. . . ." That she was in love with his brother. "And it's not fair to you."

The smile returned, and he looked confident that he would coax her back around. "I'll decide what's fair to me and what's not. I want to be married to you."

"Why?" she blurted out. She had stupidly thought this would be easier. That she would say she had doubts, that he would be hurt and retreat in anger. The wedding would be off, and she would figure out her next step from there.

"Because I love you," he said smoothly, with no hesitation.

For the first time, she thought his words had the hint of a pat answer. Was there true emotion? Or was he just telling her what he thought she wanted to hear?

"I . . ." God, she didn't know what to say. She couldn't even express her gratitude to him for the last six months knowing it was him who had taken Sebastian away from her. "What if the sex between us is terrible?"

That wasn't really what she was concerned with, but she was desperate. She had only half-truths and betrayal, and God knew, she wanted to get out of this without any sort of real confrontation. She wasn't good at conflict. She had always liked everything even.

Which was probably the very reason she had found herself engaged to Scarborough.

He actually laughed. "Given that we're two healthy, experienced adults who care about each other, I can't imagine that would happen."

Oh, she could imagine that it would be quite awful, actually.

"But if that's your main concern, we can settle that very easily, you know." His fingers moved up her leg to her inner thigh and he stroked across the seam of her jeans.

Liv jerked a little at the feel of his touch on her crotch. That wasn't what she had meant, and it felt invasive, not seductive. Panicked, she opened her mouth to say something, anything, but he was already moving in closer.

"I've wanted you for a long time," he said, eyes darkening. "Let me make love to you, Liv."

"Scarborough," she managed, clamping her legs together. "This isn't what I want. No."

"Yes." He was close to her face, intending to kiss her.

Liv shoved his hand off her leg and was about to scramble away from him, when he suddenly froze, nose wrinkling, eyes narrowing.

The transformation on his face was unbelievable. He went from calm and determined to base and ugly, his features contorting in anger.

"You have Sebastian's scent on you."

CHAPTER NINE

At the look on Scarborough's face, Liv felt the fear slam into her like a gale-force wind.

"What?" she said stupidly, even as she dropped her feet to the floor.

This wasn't going to go well.

How could he know about Sebastian? There was obviously a lot she didn't know about werewolf abilities.

"He's not dead, is he? He's not dead, and you fucked him. I can smell him on you!" Scarborough grabbed her arm and shook her. "Answer me."

She shot up off the couch and stumbled backward, tripping over the coffee table. "I don't know what you're talking about. You told me Sebastian just skipped town. Why would he be dead?"

"Don't be cute." Scarborough stood up slowly, his hands curled into fists. "You know everything, don't you?"

Though the power of his presence, his height, the strength of his arms, the broadness of his shoulders intimidated her, Liv didn't want to cower. Now she knew the whole truth, and it wasn't a pretty one. Scarborough had played her for a total fool, and none of his affection for her had been real.

"Yes. I know that I'm a werewolf too, and you didn't bother to tell me. I know you lied to me about Sebastian. That you tried to kill him." She started to back up slowly, wanting distance between them.

"Is that what he told you? Very interesting, and very pathetic on your part." Scarborough shook his head in disgust. "He just walked back into your life and you fell for his lies, and let him right back into your pants."

He was the one lying, she knew that. She trusted Sebastian.

But it still hurt when Scarborough said, "You're blind, Liv. Totally blind. How long are you going to let him keep screwing you? What's in it for you? I'd bet this house he still didn't ask you to marry him."

He hadn't. But they had talked about a future together. It was implied. She knew that.

But anything she said was going to sound stupid and defensive. So she just tilted her chin up and said, "I'm not going to discuss this with you if you're going to talk to me like that. I appreciated at the time that you helped me out and were a friend to me when Sebastian disappeared, but the truth is, I never would have needed that if you hadn't betrayed your own brother. So I owe you nothing. No thanks and no explanations."

He gave a short laugh. "So you're going to stand by your piece-of-shit man, is that it? Well, more power to you, honey. Enjoy a miserable life in poverty with an unemployed man who will never commit to you."

Liv just turned on her heel and headed for the door, not wanting him to see that he knew how to hit on all her worst insecurities. She craved commitment, a permanency, had a neediness about her because she'd lost her parents so young. She knew that. Which was why she was going to be content with whatever Sebastian offered her. If it was genuine and with love, which she knew it was, then her insecurities had no business forcing him into something he didn't need or want.

"Why are you wearing shoes in the house at eight in the morning?" he asked.

Liv didn't answer, just kept walking, grateful she did have shoes on. She wouldn't have to pause when she went through the door and got the hell out.

"I guess I should be glad you fucked him somewhere other than my own bed."

She couldn't help it. She reacted, pausing, her shoulders giving an involuntary jerk.

"Oh, you bitch," he breathed from right behind her, his voice shaking with fury.

Liv walked faster. Scarborough grabbed her arm and drew her up short. Shocked at the rough grip of his hand on her arm as he forced her to turn and face him, Liv yelled, "Let go of me!"

"Not until you give me a piece of the ass you keep letting my brother have so willingly."

Bile rose in her throat. "You can't be serious."

"Oh, I'm very serious." Scarborough yanked her purse out of her hand and tossed it fifteen feet back into the family room. "Were your keys in there? Why don't you bend over and get them?"

Disgust and fear swept over her, turning her skin clammy, and a hot anxiety rose in her mouth. She didn't know what to do. If she went for her purse, she would be nowhere near a door, and he would have her on the ground in a minute. There was no way she could fend him off if he truly wanted to rape her.

Her fear was amusing him. A sick smile was smeared across his face.

"Not your first choice? You know, you're right. I'd actually like to see your face when I'm fucking you. Back up against that wall."

Without further thought beyond the immediate desperate urge to get away from him, Liv backed up, then turned and ran, hurling the door to the garage open and darting through it. She tried to pull it closed behind her, but she just managed to hit him in the shoulder with it. Sprinting across the concrete, she expected to feel him grabbing on to her, but a glance back showed he was just standing in the doorway.

Maybe he hadn't been serious. Maybe it had just been a sick mind game.

"Go ahead and run," he told her, his voice hard and cold. "I like the chase. And you know I always get what I want."

She did know that about him.

And she also saw that as she left the garage he was shifting to wolf.

Her first thought was to run down the driveway to the main road. A car was bound to pass in a minute or two. But then that car could very well just be Scarborough. A glance at the woods as she ran across the grass showed her a lone wolf standing on the edge of the tree line. It was too far away to see who it was, but she veered towards him. If it was Sebastian, she had to assume that, angry with her or not, he would protect her. If it was one of their cousins, she would pray for the same.

But then as she got to the edge of the woods, ten feet from the wolf, she realized there were three more with the first, none of them recognizable to her in wolf form. She just knew they weren't Sebastian.

A glance behind her showed Scarborough running effortlessly behind her, keeping pace about twenty feet back.

She didn't know what the wolves could understand, having no real memory of being one herself, so she just ran past them yelling, "Help me!" hoping they would understand.

Then her dream popped into her head as she leapt over brush and a fallen log, her lungs already straining with the effort of running as fast as she could. The cold and the wind slashed her cheeks as she remembered standing in the woods in her dream, facing down the dark wolf with the angry eyes.

While the others simply watched.

Scarborough was the dark wolf.

She was truly alone. No one was going to help her.

Slowing down, she realized for the first time in her life, that being alone wasn't the enemy. Fear was.

Liv halted her steps. Whirling on one foot, she turned and confronted Scarborough.

He drew up short, obviously surprised that she had stopped running. Back twenty or thirty feet were the other wolves, moving warily as they watched.

No Sebastian.

"Go ahead," she told Scar. "Rape me, kill me, do whatever you want. But I'm going to fight you. And I'm going to spit in your face while you do it."

Scarborough stared at her, his dark eyes flashing, his teeth baring, a low growl deep in his throat causing the hairs on her arms to stand on end.

But she refused to let that stop her. She couldn't outrun him. At least she was going to have some dignity and go down letting him see the disgust on her face and the hatred in her eyes. She leaned over and picked up a stick and threw it at him.

He jumped out of the way, but it still clipped his back.

"Just do it!" she screamed.

Watching him hunch down low, she knew he was going to spring, that he would be on her in seconds and then it would all be over. Liv narrowed her eyes and focused on his canine teeth to steady herself.

Her own teeth hurt, her fingers tingled, her legs twitched.

And right as Scarborough sailed through the air and landed on her, Liv realized she was in wolf form.

She didn't know what she was doing, but instinct sent her straight for his throat.

Sebastian knew something was wrong the second he reached the house. Both Scarborough and

Liv's cars were in the garage, and the door was open. He was still in wolf form and he headed for the woods, picking up the scent of the entire pack immediately, including Scar.

He also smelled the sickly sweet smell of Liv's fear.

Damn it. Why the hell hadn't she stayed at his condo like he'd meant for her to do?

Of course, he hadn't really told her that. He'd been so angry, his shift imminent, that he hadn't communicated anything to Liv at all. She had probably been wondering what he was doing.

And now she was in danger, and if anything happened to her, he'd never forgive himself.

He got to the woods in time to see Liv shift and meet Scar's charge head-on.

Jesus.

She could never overpower Scarborough, and Sebastian's adrenaline pushed him faster. This was not a fight for domination. He could see from his brother's stance and blows that he intended to kill.

Liv got in a good bite on Scarborough's throat before he knocked her to the ground. The yelp of pain she gave infuriated Sebastian. He jumped, landing on his brother's side, shoving him off Liv and tumbling to the ground with him.

He had the element of surprise. His brother didn't immediately react, and Sebastian pinned him and went for the throat. They locked eyes, brother on brother, and for a split second, Sebastian thought about showing him some kind of mercy. Banishment. Retribution.

But then Scarborough slashed his claws across Sebastian's face, his own a mask of fury and hatred.

The pain was jarring, but minor compared to the revelation that his brother would try to kill him again. He would keep trying over and over. He hated Sebastian that much, wanted power that perversely, and maybe someday he would succeed.

So without allowing himself time for further hesitation, Sebastian bared his teeth and went in for the kill.

Liv lay on the ground naked and shivering, watching the other wolves tentatively move around Scarborough's body.

Sebastian had killed Scarborough. He had saved her from certain death.

She had almost died, and then had watched in total fear and panic as the man she loved had been locked in battle. Now it was over, and she had shifted back to human without even being aware of what she was doing.

Sebastian had moved away from the body, to the edge of the river, the very river in which his brother had tossed him six months earlier, and sat on his haunches. He gave a low, mournful howl, the sound wafting over Liv and settling into her bones like the coldest winter wind.

When she glanced back at Scar, she saw that in death his body had shifted back to man. One by one the cousins shifted, and Liv was too shocked to even think about the fact that they were all as naked as she was. But Nick had a duffel bag behind the trees, and he was dressed again in under two minutes, before silently tossing her a long sweatshirt.

She caught it, tugging it on, forcing herself to

stand up. Nick was dressing Scarborough's body with the help of his brother Jackson, and she couldn't watch. It was too appalling. The remnants of her clothes were scattered over several feet, and her jeans were torn, but she slipped into them anyway. Her boots had holes in the feet, but she put those on too, needing a barrier against the wind, and maybe against what had just happened. She walked gingerly over to where Sebastian was sitting by the water.

The air was crisp and clear, the river gurgling busily along, the smell of the water clean and pure.

Liv sat down next to him, hugging her knees to her chest, searching for the words she needed to say to him. In the end she simply said, "Thank you for saving my life."

Tiny fish hurried through the water with a vast sense of purpose and she focused on them, unable to look at Sebastian. She knew he was shifting back to human, felt the movement, sensed . . . something. The wolf that clearly lived in her had instincts she'd never even been aware of before. Didn't know how to use.

But even after she could see Sebastian's feet out of the corner of her eye, he still didn't speak. Liv took a deep breath, tried to quiet her mind, slow down her racing heart, stop the trembling in her fingers.

Then suddenly his hand was in hers, warm and strong and comforting.

The tears sprang up and she looked at him. "I'm sorry about the wedding. I understand if you don't want to be with me. I do. And I'll be fine, honestly. I think for the first time in my life I have come to terms with being alone. I'm just asking for you or Nick or somebody to help me understand how to handle the change . . . what to expect."

She would be okay. She actually believed that.

But Sebastian took their entwined hands and kissed her fingers one by one. "You don't have to be alone. Liv, I was never angry at you. I was angry at Scarborough, at the situation, at the thought of you sharing a life with another man, a life that should have been mine. I was angry with myself for not being the one to ask you to be my wife."

The tears she'd managed to contain spilled over, trailing down her cheeks. "Maybe it's time to just let some of that anger go, for all of us."

"I agree. And I hope that you'll be willing to come home with me."

She wanted to be with him more than anything, wanted the chance to pick up the pieces of their lives, together. She nodded. "Of course."

"Then let's deal with this and be on our way." Sebastian leaned forward and kissed her hard. "God, Liv, when I saw the two of you fighting like that . . . I would have died if something had happened to you."

Liv felt him shudder and she slid her hands around him and lightly caressed his back. "But it didn't. It's fine. Everything is going to be fine."

He gave a hard nod. "It is. Because I love you and always will."

"I love you too." More than there could ever be words to express.

CHAPTER TEN

The bride stepped out of the building into the moonlight, a smile of happiness on her face. She was a few years older, her gown one of greater sophistication than what she'd worn at her first wedding. Her groom was dark-haired and handsome, his hand tenderly on the small of her back, his expression one of adoration.

The evening air smelled like spring, dewy and fresh, with a damp chill in it. The grass was soggy, but the bride merely laughed and fell into the groom's arms as he danced with her in wide sweeping circles. The guests watched and clapped and laughed and chatted, until one by one they wandered off, leaving the bride and her groom alone.

When he kissed her, man to wife, the howling rose up in the distance.

It didn't bring the fear it had on her first wedding night.

It brought the comfort of being in the arms of the man she loved while family, their pack, expressed their approval to the moon in the woods around them.

Liv woke up slowly, the contentment of the dream lingering, making her sigh in pleasure as she rolled over and reached for Sebastian. The bride, Liv's great-grandmother, had been happy with her groom, her new life, and that was reassuring to see.

It was Liv's wedding day now.

It was spring, just like it was for the bride's special day in her dream.

A new beginning for both of them.

Sebastian stirred a little, reaching to wrap his arm around her, his eyes still closed. "Happy wedding day," he murmured.

Liv snuggled against his warm chest. Sebastian had proposed right after Scarborough had died, after they had dealt with all the logistics of telling the police they had all been fishing and Scarborough had been attacked by a wolf. That had been six months earlier, and while life as a werewolf has taken some adjustment, Liv was truly and blissfully happy.

"It's going to be a beautiful day." The timing was right. It felt like everything had come full circle. A year earlier she had been mourning his disappearance, now she had Sebastian forever.

"And you're a beautiful bride."

"Are you sure we shouldn't have spent the night apart last night?" Liv asked, even as she dropped a little kiss on his shoulder. "It seems weird to wake up together on our wedding day."

His eyes opened and he pulled her on top of

him, giving her a deep, long, satisfying kiss. "If we'd spent the night apart, I wouldn't be able to do this."

A little shift of her hips, and he was deep inside her.

Liv sighed in pleasure, still relaxed and sleepy, his body hard and solid beneath her. "That's very true," she breathed.

They moved together in a lazy, slow rhythm, her nipples brushing against his chest. Everything felt warm and snuggly and sexy, her heart filled with love, her body responding instantly to him as it always did.

When she had a delicious and long orgasm, her hips spread wide over him, Liv stared into Sebastian's eyes.

"I can't wait until you're my wife," he said, pumping a little more frantically inside her.

"Me, either. Just a few more hours." She clenched her muscles around him. "So I guess that was my last single-lady orgasm. It was a good one."

His eyebrows shot up. "We still have a whole hour until we have to be anywhere. I think you have another orgasm or two in you."

She laughed. "I wasn't trying to challenge you."

But he got serious. "I'll always do whatever I can to make you happy."

Her heart swelled at his sincere expression. "I am happy."

She was. Every minute with him.

As happy as a bride on her wedding day.

Smoke on the Water

BIANCA
D'ARC

PROLOGUE

"**O**h, crap."

Donna Sullivan realized her mistake almost immediately as four big Chinese guys stood up from a table in the rear of the restaurant she'd just entered. All of them were staring at her as they headed her way and they didn't look friendly.

Maybe she'd asked a few too many pointed questions in the wrong places. She was new to all this femme fatale stuff. She'd only been recruited to join a top-secret military team a few weeks ago and then, only by default. She'd earned the dubious honor because she was immune to the contagion that had the country's top scientists and a select group of Special Forces operatives scrambling to not only keep it secret but to contain it before anyone else died.

It looked like Donna had gained the attention of some of the Chinese mobsters she'd been looking for, but in a really bad way. Cursing the tinkling bell over the door, she sprinted out of the restaurant and down the street as fast as her legs

would carry her. She had to get away. She wasn't
far from the rooms her partner, CIA Agent John
Petit, had insisted on renting in a rundown building off Grant Street. Maybe she could get there before those guys caught up with her. Maybe if she
just cut through this alley . . .

Donna ran for the narrow opening, trying to
evade pursuit. Those seriously scary guys were definitely following her. A quick glance down the
street before she turned into the alley confirmed
they were running after her. She took off, looking
over her shoulder to check the mouth of the alley
when a big hand reached out of nowhere, grabbing her around the waist.

The unknown assailant dragged her into a dark
doorway. It shut ominously behind her with a soft
click. A hard male body pressed up against her as
one big palm covered her mouth and his other
arm held her around the middle. Had she gone
from the frying pan into the fire?

Pounding feet sounded just beyond the flimsy
door. She did her best not to make a sound. The
guys who were chasing her were definitely bad
guys. She didn't want to betray where she was.
She'd rather take her chances with this lone assailant than with the four who had been chasing
her. She liked the odds better, even though she
was no Chuck Norris. Hell, she wasn't even a
Chuck E. Cheese. She had zero combat skills, but
she'd go down fighting, regardless of how badly
she actually acquitted herself.

"What the hell did you think you were doing?" A
tense whisper sounded near her ear. She knew that
tone of consternation with an edge of steel.

Thank the good Lord, it was John, her so-called partner in this mess of a mission.

He let go of her mouth as she relaxed into his hold.

"I was trying to get the information you seem so reluctant to go after," she challenged, keeping her voice low.

John let her go completely and started walking into the dark interior of the hallway. He'd dragged her into the little-used alley entrance to their building. She followed him down the short hall, up one flight of stairs, and into their rented rooms.

"Who's the trained agent here?" He turned on her as soon as she'd locked the door behind them.

"Dude. Do not pull that on me." She tugged her shoulder pack off and plopped it with more force than was necessary on the console table near the door. The place had come with the bare bones of furniture. "I know you were a marine, but what do jarheads know about detective work? Your sister at least was a cop before joining this screwed-up team. If she were here, I can just about guarantee that she wouldn't be sitting on her butt twiddling her thumbs, waiting for the information to fall from the sky into her lap."

"You don't know a thing about my sister. And for that matter, you don't know a thing about me either."

She backed down, duly reprimanded. He wasn't saying anything but the truth, no matter how much it might hurt. "You're right. I don't."

He grabbed his knapsack and started gathering the few things he'd left lying around the small apartment. He was packing.

"Go change your shirt and put your hair up. Then get your stuff together. We have to leave."

"What? Why?"

"It won't take them long to figure out where you went. They lost you in the alley. There are only a few places you could have gone from there. They'll check them. All they have to do is talk to the building manager or any of the tenants who've seen you."

She hadn't thought of that. She went into the room she'd been using and tugged off her red T-shirt, replacing it with a blue tank top. "How did you know where to find me?" She raised her voice to be heard as she quickly scraped her hair into a ponytail and donned a baseball cap.

"I was watching the street and saw you run out of the restaurant. You're quick, I'll give you that. I almost didn't catch you in time. I swear, Sullivan, you took ten years off my life."

She raced around the small room, gathering her belongings and stuffing them into her knapsack. She'd packed light for this trip. John had insisted. She was glad of it now, though she'd fought him at the time.

Considering they were now on the run because of her, she thought maybe she should cut John a little slack. He might be autocratic and a total chauvinist, but he was also proving to be right about a lot of things. Damn the man.

"It's okay." She stood in the doorway to her small room, ready to go. "You returned the favor when you grabbed me like that. I thought I'd traded four goons for one possible ax murderer."

He sobered. "You could have." His gaze pinned her, deadly serious.

"Yeah, I see that now. I'm sorry, John."

"Sorry?" He smiled tightly as he checked the windows, then peered through the peephole. "I never thought I'd see the day you'd apologize for your headstrong ways." She would have argued with him about his rather insulting phrasing but she saw his entire body tense. Something was up. "Do you have everything?" His voice was pitched low and tense.

She nodded, slipping her knapsack over her shoulder.

"One of your friends from the alley is in the hall, talking to Mr. Chen." John kept his eye to the peephole. "He just flipped open his cell phone. Calling for reinforcements, I bet." His expression turned steely as he pulled back from the door and turned to her. "Hold this. I'll be right back." He handed her his bag, which was even lighter and smaller than hers, before opening the door. He shot out like a racehorse just released from the starting gate.

She heard muffled thuds through the closed door as she raced toward it. She pressed her eye to the peephole just in time to see one of the big bruisers who'd chased her go down in a heap at John's feet. She knew John was a martial arts teacher of very high rank, but she'd never really seen him in action before.

The guy on the floor hadn't even had time to draw the big gun she now saw he wore under his jacket. John relieved the unconscious goon of both his gun and his wallet, doing a fast, careful search of his pockets while he was at it. When John stood, she opened the door and met his gaze.

Gone was the exasperation she usually saw from him. All amusement had fled as well.

The man who looked at her was a hardened warrior. Intellectually, she'd known John was a tough guy. She'd just never seen him like this before. It was impressive, to say the least.

He held out one hand to her and she followed his unspoken summons without thinking. She was at his side in ten steps, holding out his pack to him. He took it, then tugged her hand into his as he turned toward the exit—not the front door, but the door they'd used minutes before. He didn't let go of her hand until they were down the alley and on the opposite street, joining the busy foot traffic prevalent in this part of town.

He let go of her hand only to put his arm around her waist and tuck her into his side. They strolled down the street, just another tourist couple out for a stroll.

"Where are we going?" Donna asked, trying to look nonchalant and no doubt failing.

"The airport. This town is too hot for us right now and I think we've learned all we can here. While you were out stirring up trouble, one of my bugs paid off. I've got a location and a name that matches one of the original research team members."

She was astonished his methods had actually worked. "Really? Who?"

"Dr. Elizabeth Bemkey. She's in Tennessee right now according to what I heard."

He looked like the cat who'd swallowed the canary as he smiled down at her. She squelched the impulse to wipe that silly grin right off his handsome face. The man could be truly infuriating at times.

"So we're going to Tennessee?"

"Looks that way. Ever been fly-fishing?"

Chapter One

They touched down in Tennessee after catching a connecting flight out of Houston. The plane dropped them in Nashville, about an hour and change from their destination. John rented a car and they were off. A straight shot across the state on Interstate 40, then a little trek on a state highway and they were there.

John made good use of the time, placing a few calls and coordinating with the folks back at Fort Bragg, where their team was currently based, while Donna drove. She had a bit of a lead foot, but was competent behind the wheel. They entered White County and turned off at Cookeville, which was a larger city, where they could pick up appropriate clothing and fishing gear at one of the big chain discount stores.

"I'll get some fishing gear while you pick out some clothes," he told Donna when they entered the giant store. "Get stuff for a leisurely vacation by the lake. Make sure you include darker colors for night work and a hat for daytime. If we go out on the water, the sun is going to be tough on your fair skin."

She had looked at him strangely when he made the observation, but thankfully hadn't remarked upon it. John had spent all too much time lately fantasizing about her skin. Was it as soft as it looked? Would she be sensitive to his merest touch?

Damn. He was doing it again. He shook himself and refocused on his task. He needed the bare bones of fishing gear. Just enough to make him look like he really was going fishing. He'd made reservations at a fishing camp that was nearly next door to Dr. Bemkey's palatial home on the lakeshore. It had been her husband's house, and as they'd been going through a very messy divorce for the past year or more, nobody had expected her to be there. They'd sent agents to check, of course, but her husband claimed not to have seen or heard from her in quite some time. Apparently they did all their talking through their lawyers at this point.

But according to the information he'd intercepted in San Francisco, Dr. Bemkey was not only staying in her ex-husband's mansion, she was working from it. It was up to them to confirm the information and figure out what she was up to.

Donna caught up with John while he was trying on vests with a few million pockets for fishing lures and tackle.

"You look like a dork in that." Her dryly amused voice came from behind him.

He turned, holding his arms out so she could get a good look at the ensemble. "You think so?"

"Oh, yeah. If you were going for the Poindexter

look, you nailed it." Her luscious lips quirked up in a half grin that he found utterly captivating.

"Question is"—he moved closer, his voice dropping so only she could hear him—"would a young hottie like you be seen cavorting on the lake with a dork like me?" His arms slipped around her waist, but he resisted the urge to pull her against his body. He could get away with just so much in the name of their cover. If he started to grope her in the sporting goods section, it wouldn't be to convince people they were together. No, it would all be for his own enjoyment.

"Cavorting?" Her tone was the slightest bit breathless as her palms settled over his chest. Damn, that felt good.

"They're a little more old-fashioned here in Tennessee than they were in San Francisco. We'll draw less attention if we show up as a married couple."

"Married?" The word whispered out of her mouth and it was all he could do to stop himself from leaning in and capturing her lips with his own.

"How does Mrs. John Pettigrew sound? Close enough to my real name that it'll be easy to remember?"

Mutely, she nodded. Something weird was going on here. She looked utterly stunned and he was feeling more than a little odd too. He'd never been on an undercover assignment with a female operative before. Certainly not one that required them to pose as lovers. Why did this feel like so much more than a simple mission?

"So what do you say? Is the vest too much?" He

stepped back, trying to resolve the weird vibes in the air with a change of subject.

"The camo vest with the camo hat is definitely too much." She flipped through the rack of vests to find something in a solid color. "How about this one?" She held up a solid green vest.

He'd automatically gone for the camo, but she was probably right. The only place he'd be wearing the vest was on the lake itself. He probably wouldn't be traipsing through the woods in it.

"It looks good." He took a quick look at the size she'd picked. It would fit. He threw it in the cart with the stuff she'd picked out. He noticed she'd gotten him some things. "You bought me shirts?"

"And shorts," she confirmed. "If you need to go for a swim, it's best to be prepared." She held up a pair of board shorts that would double as swim trunks should the need arise. They were his size too.

He shot her a suspicious look. "Have you been checking out my ass? You got all my sizes right."

"As if." She flopped the shorts back into her cart. "It's not that hard to differentiate between large and extra large, John," she protested, but he saw the slight flush of color on her fair cheeks and was oddly flattered. "Is this stuff yours too?" She pointed to a pile of gear he'd been toting around. He hadn't gotten a cart. He'd just been carrying the stuff.

"Yeah." He picked up the tackle box and gear, loading it into her cart. "Okay." He took charge of the now stuffed cart as they headed out of the sporting goods section. "Two more departments and we're done."

"Two?" she questioned, walking beside him down the wide aisle of the super store.

"Yeah, I want to get some supplies. A cooler and some food. Snacks, beer, chips. The kind of stuff people would bring for a week at a fishing cabin."

"And the other department?"

"Rings," he said simply. She didn't say another word until they started debating the merits of various kinds of potato chips in the grocery section of the store.

When they finally moved on to the jewelry counter, John picked out two simple gold bands and a petite engagement ring. They were posing as newlyweds of moderate means. The diamond was small, but it still took her breath away when she tried it on. John paid for the rings quietly and stuffed them in his pocket as they left the store.

He let her drive again as they headed for the last leg of their journey while he was busy taking all the tags off their purchases. They stopped at a fast food place on the highway for a quick meal and he got rid of the evidence of their shopping trip, throwing out the bags and tags in the garbage.

"Check out the billboard." John pointed to a big man grinning down at them from a huge advertising board that looked over the fast food joint's parking lot. The twenty-foot-tall image was of a portly man in overalls. He had a big gap between his front teeth as he grinned, holding up a giant fish on a line.

" 'Bubba's Bass Tours,' " Donna read from the sign. "'Let Bubba guide you to the best fishing holes in Tennessee. Daily and hourly rates.' " Donna took a sip of her soda. "Now I know we're in the South."

"Did you see the live bait machine near the drive-thru?" His eyes reflected humor.

"The what?"

"The bait machine. Put in a couple of quarters and out pops a plastic container full of wiggling worms."

"You're kidding."

"'Fraid not." He saluted her with his burger before taking another healthy bite.

"I guess there's not much else to do in the area but fish. Seems to be the main occupation of folks around here. Even the guys in line in the fast food place were trading fish stories."

"Yes, ma'am. We're in lake country up here. Too bad we can't enjoy any of the fishing-related activities."

"You like fishing?"

"I used to have a dune permit for my four-wheel drive," he admitted with a hint of pride. "I've been known to cast a line or two of a morning."

"I had a neighbor that was into it. He had plastic tubing mounted on the front of his dune buggy to hold the fishing poles. Don't tell me you've got that kind of setup."

"Once upon a time, I did," he admitted with a chuckle. "I'm a lot more low key nowadays."

"Thank goodness for that."

Donna finished her burger and rolled up the paper it had been wrapped in, shoving it all in the paper bag for easy disposal. John did the same and hopped out of the car to throw out the garbage. A few minutes later, they were on the road again.

She drove again as he snoozed in the passenger seat, his new camo fishing hat pulled over his eyes. She was pleased that he wasn't going all macho on her about the driving. Almost every man she'd dated had insisted on driving everywhere as if she wasn't to be trusted behind the wheel or something. John apparently felt comfortable enough not only to let her drive but to nap while she did it. She liked that about him.

In fact, she liked a lot of things about him. He could be an overbearing, pigheaded fool at times, like most men she knew, but he also had some endearing qualities. His playfulness on their shopping expedition was new and completely attractive. She thought he must finally be getting comfortable with her. It gave her a warm feeling.

She'd sensed his disappointment when she'd been assigned to work with him. He was a man of action, used to being in the field, in combat. She was an albatross around his neck. Or so he'd thought. The foolishness she had committed in San Francisco was at least partly because she had wanted to prove herself to him.

She didn't want to be an albatross. She wanted to be part of the team—a full contributor to their mission. She still wasn't sure what she could contribute. She wasn't a soldier, cop, or top scientist like the rest of the team members but she could learn. She knew how to shoot. She'd had to spend a couple of memorable hours at a firing range with John to prove she could hit a target. He'd seemed impressed, but with John's poker face, it was hard to tell what he was thinking most of the time.

He'd personally approved her to carry a weapon and had trained her in the care and use of the special toxic darts they used to destroy zombies. Years of lab work to earn her master's degree in chemical engineering had helped her get used to the strict protocols necessary for handling such dangerous ammunition.

Despite all her work to this point, if not for her immunity, she would never have been asked to join the team. She knew the truth. She understood that she was seen as the weakest link in the group. Instead of letting it annoy her, as she had in the beginning of this venture, she saw it as a challenge now. She worked extra hard to prove herself and was glad when she got those little signs of approval from her stoic partner.

As she pondered it all, the car rounded a curve on the mountain road and Donna suddenly beheld the most amazing sight she'd ever seen through a car window.

"Holy moly," she muttered, unable to keep from exclaiming at the sight that met her eyes. They were riding along the side of a mountain, about to turn onto a two-lane road that would take them over the top of a massive hydroelectric dam.

"What is it?" John roused from his nap, plucking the silly fishing hat off his face to look around.

"Sorry. I didn't mean to wake you. I've just never seen anything like this before in person."

"What? The dam?" He looked at her, one tawny eyebrow quirking upward in an amused question mark.

"They don't have these things on Long Island," she grumbled, turning onto the dam itself. To one side was a massive lake that stretched as far as she could see. On the other side was a sheer drop down the side of the dam. She put both hands on the steering wheel, feeling just a little trepidation at riding along the top of such a thing. Only this comparatively thin wall of concrete held back a massive amount of water.

"So you're a city girl?" He sat up and took a look around seeming to enjoy the view.

"Come on. I know you've seen the file they have on me. You know I was born and raised on Long Island."

"Yeah, but hearing about it from you is different than reading it from a piece of paper."

She'd give him that. "I hear from your sister that you two are from the Island too."

John nodded. "We grew up in Lynbrook. But you're a Suffolk County kid, aren't you?"

She hated the way he turned the conversation back to her every time she asked a question about him. "Smithtown. But you already knew that."

He nodded, a smug smile telling her he knew she was miffed. "We're over the dam. You can release your death grip on the steering wheel now." His words were soft. Almost . . . understanding?

She looked around and realized they'd crossed over the dam while he had been distracting her with his questions. She consciously released the fingers of one hand from the wheel. He was right, darn it. She had been holding the thing way too hard. Her knuckles were white until she relaxed her fingers.

"Where to now, navigator?" They'd come to the exit he'd told her to look for. She took it and waited at the bottom of a short ramp.

"Make a right. There should be a sign some-where up ahead for the fishing camp. We've got a cabin reserved for the week. I asked for one on the edge of the property. I told the guy we were newly-weds and wanted a little privacy." He winked at her. "So do your best to look happy when we get there, okay?"

"Don't worry. I took a few acting classes in undergrad. I'm sure I can fake not despising you for a few minutes."

He laughed out loud at her insult. They'd been trading barbs since almost the first day they started working together. It was comfortable for them and had morphed into an odd sort of affection. The more they teased each other, the closer they became.

She found the sign and turned into a wide gravel drive. "This place looks kind of rustic."

There was a main building that advertised itself as both an office and a bait shop. She could see little cabins scattered around through the woods. They were set far enough apart, and the woods were thick enough, to give the illusion of privacy.

"This place borders the Bemkey estate on one side and provides direct access to the lakefront. It's perfect for our purposes."

"Convenient." She pulled up, parking the car to the side of the office door.

John grabbed her hand before she could open her door and get out of the rental car. She looked at him, meeting his all too serious gaze.

"Give me your left hand, Donna."

She caught her breath as he took her hand in his, slipping the gold bands he'd bought onto her finger. The atmosphere was charged. The air stilled as they shared the intimate moment. She didn't dare breathe as John moved closer, placing a chaste kiss on her lips. When he pulled back, he was smiling.

"I've never given a girl a ring before. I thought the moment should be marked in some way."

His gaze held hers as he searched her expression. She didn't know what to feel. The mere brush of his lips against hers had knocked her world off its axis. It would take a few minutes to recover.

Movement over John's shoulder made her look away. An old guy in an even sillier fishing hat than John's was grinning at them through the passenger-side window. John followed her gaze. Seeing the man, John opened the door, greeting the older gent with some friendly banter. She knew her face was flushed with embarrassment at being caught like a couple of teenagers necking in her father's car as she got out on the driver's side.

The man was named Murray, she discovered, and he had an accent so thick, she had to listen carefully to figure out what in the world he was saying. John didn't seem to be having the same problem as he went into the office with their garrulous host. Donna followed behind, watching as John signed them in as husband and wife. She accepted Murray's congratulations on their supposed recent nuptials and was glad when John escorted her back outside with a wave to their new friend.

He settled her in the passenger seat and took the wheel for the first time since leaving the airport in Nashville. She realized why a minute later as he deliberately got "lost" looking for their cabin in order to check out the surrounding cabins and learn the layout of the fishing camp.

"There's a little map on the back of the rental agreement," Donna told him as they turned around for the second time on the narrow gravel road.

"I know." He spared her a withering glance as he backed the car into a three-point turn. "It's just easier to see things in person first so I'll be able to judge whether the scale of that so-called map is accurate."

Donna gave up. He knew what he was doing, even if it didn't seem like it to her. "A little communication would go a long way in this relationship, John."

He grinned at her as he started down the gravel road again. "Now you really sound like a wife."

She had to laugh. She'd heard her mother make the same kind of sarcastic observation to her dad all her life. "Yeah, I guess you're right."

"You're right too," he surprised her by saying. "I had some time to think on the plane and as you drove. A lot of our problems in San Francisco were caused by my not telling you what I was doing. Am I right?"

She considered his words and the conciliatory tone he'd spoken them in. It felt like he was extending an olive branch. She'd be a fool not to take it. She really didn't want to fight with him.

"It felt like you weren't doing anything when it turned out you had your reasons, and methods I didn't know about. It felt like I was being kept in the dark."

"Which is entirely my fault." He shook his head once as he concentrated on the road. "My only excuse is that I'm used to working on my own. I don't usually explain myself to anyone. In my current line of work, I can't. Secrecy has become a way of life for me. I'm sorry I didn't fill you in, Donna. You're new to all this and Commander Sykes made a point of asking me to take you under my wing and teach you what I could. I haven't held up my end of that bargain."

She was floored by his admission. "It's okay. I haven't been the easiest person to get along with either. I get a little sarcastic when I feel out of my depth. I've been feeling out of my depth since I woke up in the woods back on Long Island. Actually, even before that, when my boyfriend turned out to be a zombie."

They hadn't talked much about the incident that had brought her to the team of zombie hunters. She'd been doing her best to forget it, but maybe that hadn't been such a good idea after all. She knew she had to deal with the fear and pain of betrayal sooner or later. Especially if she could be confronted by the creatures again.

"How did it happen?" His gentle tone invited confidences.

"I was supposed to meet Tony at the track on the athletic field. He was part of the football team and I was going to meet him after practice. We were supposed to go to a movie, but when I got to the track, nobody was there. I walked around a little, thinking maybe they'd just moved to a different part of the field. I guess I got too close to the strip of woods that bordered one side of the field. I saw Tony there, under the trees, from a distance. It was after dark, so I couldn't really see him until I got closer. He was standing with a bunch of his friends, so I thought nothing of it when he didn't see me at first. I thought he was talking to his buddies." She paused, her mouth going dry as she remembered what happened next.

"But he and his friends were already dead, weren't they? They'd turned into zombies by the time you found them." John stopped the car in front of the cabin farthest out, along the boundary of the fishing camp. There were woods all around. They reminded her a little of that fateful night.

"It was horrible. They made this moaning sound and their faces had been mutilated. Tony was lucky—he still had most of his face, though he was missing part of an ear and his cheek had been slashed clear through. He was all scratched up and his clothes had been shredded in places." She shuddered remembering the brown stains of dried blood all over the young man who'd been so vital and vibrant.

"You must have loved him a great deal."

The question shocked her out of her gruesome memories. "Love? No. We'd only been dating a week or two. He was a good guy, but he was a year younger than me. I felt like I was getting away with something dating him, but he claimed not to care that I was a cougar." She laughed at the remembered joke. "He had a good sense of humor and he was smart as well as athletic, but I'm not sure we would have worked as a couple long-term."

John's relief at her explanation of the relationship was heartfelt. He'd been worried that she would be scarred by the loss of her boyfriend. The file he had on her gave bare facts. He hadn't been able to figure out if she was heartbroken or merely shell-shocked by the events that had led to her inclusion on the team.

"So what happened next?" He'd shut off the car's engine, but was in no hurry to go inside the cabin. They were getting to the heart of some serious stuff here. He didn't want to spoil the mood until he'd heard as much of the story as she would tell.

"He grabbed me and it felt like he was shielding me from the rest of the team. Hands reached out to claw me, but he folded me in his arms and moved away. He was a really big guy. Bigger than you, even. And strong. He picked me up and carried me off through the woods, his zombie friends following along after." She paused, a frown marring her soft brow. "I don't really know what happened next. I saw a female cop and a guy in camo. They were firing darts and I thought they had to be kidding. I mean, come on, darts? What good would that do? But one by one the guys started disintegrating." Revulsion crossed her expression. "Tony bit me before he succumbed. I'd also been scratched up pretty badly by the others when they tried to grab me away from him. I suppose he was trying to protect me in some way, but in the end, he ended up infecting me with the contagion." She gave a wistful sigh. "I passed out. I don't know for how long. I woke up in the woods just before dawn and made my way to my dorm room. I cleaned up, but I felt horrible so I checked myself into the campus clinic. Shortly thereafter I was approached and offered a position with the team. The rest, you know."

"Yes. Sarah was abducted and all hell broke loose. Nobody had a chance to check on you until much later. But I don't understand why you didn't tell anyone about what had happened to Tony." That had been bothering him. Why hadn't she told anyone about the zombies?

One sleek eyebrow rose in challenge. "You think

anyone would have believed me if I'd run to campus security babbling about zombies? They'd have thought I was coming down from an acid trip. I looked like hell. I felt like hell. All I wanted was a nice place to rest and a doctor's opinion on my condition. For all I knew, it could have been a drug-induced hallucination. I certainly felt bad enough afterward. I figured someone could have slipped me something without my knowledge. I don't do drugs, but they're easy enough to get on any college campus. I wanted a little time and perspective to think about what I'd seen before I started talking about zombies. I didn't want to be committed to a psych ward somewhere with padded walls." She laughed but he saw the wariness in her eyes.

"That was probably good thinking on your part," he admitted. "It certainly helped the team keep a lid on the operation on Long Island. I didn't find out about it until well after the fact and my own sister was involved." He still couldn't believe his baby sister had become mixed up in something so dangerous and covert.

"I like your sister. She seems like a gutsy woman."

"Gutsy enough to become a county cop in the face of our dad's disapproval," he agreed. "I have to admit, even I wasn't entirely comfortable with her choice of profession. I was raised to believe the man did the protecting and the woman did the nurturing."

"Why can't both sexes do both?" she challenged him. That was something he was coming to really enjoy about their exchanges. "After all, even in the most basic terms, the female is always involved in protecting the young as well as nurturing. And men have always been teachers of the next generation. That's nurturing in my book."

"Good point, but you don't know my dad. He's formidable and, in his little world, his daughter becoming a cop was a sacrilege. I like to think he's come to terms with it by now, but I'm not sure. I know I had a rude awakening when I found out Sarah was part of the top-secret covert team I'd been invited to join. Hell, my little sister is the reason I got this gig." He had to laugh. "It was a shocker."

"I bet." She looked amused at his expense but he didn't really mind.

He opened the car door. Their intimate talk was over and it was time to go back to work. They worked well together over the next twenty minutes, quietly moving into the small, rustic cabin. He left her organizing their food supplies while he did a circuit of the woods surrounding their cabin before it got too dark to see.

They were well situated—on the border of the Bemkey estate's lands and close to the lakeshore. The nearest cabins were somewhat visible through the trees but far enough away to give them a lot of privacy. The woods provided a natural screen that shielded their cabin from easy view of the others. It was the perfect setup to do some quiet surveillance of the estate next door.

When he was satisfied they were secure, he returned to their cabin. Donna was waiting for him on the small front porch.

"Is it okay to walk down to the lake? After all that driving, I need to stretch my legs."

John thought about it, looking around. They were reasonably close to the lake. He could see the water's edge through the trees from the cabin's porch.

"It should be okay. Don't venture too far into the woods, just in case. I haven't gotten any reports of missing people in the area, but if Dr. Bemkey really is in residence and doing research here, you never know what could be hiding in the woods."

She shivered, rubbing her arms. "I'll stick to the lakeshore. I just want to walk a bit. I won't be more than ten or fifteen minutes."

"Fair enough." John nodded at her as she passed him going down the stairs to the dirt path leading to the lake. "I'm going to check in with base and fire up the laptop."

"See you in a little bit." She waved over her shoulder as she headed toward the lake.

Sunset was just beginning over one side of the lake, casting a rosy glow over the water. It really was beautiful. John watched her progress out the front windows of the cabin as he puttered around inside. Every few minutes he looked out to see how she was doing. He couldn't help it. He was protective of her. Maybe even a little overprotective. It was part of his nature and upbringing to protect women, even those who could take care of themselves.

She'd held up well so far. Even after the fiasco in San Francisco, she'd bounced back better than he'd expected. She realized she'd made the wrong move there and learned from her mistakes. He'd done a lot of stupid things as a young marine and even on his first few ops for the agency. The critical thing was that she'd learned from the experience. He could work with that.

He made the call to their team leader, Commander Matt Sykes, at Fort Bragg. They talked for a few minutes about the setup in Tennessee and the situation at Fort Bragg, then ended the call with a promise to report immediately should anything change. John peered out the window to see Donna skipping stones on the mirrored surface of the calm lake. She was pretty good at it too.

Satisfied that she was okay, he powered up the laptop and settled by the front window to do more research into local police reports and newspapers. Missing persons reports would be a good start. They could be an indicator that Dr. Bemkey was up to her old tricks, but so far he hadn't found anything suspicious.

Night fell in earnest while he worked. He heard a commotion and looked out the window to find Donna struggling with someone—or something—down by the lake. It had her by the arm, but even as he rose from his chair, she broke free using one of the martial arts moves he'd taught her. She ran. From the way the being pursued her with a disturbingly lurching gait, he assumed the worst.

The zombies had found them.

CHAPTER TWO

John dove for the small locker that contained their weapons and the special toxic darts. Working fast, he unlocked the case, threw open the lid, and grabbed a pistol and two clips, loading the specially made handgun even as he ran for the door.

He was out in the woods before Donna had made it halfway to the cabin. The creature was about half that distance behind her. John passed her, firing on the run, being sure not to get too close. Even a scratch from that creature could mean his death.

"How many?" he asked when he realized Donna had stopped and stood just behind him, breathing hard.

"Just the one." She gulped in air as he scanned the woods. "One minute I was watching the sunset, the next that guy was next to me. Moaning." He saw her shiver out of the corner of his eye.

John walked backwards as the zombie kept coming at them through the woods.

"Keep an eye out behind us. I don't want to get boxed in if there are more of them hiding in the trees." He heard her gasp as she realized they were now alone in the darkening woods with at least one zombie on their trail. They both knew that where there was one, there very well could be more.

"I don't see anything." She was whispering, keeping pace with him as he walked backwards. He could feel her body heat against his back, though they touched only occasionally. She was facing forward, toward the cabin, watching their path while he followed, watching the zombie that continued to stalk them.

"He should be crumbling any minute if what they say is true." He backed onto the porch as the zombie drew closer, following them right up to the cabin.

"They?"

"The guys back at Bragg. I got detailed briefings and simulations, but I've never faced one of these creatures in the flesh before. I wasn't supposed to. They put me on research, remember?"

He grinned, glancing back to catch the dismay written all over her face. Damn. Maybe he shouldn't have reminded her that he wasn't the immune one on this team. He opened his mouth to say more, but the zombie chose that very moment to crumble in front of them.

It was a weird sort of end. He'd heard about it, of course, but nothing could really prepare a person for seeing a human being—or what had once been a human being—dissolve before his very eyes. The guy sort of imploded, starting at the sites where the darts had hit home, until all that was left was a small pile of rags and something that looked like slime.

He heard Donna gasp as the zombie became goo. After checking the woods visually a final time, he turned to her.

"Come here." John tugged her shaking body into his arms. "It's over now, sweetheart. You're safe." She clung to him, her slim fingers fisting in the fabric that covered his chest. He didn't mind. She was shaking like a leaf. He needed to comfort her. It was an imperative in his soul.

His head dipped lower as he nuzzled her soft hair. She lifted her face to meet his gaze and he was lost. He had to taste her. That little teasing peck in the car had cost him deeply. He hadn't stopped thinking about kissing her for real. Taking it deeper, learning her flavor, and what made her sigh in pleasure.

He lowered his head, capturing her lips with his. Yes. This was what he wanted. He pushed his tongue inward and she opened for him as if it was the most natural thing in the world. She tasted of rising passion, a hint of residual fear, and something that made him yearn for more. He'd never get enough of her.

But he couldn't do this. Not really. His life was lived fast and loose. No strings. Ever.

This girl could be a major entanglement. She had complication written all over her. Still, she was sweet to kiss and fit in his arms like she'd been made to belong there.

It was okay to offer her comfort. If he got a rise in his Levi's out of the deal, no harm done. He could help her forget the trauma of the last few minutes and taste the forbidden fruit of her luscious young body while he was at it. He wouldn't let it go too far. A few kisses was all he'd allow. That's all he *could* allow.

A few more minutes of her soft, yielding body against his. That's all he could take. Then he'd let her go and never touch her again. It was better for her. Better for his peace of mind too. Donna was too young for him, too innocent. He'd seen too much of the seamy side of life. He'd done too much. Killed too many people. He was no good for her. Never would be.

He let her go by slow degrees, pulling his lips from hers with great difficulty. Damn, she was sweet. He could almost taste the innocence of her. It was a dangerous flavor. Nothing for him to mess with. He could only tarnish her beauty.

He looked down at her, taking a few moments to gaze into her eyes. It would be the last time he saw that glazed look on her face if he had any willpower at all.

"We'd better go inside, patch you up, and call the cavalry." The change of subject worked. She looked down at herself and the deep scratches on her arm in dawning horror.

"Oh my God, John. You shouldn't have touched me. I need to decontaminate everything." She looked at him with wide, terrified eyes. "I bled all over you. Take off your shirt."

"Now that's what I like to hear." He gave her a wink to lighten the mood as he unbuttoned his shirt. "I'll strip for you anytime, baby."

"Be serious. This could be really bad, John. Go inside and get the decon kit. It's in the red bag. Don't touch anything else. Just get that and come right back out. I'll decontaminate you, then do the rest while you call for a real decontamination team."

"Yeah." He looked around at the remains. "I guess we're going to need a decon team all our own if this is any indication."

He loped into the cabin and spotted the red bag. He picked it up with two fingers and returned to the porch as ordered. It amused him, the way she'd taken charge. He knew she'd been trained in proper decontamination protocol. She had a science background, so he guessed the procedures hadn't been too hard for her to pick up. He'd had a rudimentary course in the same stuff, but he wasn't immune and he wasn't part of a combat or decon team, so he hadn't really paid much attention.

"Open the bag and spill the contents onto this chair." She pointed to one of the plastic patio chairs that graced their tiny front porch. He did as she asked and stepped back as she decontaminated her hands first, using two of the wipes that had been supplied in abundance. She disposed of the specially prepared wipes, putting them in a neat pile to deal with later, then turned to him. "Some of my blood seeped through your shirt. Let me just wipe the area. Hold out your right arm, please."

He did as ordered, trying not to laugh when she started at his ribs and worked her way upward. Few people in the world knew he was ticklish.

"Sorry. I know this is cold. It's the alcohol base in the cleaning solution." She looked up at him as she worked, touching his bare chest and arm with her delicate fingers. It was all he could do to not tug her back into his arms and finish what they'd started.

She was done before he lost total control, thank goodness.

"Could you start a fire in the fireplace? I need to burn these wipes when I'm done and your shirt. And my clothes." She looked at her torn blouse with distaste as she stepped back, out of his personal space. "I can check the remains for I.D.," she offered.

"Only if it won't put you at risk, Donna." He was adamant on that point.

She shrugged. "I'm immune. Hell, the first time, I woke up in a pile of goo. I don't think the remains can hurt me. But I'll be careful to decontaminate everything before I bring anything inside. Because this could really hurt you, John. Hurt as in kill you dead and turn you into one of them. I won't let that happen if I can help it, so you follow my orders when it comes to decon, okay?"

He gave her a jaunty salute. "Yes, ma'am. I like it when you go all militant on me."

She laughed, as he'd intended, and he left her on the porch while he got the fire going and called in the incident to their base. He kept one eye on her the whole time, wary in case there were more of the creatures out there. She'd done well tonight, but she'd gotten injured. He didn't like that at all. The deep gouges in her arm pained him to look at, yet she carried on, doing her job and not complaining. She had more grit than he'd thought. She soldiered on when she had to, which was important. The more he got to know her, the more he found to admire in her character. Not only was she beautiful, she was smart and brave too.

John's eyes almost bugged out of his head when

she stripped down to her underwear right there on the porch. Her bra-and-panty set covered her reasonably well, but the sight of all that bare skin sent his pulse into overdrive. She was even more gorgeous than he'd imagined. Full breasts, a tiny waist, and the most delectable ass he'd ever seen. Damn. She'd been hiding that figure under loose clothing. He'd known she was fit, but her body was that of a goddess. At least to him. He'd always been an ass man and hers was about as perfect as it could get.

She carried the bundle of used wipes into the room, going straight to the fireplace. The blaze was going really well and she wasted no time placing the used white squares on the fire. They went up in little blazes of blue-green flame, powered by the alcohol and whatever other chemicals were in the wipes. He'd made sure the chimney was working properly, taking the smoke well away from them to dissipate harmlessly in the dark night sky.

The way he understood it, once the contagion was exposed to high temperature, of a fire in this case, the virus came apart and could not reconstitute. It was rendered harmless. So burning was the method of choice for getting rid of anything that could possibly be contaminated.

Donna bent over, poking the fire, and John's mouth watered at the view. She straightened and went back out onto the porch before he could make a total fool of himself. Then she came back with his shirt, dumping that onto the fire in small pieces.

"How did you rip that up?" he asked, curious. The shirt had been heavy cotton. He'd have had trouble ripping it. There's no way she could have . . . unless there was more to this immunity thing than he'd been told.

"There was a small scissors in the decon kit. Thick cotton like this rips pretty easy once you get it started. See?" She held up a bit of the sleeve and tugged on a tear. The fabric made a soft ripping sound as it tore easily for her. "I figured it would be easier to burn this in small sections rather than dumping it all on at once. It could have smothered the fire."

"Good thinking." His mouth was as dry as a desert. Seeing her prance around in her undies had that effect. That effect, and others. He kept the couch between them so she wouldn't see his rather blatant response to her near nudity.

"I found a wallet in the pocket of the man's trousers." Her words diverted his attention. "I took out his driver's license and something called a 'Frequent Fisher Card' issued from this place. He's a regular. It's got stamps from the last three years, all around this time of year." She headed back to the porch. "I'll wipe the items down as a precaution, then you can have them."

He went to the laptop computer he'd set up by the window. "What was the guy's name?"

"Bill Wallace." She carefully wiped each card and bill that had been in the wallet. He could see her through the open window as she paid strict attention to detail. Her science background was showing. "His business cards say he was an assistant vice president for something called Praxis Air. The office address is in Lexington, Kentucky."

John pulled up the man's background information on the computer. "He looks clean as near as I can tell from a quick search," he told her through the window screen. "Poor guy. Probably a bad case of wrong place, wrong time."

"Everything is wet. Don't you think that's odd?" she asked, finishing up. She came back inside and deposited the now clean articles from the wallet on the small table next to the laptop. "It's like the guy went swimming before he decided to hassle me."

"I have no idea what it means. I just hope we won't have a bunch of zombie fish menacing the lake." He chuckled at his own joke.

"It doesn't work that way, from what I've been told. It's human-specific gene altering. It can't cross species. They made sure of it when they designed it. Humans only."

"Lucky us."

"Well, in a way it is. Those zombie fish could cause quite a problem otherwise." She went back out to the porch a final time and brought in the last pile of refuse. The man's remains would stay on the porch until the cleanup team arrived the following day.

Donna squatted before the fire, sending the new stack of used wipes up in flames a few at a time. When she was finished with the used wipes, she took out a few fresh ones and did a final cleansing of her hands and arms, burning those as well.

John settled on the couch behind her, unable to stop himself from looking his fill. She glared at him over her shoulder as she worked.

"Stop staring at my ass," she muttered in warning.

He had to laugh. "How can I help myself when

you're prancing around half naked? I'd have to be dead not to notice your smokin' hot bod."

A tingle went down her spine at his words. That hadn't sounded like teasing. His words had been edged with frustration. Had she caused that?

Wow.

Maybe she wasn't the only one having a hard time concentrating with all the bare skin around here. The moment he'd taken off his shirt, her body had begun to purr. The man was gorgeous. He had biceps to die for and the lean, muscular build of a martial artist. She knew he was a highly ranked *sensei*. She'd even participated in a few classes he'd run for the team back at Fort Bragg. But she'd never seen him without his shirt.

Her mouth went dry at the masculine perfection of him. Not too bulky, not too skinny, he was chiseled perfection, like one of those famous marble statues of a young Greek god. She wanted to run her hands all over him and had to clench her fists to keep from reaching out and doing just that.

"I'm covered more than I would be in a bikini," she pointed out, working steadily at the fire.

"For some reason, knowing it's underwear and not swimwear makes a difference. I love the cut of those panties, how they go high up on your hip and make your legs look a mile long." His voice had dropped to intimate tones that sent shivers down her spine. "Of course, right now, I'm sort of wishing you were a thong girl."

"A thong?" She brazened it out, turning to shoot him a daring look over her shoulder. "Do you have any idea how uncomfortable it is to wear butt floss?"

He laughed out loud at her irreverent question, lightening the mood. "Can't say I do. It looks sexy as hell, though."

"Well, it's like walking around with a wedgie all day." She chuckled as she put the last bit on the fire.

"Hold still. I'm dying to know." That's all the warning she got before a warm hand insinuated itself between her skin and the back closure of her bra. She could feel him flipping the fabric over, then tugging on the little pink label that was sewn underneath.

"Ah, it's not a *secret* anymore. Thought so. And may I compliment your taste in lingerie?" Satisfaction laced his voice as he removed his hand from the fabric, skating his warm fingers down her spine.

"John." She tried to object, but it came out too whispery and needful.

"You have a sweet, round, luscious ass, Donna."

That snapped her out of the sensuous spell he'd put her under. "Did you just say I had a fat ass?" She rocked forward on the balls of her feet, out of his reach as she glared at him over her shoulder.

His smile was pure sin. "Round, Donna. Not fat." He sat up on the couch and scooted forward, reaching for her waist only to slide his big hand downward to cup one butt cheek. The warmth began to return. An aroused tingling awoke in the pit of her stomach.

"Round and womanly," he whispered, moving closer. "Perfect." He slid off the couch to kneel behind her. She could feel his hot breath wafting over her back, making her tremble. "The perfect size and shape for my hands." His voice dipped lower as his fingers squeezed. Her traitorous body pushed into his touch. "I've wanted to touch you for days."

Both big hands moved to her ass, squeezing and shaping her flesh. When he slipped one hand beneath the edge of her panties, she couldn't find the breath to stop him.

"A thong would land right about here." His index finger rubbed over her tailbone as his words whispered past her ear, making her shiver. His finger dipped lower, following the valley between her cheeks. He paused only slightly before dipping lower, all the way inside her panties, to cup her mound from behind.

"John," she whispered in warning. His head bent closer to hers, his breath wafting over her ear before his lips captured her earlobe, teeth biting gently. She tilted her head, giving him greater access and implicit permission to do what he wanted. The way he made her feel at the moment, she'd give him anything he asked.

"Yeah, baby. This is what I wanted each and every time I've looked at you," he murmured as he let her earlobe go. "You're wet for me, Donna." His tone was almost chastising as he slid his finger between her lower lips. The tip of his finger teased her distended clit, making her moan. She tried to bite back the sound without success. John Petit lit her on fire with just a touch and she was powerless to resist. She didn't want to resist. She wanted whatever he'd give her, if only for this short space of time.

She knew it couldn't be anything more. John wasn't the kind of man who did long-term. She'd intuited that about him from the very beginning.

She gasped as his finger slid into her without warning, pushing deep. Her body made room for him, accepting him as if he belonged there within her tight core, touching the deepest heart of her pleasure.

"Will you let me, Donna? Will you let me have you?"

She didn't need to think. She didn't want to think. She knew what her answer would be and had known it almost from the moment she'd laid eyes on him.

"Yes."

Things happened fast once the word was out of her mouth. He removed his hand from her panties and turned her toward him, assisting her from her crouch into a much more comfortable kneeling position opposite him. His hands went to her shoulders and down her back, following the line of the silky straps of her bra. He unhooked the catch with deft movements.

"You've done this before," she teased.

He gave her a lopsided grin. "A time or two."

The bra came off slowly, guided by his gentle hands. His eyes followed it as she was revealed to him. She felt a momentary pang of shyness that was quickly smothered as he dipped his head and kissed all ability to reason right out of her mind. His mouth was hot and tangy, his flavor divine, his skill undeniable. He coaxed her tongue into a duel of the most sensuous nature that left her breathless when he finally left her lips, only to trail kisses down her throat.

He licked her nipples, each in turn before selecting one to suck and one to roll between his skilled fingers. She writhed against him as he plied

his skills on her willing body. Never had she been
so inflamed by a lover's touch, or made so hot by
such a simple act.

With John, everything was new and even more
exciting. He knew just how to touch her to make
her cream. Every time. No exceptions. She'd been
in a state of semi-arousal since they had started
working together. Since he'd kissed her in the car,
she'd been aching for him like she'd never ached
for a man before.

He switched things up, licking and nibbling his
way across her chest. While his tongue and teeth
teased her other nipple, his hands moved downward to cup her ass. He went under the waistband
of her panties, pushing them down so he could
claim her completely. The fabric fell to her knees
as his hands rubbed over her cheeks, and inward
as he grasped and lifted. He lifted his mouth from
her breast, sucking as he let go with an audible
pop. He straightened his spine to face her, his arms
wrapped around her body, caging her, yet making
her feel safe.

"I love this luscious ass, Donna. I can't wait to
sink my teeth into you."

"Teeth?" She lifted one eyebrow in question.

"Figure of speech, though I will admit to wanting to lick you all over."

"I think I can live with that." Even if it killed her.
Damn, just the idea of what he would do made her
want to faint with pleasure.

"I'll make it worth your while, Donna. I promise."

She had no doubts about his intentions. The
man was sex personified. Every wicked thought—
and she'd had quite a few since teaming up with
him—centered on him. John was the epitome of

virility in her eyes and there was no question in her mind that he could live up to the advertising of his scrumptious body. This was a man who could deliver.

And it made her shiver to think she'd learn the ultimate truth of that belief any minute now.

"Ready?" His eyes dared her.

"Depends on what you mean?"

"I want to lay you down and begin that licking I was talking about. I warn you, it could take a few days to do properly." The joyful, teasing light hadn't left his eyes and it drew her in.

"Well then." Was that breathless voice hers? "I suppose the sooner we start, the better off we'll be."

"Oh, yeah. And the sooner we can start all over again."

"I'll hold you to that, Romeo."

He chuckled as he lowered her to the soft rug before the fireplace. The flames continued to lick upward into the chimney and gave off a pleasant warmth. She watched the almost mesmerized expression in his eyes as he viewed her naked body.

"How soon she forgets." He shook his head, making a comical *tsk*ing noise. "I'm John. I don't know who this Romeo guy is but, if I do my job right, you won't be able to even think of another man when I'm through with you."

She laughed at his boast. The thing was, she feared he was right. She'd only known John for a few weeks and already every other man she'd ever known faded in comparison to him. She reached upward and twined her fingers around his neck as he moved over her. His eyes met hers and she could've sworn lightning flashed between them.

"Donna, I . . ."

She stopped him from speaking, placing one finger gently over his lips. She didn't want to hear platitudes, or worse, words he'd spoken to a dozen other girls. She wanted the illusion that this meant as much to him as it did to her. In the bright light of day she couldn't fool herself into thinking a man like John could really be interested in anything serious with a girl like her. But for this moment out of time, she wanted to live the fantasy. She wanted to believe—if only in her own heart— that he could love her, desire her, and want her for longer than a fling.

But if a fling was all she could have with him, she'd take it and be grateful. Men like John Petit didn't saunter into her life every day. Well, not until recently, anyway. He was a man apart. The kind of guy she daydreamed about but had never really believed existed in real life.

And now here she was, living the dream. She wouldn't let anything ruin it. Especially not a few offhand words.

"Come here, John." She pulled his head down so she could kiss him. It was the first move she'd made on her own initiative in this little drama and it felt good. Freeing.

This time, she kissed him. He was panting when she finally let him go and she felt the first stirrings of her feminine power. She smiled, knowing there had to be a wicked glint of satisfaction in her eyes. John answered her with a knowing grin of his own before he dipped his head once more, his tongue riding over her collarbone before it slipped downward.

She held on to his shoulders as long as she

could while he worshiped her breasts again, lest they forget the way he'd toyed with them minutes before. She writhed under him, her fingers coasting over his muscles as his head drifted downward, his hands leading the way, touching her, testing her, spreading her legs for his passage.

"Look at me, Donna," came the gentle command in John's gravelly voice.

She raised her head a few inches to see him resting on his stomach between her splayed thighs. His hands were poised over her, as if waiting only for her to watch. Their eyes met for a moment and then he struck.

Callused fingers parted her nether lips, spreading her for his inspection. She quivered as he broke eye contact to look downward at what he'd uncovered. She'd never been this exposed to a lover in her life. A moment of insecurity gave way to a pleasure-filled sense of freedom as he lowered his head, his talented tongue homing in on her exposed clit for a fast swipe that nearly undid her.

"Mmm. You like that, do you?" His words made her squirm as his breath drifted over her skin. "I like it too, sweetheart. You taste like passion and it's all for me." He sounded so self-satisfied she felt a little tingle of amusement snake down her spine. Or maybe it was rapture. John made her feel good in so many ways, it was hard to tell.

"More, John," she whispered daringly.

He grinned at her. "Your wish is my command, baby. This first one is for you."

First one? Did he mean what she thought he meant?

As his mouth settled over her clit and his fingers teased inside her core, she quickly learned the answer to her question. She went off like a rocket with very little provocation, riding John's fingers and mouth like a bucking bronc while he hummed against her, the vibrations going straight to her core.

When she finally began to settle down from the unexpectedly intense climax, she looked downward to meet his gaze. He had a self-satisfied grin on his face that made her want to laugh.

"Ready for more?"

"More?" she panted. "I think I may need a minute to recover."

He laughed outright. "That good, eh?"

"Wipe that smug grin right off your face, Petit."

He only grinned wider. "How can I when you look so cute and flushed and . . . satisfied? I bet I can make you look even more satisfied, though."

"You're trying to kill me." Her head flopped back on the rug as she closed her eyes.

Wrong move. John must have taken her words as a challenge. A moment later, she felt a light, flickering touch on her clit that stirred renewed interest in places she'd thought wouldn't be up for anything else for a good long while. She lifted her head again to look and saw the tip of his tongue flicking in a move she'd only ever seen once before. And that was in a porn movie she and her friends had watched in freshman year.

Only now did she understand why the woman in the porno flick had writhed like a cat in heat. Within moments, she could have given that actress a real run for her money in the gasping and moaning department. No doubt about it. John Petit knew how to make a woman come. And come again, if he had his wicked way.

"John!" she called out to him as he pushed her pleasure higher. He seemed to take that as a sign to stop what he was doing. Totally *not* what she'd wanted him to do. They'd have to work on their communication skills.

He moved, stalking up her body on hands and knees and she suddenly didn't mind that he'd stopped licking her. He kissed her and she tasted the faint trace of what must have been herself on his lips. It was exciting in a forbidden way.

Her hands stole around his back, enjoying the play of his muscles as she swept downward. She drew up short when she encountered the waistband of his pants. Damn. He still had his pants on. She drew back from his kiss and grasped the waistband, tugging.

"These have got to go."

He pulled back to meet her gaze. "I'm all for it. Want to pull the zipper down with your teeth?"

"I would," she purred, playing along, "but it's a button fly."

They both laughed as he lifted away to kneel between her thighs. His fingers went to the fly and began a slow, sensual display. He unfastened the garment one button at a time. The last barrier between them. She didn't see underwear. He was going commando under those soft cotton fatigue pants.

Hubba hubba.

"Lick your lips like that one more time, baby, and I'll give you something else to lick."

Her gaze rose from his hips to meet his eyes. "Is that a promise?" She licked her lips deliberately, liking the fire in his gaze. It leapt, flaming higher as she watched.

"Next time." He made short work of his pants, pausing only seconds to retrieve something from one of the pockets. It was a square bit of foil. A condom.

Thank goodness one of them was thinking clearly. She reached for it, but he pulled back, tearing the thing open with jagged motions and rolling it over the most magnificent erection she'd ever seen in person. He was long and thick and, suddenly, she didn't want to wait anymore. She wanted him in her. Now.

He appeared to be on the same wavelength. Once he was sheathed and his pants out of the way, he settled between her thighs like a man on a mission.

"Are you ready for me?" He let the fingers of one hand ride through the wetness gathered between her legs for him. All for him.

"Yes," she whispered. "Don't make me wait, John."

"No more waiting." He positioned himself swiftly and slid inside as he lowered over her. He held her gaze as he pushed home, joining them for the first time. If she had her way, it definitely wouldn't be the last.

She was caught up in a whirlwind of sensation as John began to move. He stretched her to her limits, reaching a place inside her on every thrust that made her head reel in pleasure. Damn. He'd found her heretofore missing G-spot without even trying. Now that was talent.

"You're tight, baby. This is so good," John praised her as he settled over her, running his mouth over her neck and shoulder. She loved the feel of him so close to her as he made love to her for the first time. There was nothing standoffish about John. He was an all-or-nothing sort of man. That carried through to the way he made love, she was pleased to learn.

"John." She couldn't string two words together as her passion rose even higher than before, but she could whimper his name as she rode a crest of intense pleasure. He stroked her higher and higher still as he rode her through her second climax of the day and pushed her toward an unbelievable third.

"That's it, baby." He increased his pace, praising her as he moved more forcefully within her body. She loved the feel of him. The commanding presence and the undeniable skill he had made her insane with bliss. "Come one more time for me, sweetheart. Just once more."

"I . . . don't know. . . ." She panted, her breath coming in quick gasps as her body soared.

"Do it, Donna. Do it now." It was an order and her body didn't dare refuse. His gaze holding hers, she tipped over the edge into a third glorious orgasm. This one was mightier than the last two combined. She hadn't known she could fly so high or feel so much. She cried out as she came and felt the answering spasms of John's big body inside her.

They'd come together in a rare moment of communion. She'd never had such a powerful simultaneous climax. The thought of it pushed her higher as the pleasure spiraled upward and outward, growing and not diminishing for long, long moments. John held her throughout, fire in his gaze and pleasure washing over them both as they lay entwined, unspeaking.

A long, pleasurable time later, they began to come down from the peak. John smiled his bad-boy smile at her and she answered with a tired lift of her lips.

"Was it good for you?" he asked, the inflection in his voice making her laugh.

"You know the answer to that one." She flexed around him, making them both give a sharp intake of breath as their bodies echoed the pleasure that had claimed them so completely.

"You rocked my world, sweetheart." He rolled with her in his arms, disengaging them as he got to his feet with her held securely in his arms. The man was strong in ways she'd never experienced with another man. Of course, she'd never dated a superhuman sort of ex-soldier before.

He started for the bedroom, a mischievous expression on his handsome face.

"Where are we going?" she asked out of curiosity, though she knew darn well there was a soft mattress in her near future.

"Taking you to bed."

"Bed? Why?" She toyed with the light dusting of hair on his chest, acting coy.

"I told you, Donna. You rocked my world." He paused at the door to the bedroom to look into her eyes. "Let's do it again."

In the hour before dawn, Dr. Elizabeth Bemkey looked out from her balcony at the corpses gathered in her backyard. It was marvelous to have them follow her orders. Especially him. The bastard. Her husband and his so-called girlfriend, Claudette.

Lizzie had killed the bastard first with a quick injection to the jugular. She'd enjoyed watching him writhe on the ground, all the while knowing who had brought him death. She'd laughed as he died, holding her gaze. But it wasn't enough. Nothing would ever be enough to repay the pain he'd given her.

She'd stalked the bimbo out on the patio next. Skinny Claudette with her massive breast implants had been easy to surprise. A quick jab to the chest and not only had Claudette been injected with the deadly contagion, but Lizzie had taken great joy in deflating one of the bimbo's boobs a full cup size with aid of the needle and a lovely, spurting, slow leak.

Since then, the other zombies had had their fun with weak little Claudette. She was looking much worse for wear nowadays. The string bikini she'd been wearing when Lizzie had killed her was dirty and torn. Those prize melons had been gnawed by half the zombie population and her once pretty face was pretty no more.

Served the bitch right for stealing Lizzie's husband.

She looked out over her creations, gathered to receive her orders in the backyard. Besides the bastard and the bimbo there was fat Bubba from the infamous Bass Tours, the gardener, and a few odd fishermen who'd been savaged by her pets over the past day or two.

"My little army is growing. Soon, my friends. Soon you will be unleashed on the world." She laughed to herself, the creatures looking up at her with blind devotion.

She liked this change her friend Sellars had engineered in them. Where he'd found the brains to alter the original formula, she didn't know. She never would know now. Last she'd heard, their colleague Dr. Rodriguez had gotten impatient with Sellars and had him killed. Pity that. She would have liked to pick his brain about the improvements he'd already made to the formula. It was her goal to make it even better.

For one thing, she didn't dare go near the creatures. She kept them locked out of the house and only addressed them from up here as a precaution. They seemed docile enough for now, but she wondered when or if they'd tire of following her orders. Still, it didn't matter. They were hers for now and she was enjoying tormenting the bastard and his bimbo especially.

Those two really made her mad. She paced as she fumed, her anger growing. She hated her husband with every last fiber of her being.

"Go jump in the lake!" she yelled down to them. She began to cackle hysterically when they turned and followed her orders, walking slowly in their shuffling gait until they were all fully submerged in the water.

With any luck, they'd stay there until tomorrow night. She had plans for them, but she had to put a few things in place first.

Chapter Three

The phone woke John not long after dawn. He wasn't scheduled to check in with base until later in the day. Unscheduled phone calls were never a good sign.

"John, it's Matt Sykes. Things have changed. All hell broke loose here at Fort Bragg last night. I can't spare any personnel to assist you, but we may have another solution. Do you still want in on the combat team?"

"More than ever." John was confused. Matt Sykes had been adamant about not allowing any but immune personnel on the combat side of the team. "But how?"

"Can you two get to Knoxville by oh-nine hundred?"

John did a quick mental calculation. "Yes, sir. I believe we can."

"Good. I'm sending Dr. Daniels to meet you there. She'll explain. And I'm giving you a two-man cleanup team. They should be arriving in Cookeville in a few hours. They'll stay there and commute out when needed."

John didn't need to be told why the cleanup team was positioning themselves in Cookeville. The town was big enough that no one would question their presence. Out in the countryside by the lake, they would probably stick out like a sore thumb. For secrecy's sake, it was better to have them stay in the larger town.

He ended the call with Commander Sykes after being given detailed instructions on where and how to meet Dr. Daniels. John knew Mariana Daniels. They'd been introduced when he joined the team. She was a general practitioner who had been sucked into this mission during the initial infestation at Quantico. She'd been working with the research scientists ever since and John knew her to be a competent professional with a good head on her shoulders. She was also engaged to one of the combat team members, a former Navy SEAL named Simon Blackwell.

When he returned to the bedroom to get his clothes, Donna was awake—just barely. She rubbed her eyes as she blinked against the dappled early morning sun coming in through the window.

"What time is it?" she asked.

"Time to get up." He leaned in to kiss her awake, taking his time but not giving in to the impulse to lay down with her again. If he did that, they'd never get on the road. He straightened and reached for his clothes.

"Did I hear the phone ring?"

"Yeah. It was Commander Sykes. We have to go

to Knoxville today. We're meeting Dr. Daniels there at nine."

Donna sat up in the bed, looking adorably rumpled. "Why?"

"He said she would fill us in. Apparently the problems have escalated over at Fort Bragg. They're not going to be able to send us much help, though he did promise a two-man cleanup team would be here sometime today. Dr. Daniels is supposed to explain more when we meet her."

"I don't think I like the sound of that." She shot him a worried look.

He smiled at her, tugging her hand to help her stand. He put his arms around her, settling his hands on the warm skin of her back and that luscious ass of hers.

"It'll be okay."

"If you say so."

He let her rest her head in the crook of his neck for a moment. It felt so good to have her in his arms, he couldn't complain. But time was short. They had to get on the road. Pulling away, he tried to calm her unspoken fears, but only time—and discovering what awaited them in Knoxville— would really solve the problem.

They were able to relax a little on the drive to Knoxville. They made it in plenty of time with a stop for breakfast along the way. Donna was subdued. He could tell she was worried about the unexpected detour to Knoxville. He tried to draw her out as they sat in the waiting room of the VA clinic waiting for Dr. Daniels to arrive.

"What has you tied up in knots, sweetheart?" He

took her hand, lacing their fingers together. John liked being able to touch her whenever the mood struck him. After being so careful to keep his hands to himself for the past days, it was a relief.

"I'm not crazy about hospitals and doctors' offices. Even after I woke up in the woods, I thought long and hard before I went to the campus clinic."

"Why? I mean, I don't find hospitals particularly pleasant either, but when you need help, you need help."

"My dad went in for a simple hernia operation a few years back and ended up with a staph infection it took months to cure. They say hospitals are clean, but you can catch some really nasty stuff in them."

He nodded. That explained a lot. He would've said more but Dr. Daniels walked through the door and spotted them. She came over, greeting them both, and taking them back with her into the treatment area.

"They've given me a private room for the day. Longer, if we need it," she explained as they went into a room and she shut the door firmly behind them. She dropped her big briefcase and a cooler bag on a side table and leaned against the bed, facing them. "Here's the deal. Some very bad stuff went down at Fort Bragg last night. Commander Sykes really can't give you any of the immune combat team. He's not being stingy. He really can't spare them right now. Dr. McCormick and I have been running tests on your blood, John. We've been comparing it to your sister's blood. Her natural immunity versus your very close blood match is helping us figure out the way the immune response is triggered. While it's possible you might also prove to be naturally immune, Dr. McCormick and I think we can speed up the process and also make it considerably less painful."

John brightened. "You can make me immune to the contagion?"

If they could manage to do that, his problems would be solved. He could go out in the field and face the zombies head-on. No more pussyfooting around behind the scenes. He could join the combat side of this mission, where he really belonged.

Dr. Daniels nodded slowly. "I believe so. We've done extensive testing and if you're willing, we can do the treatment today. There are some risks, of course. Worst-case scenario, you could die and rise again, at which point, I'd dose you with toxin and you'd end up like the other zombies."

Donna's hand stole into his, squeezing. She was trembling and he knew she was afraid for him. The thought of it touched him deeply.

"What are his chances, Doctor?" Donna asked quietly.

Dr. Daniels looked from their joined hands to Donna's worried face and John knew it was clear they were involved. Oddly, he didn't mind that the doctor knew. He'd have shouted it from the rooftops if he could. The night spent with Donna had changed him. He usually ran when women got the least bit proprietary, yet every second of Donna's concern made him want her more.

"I believe the process will work. I'd estimate he has about a seventy-five-percent chance of walking out of this immune and healthy. There's about a twenty-percent chance that we've made a miscalculation somewhere and he might end up ill, but not in fatal condition. And a five-percent chance of the worst."

"I can live with those odds." John wanted to do this. He felt useless being kept out of the field. The small taste of action he'd gotten when Donna was in trouble had only driven home how badly he wanted to be able to fight these bastards and keep her out of the line of fire, if at all possible. He felt strongly that if his baby sister was immune, he should be too.

Dr. Daniels smiled at him. "I think you can live with them too, John. I would never have suggested this course of treatment if I really thought you'd die from it. Dr. McCormick and I have a strong belief in this and if it works the way we think it will, your experience will also go a long way toward helping our research."

"So he's a human guinea pig?" Donna's tone was challenging. His little vixen had sharp teeth when provoked.

Dr. Daniels sighed. "In a sense, yes. But it's his choice." Her attention turned back to him. "What do you say, John?"

He looked at Donna's worried face and decided to at least pretend to think about it for her sake. "How long will it take?"

"I can administer the shots this morning and monitor you through the process. It shouldn't take more than a few hours. You can probably go back to the lake by tonight. It's likely you'll sleep most of the day while your body adjusts. I'll have to wake you every few hours to take blood samples, but otherwise, it should be relatively painless. We're operating on the theory that a small amount of a watered-down version of the contagion will provoke the immune response in your body. Like a vaccine. Since your blood chemistry is so similar to your sister's and she's already proven immune, we expect you to do well. Just in case, I'll be administering a series of antigens first that we refined from your sister's blood. Since you're the same blood type and genetically very similar, the chance of rejection is incredibly low. We'll wait for them to circulate through your blood, then administer the inactive version of the contagion and monitor your blood for developments. Since this contagion inspires such a rapid reaction, it should be over within a few hours at most."

John turned to Donna. "I want to do this."

"I'm worried," she admitted, breaking his heart with the expression in her beautiful eyes.

"Don't worry, sweetheart." He brushed a stray lock of hair away from her face. "It'll be okay. I have every confidence in Dr. Daniels and Dr. McCormick. If they both agree this will work, who am I to argue?" He gave her a smile, glad when she returned the gesture.

"You trust them with your life?" Her voice dropped to a whisper as she stepped closer to him.

John thought about it and realized he did. "I've researched every member of this team. You know how I love to research." He rolled his eyes, and was pleased when she smiled back faintly. "McCormick is brilliant. She saved one life already with her magic serum."

"But Dr. McCormick was part of the original science team that started this whole nightmare. How can you trust her with your life?" Donna's expression was agonized.

"I wasn't on the team," Dr. Daniels's voice intruded on their moment, but he didn't mind. He could use her help convincing Donna this was the way to go. "I was a general practitioner until I got involved in this. I wouldn't endorse this course of action unless I thought it was the right thing to do. I wouldn't have even come here if I thought this was just another experiment. It's not. Not to Eileen McCormick. And not to me."

"Thanks, Doc. That means a lot." John turned back to Donna. She looked skeptical but better than she had before. He reached down and kissed her lightly, reassuringly, despite the doctor's presence. "It'll be okay. You'll see."

Donna threw her arms around him, hugging him tight for just a few seconds. She drew back and her eyes were suspiciously bright. "If you die on me, I'll haunt you, John Petit."

"Isn't that supposed to be the other way around?" He enjoyed her tough spirit.

"You die on me and I'll change all the rules. See if I don't."

"Then I'll have to be sure not to die, won't I?" One last hug and she let him go. "All right, Doc. Let's do this."

"Okay." The doctor straightened from her leaning position and got to work. "Strip down to your boxers and get on the bed."

"Now that's a sentence a man doesn't hear every day with two pretty women in the room."

Both of the women in question laughed and the serious mood was tempered. He stripped quickly, throwing the clothes at one of the chairs in the room. He didn't complain when Donna—bless her tidy little heart—took each piece and folded it neatly, placing his clothes in the small closet built into one wall.

"We'll start with the antigens and wait a bit for them to spread through your system. If you change your mind after that, no harm done. The point of no return will be after the nonactive contagion is administered."

"Okay, Doc." John got on the bed and held out his arm. "Shoot me up."

Dr. Daniels laughed at his antics and gave him a series of three shots in rapid succession while Donna watched from the foot of the bed.

"How are we doing, John?" Dr. Daniels asked as she took his blood pressure and checked his pulse.

"*We're* just fine and dandy, Doc. What's next?"

"Whoa, tiger." She put her hand on his shoulder when he tried to sit up. "You're staying prone for now. Give the antigens a chance to circulate. If you aren't dizzy in a few minutes, you can stand up and do some stretches to help increase blood flow."

Dr. Daniels stayed in the room, as did Donna, checking his vitals every few minutes and making notes.

"This is getting old, Doc," he groused good-naturedly. "I'm not used to all this boring inactivity."

"Think of it as the calm before the storm, John. Once we boost your immunity to the next level, you probably won't have another free moment until this is all over."

"Will I gain all those nifty side effects like the super-healing?" The thought occurred to him belatedly.

"We believe so. We're basically re-creating your sister's immune response, only speeding it up."

"Would this work for other people?" Donna asked. "Is this a way to make the contagion work the way it was supposed to? I mean, wasn't the original intent to create something that would boost healing?"

"Unfortunately not. This is a one-shot deal. It'll work on John—and maybe on other members of his close family, now that I think about it. Nobody else." She took his pulse again and stepped back. "You can sit up, but take it slow." He sat up as she observed. "Any dizziness?"

"None," he reported.

Dr. Daniels had him stand and then walk around, each time checking him over before she'd let him do the next thing. Eventually, she sent him back to bed.

"Rest up for a little while. You're making good progress. We'll just wait a few more minutes before we take the next step."

"John, are you sure about this?" Donna couldn't help but ask. The closer he got to taking that final step, the more she worried.

Dr. Daniels looked from Donna to John and back again. "I'm going to step outside. When I come back, I'll confirm your readings and then if you're still prepared to proceed, we'll do the final injection."

"Sounds good, Doc." John watched the doctor leave, then patted the spot next to him where he sat on the edge of the bed, inviting Donna to join him. She walked over and sat down next to him.

John's strong arm slid around her shoulders, drawing her into his side. He felt so good. So warm and stable and strong. That could all change in the blink of an eye—or in this case, because of a shot in the arm.

"I'm worried."

"I know." He leaned down to nuzzle her hair. "But I'm not. You should take some comfort from that. Despite appearances to the contrary, I'm not cavalier with my own life. It's precious to me and I wouldn't do this if I didn't believe it would be okay. Plus . . ." He seemed reluctant—almost uncomfortable.

"What?" She turned in his loose embrace to search his eyes. They were troubled.

"My sister was exposed to this contagion. So were you, Donna. I . . . I feel like this is my chance to be there for you both. If either of you have problems down the road because of this, I want to be there with you—for you. I want you both to know that you are not alone. I see this as a way to help. The more people the scientists have to study, the better their chances of finding a solution."

She read the truth in his eyes. A tear rolled down her cheek, unheeded. She touched his face with trembling hands, brushing his short hair back. "You are the best gift I have ever received in my life, John Petit. I don't want anything to happen to you."

"It won't. Trust me." He winked at her and she had to smile at his unstoppable confidence. If that alone would bring him through the treatment, he had it made.

She wiped her cheek self-consciously. "And here I thought the only reason you wanted to do this was to go out in the woods and shoot zombies."

"Well, there is that." His smile was contagious. "I've felt pretty useless sitting on the sidelines."

"Never that, John. If . . ." She couldn't bring herself to say it. "I've enjoyed every minute of working with you, John. Of being with you."

He put both arms around her and drew her close. "Ditto, sweetheart."

He captured her lips in a sweet kiss. It was a kiss that promised more. It wasn't an ending, but a beginning that held hope for times to come. She took heart from his kiss, knowing it was a reflection of the man. He drew back and the feeling remained.

The door opened after a perfunctory knock and Mariana Daniels came back in. John let Donna go and she hopped off the side of the bed, moving to her former position, standing opposite the foot of the bed, against the wall, by the chairs.

Dr. Daniels took her readings and seemed satisfied.

"Moment-of-truth time. Are you still up for this, John?"

"Hit me with it, Doc." He held out his arm eagerly, but his eyes never left Donna's face. Even as the plunger depressed and the dormant contagion entered his bloodstream, his gaze held hers.

The hours that followed were harsh. At first, the contagion didn't seem to have any effect. Then, suddenly, John's muscles began to spasm. It wasn't quite a convulsion, but it wasn't pretty and it couldn't be comfortable. John remained stoic throughout. Between episodes, he began to drift asleep.

"Is that normal?" Donna asked the doctor in a whisper.

"We're charting new territory here, I'm afraid, but his readings are strong and his blood appears to be adapting. Most of the naturally occurring cases of immunity we have seen produced very strong convulsions as the host body adapted. You probably don't remember it because you were unconscious at the time and nobody was around to witness it. Sarah Petit, John's sister, went through it at a hospital and we have very detailed records of her reactions. My fiancé, Simon, had a similar experience, as did the others. Compared to them, these muscle spasms are really nothing."

"Yet you believe he'll have the same immunity and speed healing when he recovers?"

"Yes, I believe so." She'd been taking blood samples throughout the procedure and examining them under a microscope. She also had some other instruments and testing apparatus she'd been using. It looked like she was monitoring the changes almost in real time. "His blood gives every indication of the full immune response. I'll know more when it settles down. The initial reaction is violent with this contagion. After a few hours, it levels out and he should reach his new normal fairly rapidly."

"Do you foresee any long-term problems with the way we are now?" Donna found the courage to ask. She hadn't asked the question before, more interested in the immediate effects. But John's thoughts about the future sparked her own.

"None that I can see." The doctor's words lifted a weight off her shoulders she hadn't known she'd been carrying. "I've done as much research into this as I can because of Simon. We're getting married and he was understandably concerned about his future—about our future. From everything I've seen so far, the new structures in his blood stabilized rapidly and show no signs of deterioration. It's the new normal for him. And for you now. Unless something radical happens, this'll be the way you are for the rest of your lives."

"You almost sound envious." Donna was puzzled by the doctor's reaction.

"I am in a way. You have a lot of advantages. Very little can hurt you permanently now. Including those horrors in the woods." The doctor shivered.

They fell silent for a time, watching John as his body went through another round of spasms. He didn't wake this time and Dr. Daniels monitored him throughout.

"He's a good man, you know." Dr. Daniels removed her stethoscope from her ears and let it dangle around her neck. "And he cares a great deal for you."

"How do you know?"

"It's in the way he looks at you, Donna. The man is smitten." They both laughed at the old-fashioned word. "And you are too. Am I right?"

Donna thought about it. "Yeah, I guess I am. He's not like any other guy I ever dated. He's infuriating and funny and incredibly noble." She took his hand as she stood beside his sleeping form.

"You're in love with him," Dr. Daniels whispered.

Donna wasn't as shocked by the idea as she probably should have been. She hadn't admitted the depth of her feelings, even to herself, but hearing Dr. Daniels say it didn't trouble her. It was true. She loved him. She was in love with John Petit.

How in the world had that happened?

"I can see that's a new concept for you." Dr. Daniels laughed at Donna's expression. She had no doubt she probably looked like a landed fish.

"Yeah," Donna admitted. "I don't know when or how, but I think you're right. Damn." She shook her head and laughed at herself.

CHAPTER FOUR

John had short moments of lucidity between long bouts of being dead to the world. He was aware of the passage of time only peripherally. They'd started this odyssey around eleven in the morning. By the time he was feeling like himself again, it was closer to dinner than lunch.

"How are you feeling, sleepyhead?" Donna was at his side, holding his hand. He squeezed her fingers, looking up at her beautiful face.

"I'm good." He yawned but the fierce exhaustion that had weighed him down for hours had passed. "What time is it?"

"About four," Dr. Daniels answered from his other side. "Any soreness?"

John tested his limbs as he lay in the bed. "I'm a little stiff, but otherwise okay. I feel like I had a workout, but all I did was sleep, right?"

"Your larger muscle groups spasmed more than a few times," Dr. Daniels informed him. "That's probably why you feel some muscle soreness. How about your joints? Any pain in the knees or elbows? Hands, feet, hips?"

He tested each area as much as he could lying down. "Everything feels okay, Doc."

They went through a lengthy checklist before she would allow him to even try to sit up. He managed it on the first try, though he had a sensation of lightheadedness for a moment. It quickly passed and as time went on, he began to feel more like his old self. Dr. Daniels took blood samples at intervals, pausing to study the results under her microscope or on one of the other instruments she had set up at the side of the room.

After about a half hour, she finally let him stand up. He was more than ready to waltz right out of there at that point. Only Dr. Daniels's quiet appeals kept him there, answering her seemingly endless questions.

"All right. I think that should do it. Your blood has remained stable for the past three hours," Dr. Daniels informed them. "If it's stable now, it should stay that way. This reaction is a fast one. Your results mirror what we've come to expect and you've confirmed a lot of our hypotheses, John. Thank you."

"So I'm good to go?" He was relieved it was nearly over and he could get out of the desk job and into the field.

Dr. Daniels smiled at him. "You're good to go, John. I know you guys like to patrol at night, but you should probably stay in tonight if you can. You can start your night watches tomorrow night. I don't expect any problems, but if you have discomfort of any kind, give me a call, okay?"

"Yes, ma'am."

* * *

John was content to let Donna drive them back to the lake. He dozed off and on, but felt a lot more alert than he had during most of the day. They said little and he sensed Donna was still upset with him. It all came to a head as they drew closer to their destination. He put his hand on her thigh, unsurprised to find her muscles stiff and quivering. She was on edge and he had the disturbing notion that he was the reason.

"Come on, babe. It wasn't that bad."

She glanced at him, and he was shocked to see the brightness of tears in her eyes.

"You didn't have to take the chance with your health, John. I had no choice. I was attacked. You walked into this willingly. Hell, eagerly. I don't understand you. They say we'll be okay, but they really don't have a clue about how this will affect our future."

"Oh, honey, is that what's got you worried?" He tried his best to soothe her. "To be frank, that's why I did it. I meant what I said. I don't want you, or my sister, to go through this alone."

"I bet it didn't hurt that you get to go into the field now and play shoot 'em up with the zombies?" Her tone was accusatory.

"Hell no. I'm a marine, Donna. My place is in the field. I've trained for combat most of my life. It goes against the grain to have to sit back and watch others fight my battles."

"Especially women?" she challenged.

He took her hand. "Especially you, Donna." His voice dropped to a low tone as he spoke the truth from his heart. "It scares the hell out of me to think of you fighting those things all alone."

"Well, I haven't done a very good job of it so far, have I?" She chuckled brokenly, still fighting the emotion that showed on her pretty face.

"You were never meant to go hand to hand with the bastards. This wasn't supposed to be a mission where we'd go up against them. It was only supposed to be recon. It's not your fault we got way more than we bargained for out here."

"Yet because I can't fight them—and up 'til today I was the only one who could face them without fear—you took a terrible chance with your life and your health."

"You feel guilty?" John was amazed. Nobody had ever taken his worth so seriously before. Well, nobody outside his immediate family. A marine got used to being one of many. It was disconcerting, and touching, that she thought of him as an individual worth worrying about. "Sweetheart, that's . . . well, it's flattering. But you have nothing to feel guilty about. Even if I hadn't met you, if I was offered this same opportunity, I would've taken it. Fighting bad things is what I've made my life's work. Being given the opportunity to stop these creatures is an honor I don't take lightly. These things are probably the worst threat to humanity I'll ever come up against. Fighting to preserve innocent lives is what I do. It's who I am."

He'd never articulated his thoughts so well or so wordily before. Belatedly, he was self-conscious about it until he saw the single tear trickle down her cheek. He cupped her cheek, wiping away the moisture with a gentle touch.

"You're a special man, John Petit."

She let it go at that. He moved back and released her hand so she could use both to drive.

"Let's pick up some dinner on our way back so we don't have to cook." He decided a change in subject was in order and he was hungry as hell.

"Good idea. I saw a sign for a chicken place near the turnoff." The atmosphere in the car lightened considerably.

"Sounds good. It's getting too close to dark, or I'd suggest we eat at the restaurant, but I think it's better if we get it to go."

She agreed and they picked up enough food to feed a small army before heading for their cabin.

When they arrived back at the lake, it was clear the cleanup team had come and gone. The tracker and debris were removed from the porch and they'd left a cryptic note to confirm who'd been there. John was glad they'd been discreet. During the day they did see a few people from time to time, though it was isolated out here. Isolated enough that a few zombies running around hadn't been heard and Bill Wallace, the missing fisherman, apparently hadn't been missed yet.

They'd made a quick stop at the office on their way in and John had asked a few subtle questions about Bill Wallace. The owner, Murray, knew the man, but clearly had no idea he was missing, much less that he'd become a zombie. Wallace's reservation had him booked 'til the end of the week. John supposed Murray would find out then that the man had disappeared when he didn't move out of the cabin he'd rented and didn't show up to pay his bill.

"Dr. Bemkey couldn't have been in the area too long or someone would have noticed more missing people by now. Bill Wallace had been attacked," John reasoned as they dug into dinner.

"The condition of his face and skin made that clear. So there had to be a primary creature that killed Wallace. And Wallace didn't get here until four days ago. So he had to have been attacked very recently. Within the last three to four days considering he'd need time to rise."

"Can we not talk about that part while I'm trying to eat?" Her tone was clearly teasing and he was glad she'd bounced back from the emotional storm that had gripped her earlier. He wasn't good at dealing with female emotions.

"Sorry. I forgot you had a weak stomach." He stole a chicken wing from her plate and barely missed the fork she swatted halfheartedly in his direction.

"I don't have a weak anything. I'm tough as nails. Ask anyone." The false bravado was as obvious as was the grin on her pretty face.

"Okay, tough guy. Are you up for a little recon in the woods, marine-style?"

"Is that what they're calling it these days?" She batted her eyelashes at him and he had to laugh out loud.

"My, my. What a one-track mind you have, Little Red Riding Hood. I like it."

"Does that make you the Big Bad Wolf?" She sounded breathless. He felt the tension rise just like that between them.

He set down his fork and swiped at his mouth with the napkin before tossing it aside. He held her gaze as he stood and held out one hand. It was a clear command and she responded as he'd hoped.

She took his hand, her own trembling as she placed her palm against his. He helped her rise from the chair and pulled her into his arms. They came together in a tempestuous kiss, a melding of mouths and hearts and breaths. He couldn't get enough of the feel of her against him, the taste of her against his tongue, the soft scent of her hair in his lungs. She was vital to his continued existence.

"Donna . . ." He whispered her name as he broke the kiss, only to stroke his hands down her back to cup her incredible ass. Dipping his knees slightly, he lifted her right off her feet, surprising a little yelp from her lips. He liked it. He liked everything about her.

John lifted her onto the countertop in the small kitchenette, urgency riding him.

"Here?" He loved the scandalized note in her voice.

"Yeah, baby. Right here. Right now." He spread her legs and stepped between them. As he'd thought, the small countertop was the perfect height for what he had planned. "That a problem?"

She looked cute as she considered. He could see her thought process written clearly on her beautiful face. Should she get wild with him? Should she let her hair down? Silently, he rooted for her to let go and be daring.

"No. No problem," she said finally, a hint of shyness in her voice. "I've just never done it in a kitchen before."

"Stick with me, babe. I'll take you all kinds of places you've never been before." He crowded against her, nibbling on her lips as she giggled. He liked the sound. It was young, fresh, and sexy, just like her.

He felt like he was getting away with something,

having this comparatively innocent young woman in his arms, but he was powerless to resist her. He would take care of her and treat her like a goddess for as long as she'd let him. The future would take care of itself.

"John."

It drove him nuts when she said his name like that. Her breathy, needful voice did things to him. Unexpected things. Things that made him feel . . . Too much.

"You make me crazy, baby." He breathed the words against her skin as she pushed her clothing off. It wasn't neat and it wasn't orderly, but he wasn't in a very neat and orderly mood at the moment. Judging by her response, she wasn't either.

Within moments, she was mostly naked. All the important parts were uncovered and ready for him. She'd pushed his shirt off and was working on his fly when he had a single moment of clarity and reached into the cargo pocket on his pants for one of the foil squares he had stashed there.

She practically ripped the package out of his hands. She pushed his pants and shorts down over his hips, freeing him.

"Oh, yeah." The words came out of his lips involuntarily as she wrapped her fingers around him, squeezing with exactly the right pressure.

Her other hand brought the foil packet to her mouth. Taking one corner between her teeth, she ripped the wrapper open, allowing the rolled condom to fall. Before it could be lost, she grabbed it, throwing the empty wrapper to the floor instead.

She gave him a tilted smile as she reached downward to roll the rubber over him. She took her time, her light touch driving him higher as she toyed with him deliberately. When the condom was all the way on, she cupped his balls and gave a gentle squeeze. He sucked in a quick breath.

"Like that?" She gave him a blatantly mischievous look.

"You know I do, vixen. But much more of that and I'll start the party without you."

"We can't have that." She removed her hand and he was almost sorry he'd said anything. Then she scooted forward on the counter and put her soft hands around him. It was obvious what she wanted, but he had to hear it from her lips. Her sexy, almost shy way of speaking made him hot every single time he heard that special turned-on tone.

"What do you want, baby? Tell me exactly." She shot him a surprised look.

"You know."

"I won't let you off that easy, sweetheart. I want to hear it." His voice dropped. "Tell me."

A small flush rose up her cheeks. Man, she was something else.

"I want you, John." She moved closer, running her hands over his back as if she couldn't get enough of touching him. "I want you to make love to me. I want you inside me."

He grinned, hearing that perfect tone in her voice. The tone that made his balls ache with need. Yeah, that's what he wanted. He could die a happy man having heard those words from her luscious lips.

"All you had to do was say so, baby." His hands went to her thighs, stroking upward toward the apex between them, rubbing with circular motions as he moved higher and higher until he reached the promised land. The place he would soon possess with an eagerness he hadn't felt since he was a teenager.

He was more than ready to take her, but he had to make sure she was with him. He didn't want to hurt her. He never wanted to hurt her in any way.

"You're nice and wet for me, aren't you?" He met her gaze as he rubbed closer to the opening that wept for his touch. She gasped as he slid one finger inside her. Damn, she was hot. He wouldn't last long. He had to drive her closer to the edge so he took her with him when he blew.

John's finger pressed deep within her, lighting her fire and sending her senses spinning. Then his other hand moved in and those talented, callused fingers found her clit, rubbing in slow circles that sped up as her breathing increased.

"How's that, baby? Are you close?"

"Yes." She threw her head back as her peak neared, closing her eyes as bliss descended on her. Before it could sweep her away, he removed his hands. Her eyes shot open as she searched his expression. He gave her a quick grin as he stepped up, moving into position. "Now, John. Do it now."

John pushed in with little delay. She scooted forward on the countertop to help and they met in the middle. She moaned as he bottomed out within her. Damn, that felt good. No man had ever fit her like John did.

He began to move almost immediately, his big hands anchoring her on the edge of the countertop. Without his support, she probably would have tumbled from her precarious perch, but John was big and strong. His body blocked her from the front and his muscular arms bracketed her. She felt safe and protected . . . and well loved, if only in a physical sense.

The way he protected her and his gentle touch made her almost dare to hope there was some emotional component in their relationship, but she couldn't be absolutely sure. John wasn't one for discussing his emotions and she didn't dare bring up the subject. Their relationship—if that was the right word for this crazy fling—was too new to test with such a weighty topic.

"Won't be long," he warned her, panting as he sped up his pace. She moved with him as best she could in her position, adding counterpoint that drove them both higher. He was right. It wouldn't be long. She was so close to rapture she could taste it.

"John!" She cried out his name as she came hard, a series of spasms rocketing through her body. His hands gripped her, fingers tightening hard enough to leave bruises, but she didn't care. His strength only added to her pleasure as she heard his harsh groan and felt his body join hers in bliss.

Long moments later, John disengaged and lifted her into his arms. She was half asleep as he carried her into the bedroom and deposited her on the bed. She thought she felt him kiss her brow as he tucked her beneath the blanket.

CHAPTER FIVE

Donna was sound asleep in his arms when night fell in earnest. She'd had a long day of worry and travel. He decided to let her sleep as he slid out of bed and suited up for a quick look around the woods. Now that he'd been cleared to join the combat team, he wanted to get a bead on the area, strategizing in his mind the most likely avenues of attack and places to hide. He had to see the surrounding forest at night. The way the enemy would see it.

Now was his chance. And if he ran into one of the zombies while he was out, so much the better. He'd take it out before it could threaten anyone else. Donna would be safe enough in the cabin. John wouldn't go far. He'd left her a weapon and locked her securely inside. She'd be okay until he got back.

John headed down to the lake first. That would be his point of reference. The moon had risen over one side of the haunted lake. A thick blanket of fog lay on the surface, like smoke rising from the water. It rippled as a precocious wind tickled the surface here and there.

"That's certainly creepy enough," John muttered under his breath, taking a moment to appreciate the full effect.

He dismissed the strange weather from his mind as he turned back to locate the cabin through the trees. He'd left a night-light on in the front room, and with that faint glow as his guide, it was easy to spot their temporary home away from home.

Triangulating from the cabin and the lake toward the boundary with the Bemkey estate, John did a thorough walk-through of the woods. He'd done it before in daylight, but everything looked different at night. Somewhat to his disappointment, he didn't come across any zombies. For whatever reason, there was none to be found in the area at that moment.

Deciding he'd been gone long enough, John went back to the cabin and let himself in. Donna was still asleep when he slid back into bed next to her warm body. She had the softest skin. He remembered stroking her hair and shoulder for a while before sleep claimed him again.

Something woke Donna in the middle of the night. For a moment, she was surprised by the warm, hard body in the bed next to her. Then she remembered the night before with John. She could feel her cheeks heat in the cool night air as a little thrill of memory shivered through her body.

It turned to something else when she realized

what had woken her. She heard something. Outside.

Tip-toeing out of the bed, Donna went to the window to see what she could out in the darkness under the trees.

She gasped. A zombie faced her, not five feet from her window. Then she recognized the sound. It was that inhuman moaning sound that had woken her, growing nearer the cabin. She froze for a split second before her brain kicked in.

She jumped back from the window and turned to the bed to wake John, but he was already up. He had two pistols in his hands and was loading them with the special dart ammunition. She hadn't even heard him get out of the bed.

"Here." He handed her one of the pistols and she took it automatically.

She was becoming more comfortable with the pistol the more she handled it. She'd shot rifles with her father and other weapons from time to time but never something like this. Luckily, she'd proven herself a decent shot when they'd tested, then trained her back at the base.

"Guard the door. I'll take care of this and then we'll go together to check the rest. Dress if you can. Shoes are most important." John stepped in front of her as he spoke in a rapid, urgent voice. He wore only his boxers and partially laced boots. He raised the window sash enough to get the barrel of the pistol out and began to fire.

After hitting the creature with four darts in rapid succession, he turned back to her. She'd tugged on her T-shirt and sneakers in record time.

"What now?" she asked, her voice noticeably shaky despite her best attempts to pretend she was as calm as he was under fire.

"We check the rest of the windows first. See if we can get them—if there are more—from here before we go out in the open." He opened the door and eased in front of her, striding boldly forward, checking each window.

When they reached the main room of the cabin, he went to the largest window and sent her to the smaller side windows with a pointed glance. She caught her breath as she noticed two more zombies emerging from the woods about ten yards away. She looked at John for guidance, but he was already firing out his partially open window. She followed his example.

Reaching out with trembling hands, she raised the window sash, fumbling only a little. She sank down and took aim, firing as quickly as she could. They were getting too close.

"Split up your shots if you can," John instructed. "Four shots in each and spread them around."

"Got it." She was proud when her voice only quavered a little. She set to work, doing her best to make every dart count. She had just plugged two darts in each of her targets when another started walking toward the cabin through the woods. "John, there's another one." She heard the fear in her own voice.

"I see him." Their windows were at ninety-degree angles to one another. John was firing at multiple targets, but she didn't dare spare a glance to see how many. She had enough work cut out for herself with the two she was working on and the third on the way.

She gave each of the first two one more round each. She had two more darts in the clip. Should she use the last two darts in the clip for the first two zombies or try to get them into the other one? The moment of indecision cost her. All three were getting closer.

"Four in each, babe. Finish off the first two and we'll work on the third together." John took the decision out of her hands and she was thankful. She followed his directions thankfully.

"I need to reload." She was still breathing rapidly, but John's steady presence helped her focus.

"Catch." He tossed her a fresh clip and only then did she realize he'd clutched a few spares in one of his hands.

It took her longer to reload than John. She wasn't a marksman like him, but she managed. When she looked up again, the third creature was nearly to the front porch. Her racing pulse spiked up a notch. The other two were gone. Thank heaven. She hadn't seen them fall, but there was no other explanation for where they might've gone. She'd hit them with the toxin from far enough away that there'd been time for the toxin to work.

Not so with the third zombie. He didn't even have one dart sticking out of him yet and he was altogether too close if she was any judge.

"John?" He must've heard the fear in her voice.

"Hang in there, baby. I'm almost done with these five. We'll get the other one together, just like I promised, but we need to get the rest under control first or we'll be totally overrun before we can blink."

She fired as he talked and hit the third zombie twice in rapid succession. The shots weren't too widely spaced, but she'd do better. She had to do better. From what she'd been told, spacing the shots out around the torso and legs helped spread the toxin faster. At least, that was the theory. She'd hit her target twice near the left shoulder. It would take awhile for it to spread from there and she needed at least another two darts in the thing before there would be enough of the toxin to take it down.

"John." His name dragged out as she fired another round, hitting the creature in the stomach this time. Better.

The creature veered off, away from her. She couldn't get another shot. "John, he's—" She looked toward him, but he was gone and the front door stood ajar. "Oh, no!" She ran toward the door only to find John facing down the zombie, darting him from point-blank range.

The zombie swiped at him, advancing on John. It was a hell of a sight. John wore only half-laced combat boots and a pair of bright white boxers. He walked backward as the zombie advanced, staying a foot ahead of the ugly yellow claws that had once been fingernails.

Donna scanned the trees behind him, but thankfully there were no more of the creatures. At least none that she could see from her vantage point. She stepped onto the porch and perched at the edge of the top stair. John had led the creature away from the cabin a few feet, off the main dirt pathway that led to the lake and into the grass that bordered the tree line. John walked backward, a step at a time, keeping a vigilant eye on the zombie as it followed his lead.

"Stay back, Donna," he ordered. "Stay on the porch in case there are more of them. This guy should be going down any minute now."

"Be careful, John." She dared not talk above a low whisper.

Her warning came a moment too late. As if in slow motion, she saw John's loose bootlace get caught on a fallen branch, tripping him up. He fell hard on his ass and the zombie bent over him, clawing his chest as John scrambled to recover.

"John!" She came down off the porch, raising her pistol but she didn't dare fire until she had a clear shot. She couldn't take the chance of hitting John. Besides, the thing already had the required four darts sticking out of his gray flesh. Shooting him with another dart wouldn't do any good. The toxin still required a certain amount of time to work.

The zombie appeared to be winning. As she ran toward the struggling pair on the ground, she saw that the creature had John pinned. Her heart in her throat, she tried to think of a way to help. The monster had been a big man in life. He easily weighed twice what she did. There was no way she could pull him off John, but she had to try.

Just as she approached to give what little help she could, John pulled his knees up for leverage and rolled, throwing the zombie off him.

A second later, it dissolved on the ground, leaving behind a pile of ruined clothes and a sticky residue. John lay on the ground nearby, catching his breath for just a second before he climbed to his feet. He had slashes diagonally down one side of his chest that were bleeding, but not heavily, much to her relief.

"Are you hurt anywhere else?" she asked quickly.

"Just my wounded pride. Damn, my butt hurts." He dusted off his now dirt-stained boxers and gave her a rueful, lopsided grin. "Get up on the porch and keep a lookout while I do a sweep of the area. It's close to dawn. Chances are they're going to ground for the day."

"What about your chest?"

He dismissed her question with a shake of his head. "It's not bad." He ran one dirty finger over his chest near the quickly closing gashes. "Son of a gun. I heal fast now. Guess that answers the question about whether the immunity treatment worked." That lopsided grin was back, stronger than before. "Get up there now. I'll be back in a few minutes. Stay sharp. Just don't shoot me when I come back. I'm the one with the white flag on my ass."

He pointed to his boxers and she had to admire his humor. Grace under fire was this man's middle name. He took a moment to secure his trailing bootlaces so they wouldn't trip him up again and set off silently around the perimeter of the building, his pistol leading the way.

Donna waited for him on the porch, fear in every breath. The sky was beginning to lighten, which gave her hope. So far, the creatures had shunned daylight. When the sun came out, they should be safe.

He came back, making more noise than he usually did. He probably knew she was still jumpy and was making certain she wasn't going to shoot him accidentally.

"Clear," he called softly through the grayness of predawn as he approached the cabin. His steps were calm, yet smooth and rapid. He mounted the small staircase and reached for her arm. "You okay?"

She looked upward to meet his concerned gaze and nodded. "Are they gone?"

"Yeah. Either that was all of them or the dawn scared away any others that were with them. We should be okay now."

She led the way back into the cabin. He locked the door behind them and followed her to the small kitchen area. She dampened some paper towels and turned to swipe gently at the stripes of blood on his chest. The blood was all that was left of the gashes. Not even a red line hinted that he'd been clawed. His skin had healed completely in the short time since the attack. Even though she'd seen similar speed-healing on her own body, she was still taken aback by it.

She said nothing as she bathed his chest, washing away the blood. When he was clean, she stepped into his open arms, needing the hug he so freely gave.

"I'm such a wimp." She hiccupped once as she buried her face in the crook of his neck.

He burst out laughing.

"Sorry." He bit back his laughter. "You are the most unwimpy woman I know, Donna."

"Yeah, right. Any woman on the team is way braver than me."

"They're all pretty formidable, but you're no slouch, Donna. I've fought at your side. I know."

She drew away from him to meet his gaze. "If you say so. I think you're just being nice. But I will admit I'm getting a little better. I only froze for a few seconds before."

"You did good, sweetheart. You took out your targets and followed direction. You're a good little soldier."

She chuckled at his teasing tone, but his words and the look in his eyes made her feel better. She reached up and wove her fingers through his hair, coaxing his head downward. Their lips joined. She may have initiated the kiss, but John deepened it, making it grow from something innocent and light to something hot and molten. When he finally lifted his head, she was breathless.

"Come on." He tugged on her hand as he led her toward the bedroom. "I doubt we'll be able to go back to sleep after that, but it's worth a try."

"Are you sure we're safe?"

He looked out the window. "It's dawn. They're gone." He snagged his phone out of his shirt pocket as they entered the bedroom. He'd left it hanging over a chair back earlier. "I should call in the cleanup guys. It'll take them the better part of an hour to get here. I should also report the increased activity to Commander Sykes. It won't take long."

He kept her hand in his as he sat on the edge of the bed and hit the speed-dial with one hand. He spent less than a minute on the line with the cleanup guys, then disconnected and hit another speed-dial button. This time, the call connected with Matt Sykes, back at the base in North Carolina.

She sat next to him as he talked, unabashedly listening in and letting his warmth calm her more. It wasn't every day she faced zombies and shot them down. Nothing had been normal since her ex-boyfriend had become one of them and savaged her.

It sounded like Sykes still couldn't spare anyone to help them, but John assured him they had the situation under control. She wasn't so sure, but she knew if anyone could handle himself in a crisis, it was John. She'd do her best to hold up her end of the deal, though she wasn't as highly trained.

John ended the call after a few minutes and tossed the phone onto the bedside table. He scooted onto the bed and he pulled her into his arms, spooning her from behind.

"You okay now?" His hands wrapped around her middle, he spoke in a low voice, next to her ear.

"I'm good," she said softly. "You were great out there tonight, John."

"Don't forget your part. You were a big help, babe. I was glad you were there to watch my back."

"You're just saying that." She rolled over to look into his eyes as they lay facing each other.

"I'm not." He raised one hand to cup her cheek, moving eventually to gently stroke her hair back from her face. "I think you're gorgeous and smart and funny. And very capable. You were a big help, Donna."

She didn't know how to respond to the honesty she read in his gaze, so she closed the distance and kissed him. He responded so well, it encouraged her to be more aggressive than usual. She pushed on his shoulder, urging him to lie on his back beneath her. She straddled him, holding his gaze as she tugged her T-shirt off over her head. She was naked beneath and she read the appreciation in his eyes as she knelt over him.

"You hunt zombies in nothing but a T-shirt?" he teased. "Man, when you go commando, you really go commando."

"Well, I had my sneakers on too." She glanced toward where she'd kicked off her shoes when she'd come back into the bedroom.

His hips rose and jostled her higher, but it was worth the momentary fear of falling when his shorts disappeared from between them. His hands reappeared from behind her after completing the task and he wrapped his warm fingers around her waist, just over her hips. She liked the secure feel of his heavy hands anchoring her to him.

"Now we're even." He smiled at her in that devilish way that promised hours of pleasure. She couldn't wait.

"Oh, I like that." She bent over him to place little kisses along his strong jaw. Her hair fell forward to cocoon them in intimacy. "As much as I like you," she dared to whisper near his ear. It was as close as she could come to admitting the growing feelings she had for him. She'd tried to convince herself this was a temporary arrangement. She'd tried to keep it light and she'd failed miserably.

Facing danger with him and fighting at his side had made her feel closer to him in a shorter amount of time than anyone she'd ever known. He'd saved her in San Francisco. He'd saved her again here in Tennessee. Twice. No doubt he'd do it again before this was all over.

She admired his skills. She loved his sense of honor. And she couldn't resist his easy charm. John was all she'd ever looked for in a man and didn't think she'd find.

And she couldn't have him. Not to keep. He had "love 'em and leave 'em" written all over him. She'd known that from the start and she still hadn't been able to protect her heart. She was very much afraid she'd already surrendered her heart to him, lock, stock, and barrel. It was too late to stop herself from loving him now.

But she'd never let him know. That would only send him running for the hills. She wanted to enjoy this while it lasted. She'd deal with the heartache later. Somehow. For now, she had him exactly where she wanted him.

"Where are the condoms?" she whispered in his ear, liking the way his muscles tensed under her thighs.

"Right thigh pocket of my pants." The growl in his voice set her on fire. She looked around the bedroom to see if she could spot the pants. There they were. Flung over the chair next to the bed. Thank goodness.

Donna stretched and nabbed the pants while John placed one of his hands over her breast and squeezed, making her shiver in delight. His action drew her gaze as she pulled one of the dozen foil packets out of his pocket and threw the pants away, uncaring where they landed.

"So many?"

"Call me an optimist." He gave her a cocky grin.

She dipped, pushing her breast into his hand as he rubbed obligingly over the distended nipple.

"Judging by the way you make me feel, I'd say you've got a good chance of being right."

"Now that's what I like to hear." He pinched her nipple, moving his other hand down from her hip to tangle in the curls at the apex of her thighs. He held her gaze as he slid one finger into her folds, finding the nub that craved his attention. He stroked her clit and her breath came in short gasps as her temperature rose.

She sat over his thighs, enjoying the wicked sensations for a moment before moving away. "No more of that for now. I want to come with you inside me, John." She almost blushed saying the words aloud, but the fire in his gaze told her he liked hearing her say such things.

She drew out the process of covering his cock with the condom, making sure John watched every step of the process. She wouldn't let him participate. When he tried to help, she pushed his hands away with a *tsk*ing sound. He gave in with good grace, letting her call the shots. She liked that. And she loved having him at her mercy, so to speak.

Before she finally rolled the condom over him, she took him in her mouth, just briefly. She would've spent more time there but he seemed too eager to let her play very long. Besides that, she wanted him desperately. There was something about the danger they'd shared earlier that spurred her libido to new heights. She didn't want to waste time. She wanted him now. Urgently.

Once he was covered, she rose over him, positioned him, and pushed downward. Damn, that felt good. He filled her so completely, so wonderfully. It was sheer bliss when he was inside her fully.

"Oh, yeah." The words popped out of her mouth without thought, without intention.

"Yeah," he echoed, drawing out the word, his expression intense as their gazes met and held. She began to ride him, slowly at first, then picking up speed as her passion increased.

John helped her when her thighs began to quiver under the strain. His hands gripped her hips, the muscles in his arms rippling as he lifted and lowered her. Even though she was on top, at some point, he'd taken control of the pace.

"Just like that, baby," he urged her in the sexiest voice ever. His eyes were half-lidded, his body hot beneath her and inside her. She loved the way he made her feel. The way he looked at her. The way he rocked her world.

"John! I need—" She couldn't finish the thought as her teeth clenched. She didn't know what she needed. She only hoped John did. She strained toward completion that was just out of her reach.

Until he reached down with one hand, his fingers stroking between her legs, rubbing her clit with urgent motions. Yes. That's just what she needed.

Donna screamed as she went off like a rocket, coming hard over him. John joined her a moment later, his body lifting hers as his muscles went rigid beneath her. She felt his spasms through her own as they joined in an orgasm that left her utterly replete.

Sighing as she floated downward, she settled her head against his chest and drifted for a long, pleasurable moment. Eventually, she was vaguely aware of John disengaging from her body and rolling them to their sides. She watched wearily as he took care of things quickly, then returned to her, tucking her back against his heart as she drifted off for a nap.

CHAPTER SIX

The sound of a car parking behind theirs on the gravel drive under the trees alerted them. John rolled out of bed and began to dress.

"Go take your shower. I'll deal with these guys." John buttoned his shirt as he went out to meet the cleanup team.

The shower was lovely and restorative. She took a few minutes longer than she usually did, knowing John was occupied with the cleanup team. When she came out of the bathroom, she took a moment to tidy the bedroom.

Dressing in a fresh T-shirt and jeans from her knapsack, she headed out into the main room to find John. She paused to look out the window to see two very unfishermenlike-looking fishermen working near the porch. They had brand-new boots and clothing that looked as if they'd only snipped the tags off five minutes before they'd gotten there. Not only that, the clothes were ill-fitting as if someone else had bought them without regard for sizes. Donna stifled a laugh as she went toward the kitchen area where John stood.

"Are those guys for real?"

"Yeah, I know. They're not real good at camouflage, are they?" John chuckled as he handed her a cup of coffee. "If anyone asks, they're friends of ours from the city, just down for a little visit."

"They look more like city slickers than we do and we're both from New York." She chuckled and took a small sip of her coffee.

"Buzz there—the taller one—is from Georgia, and Willie is from New Orleans. Seems like neither one has ever been fishing before. They're both dyed-in-the-wool science geeks."

"Hey, you better watch that, bud. I'm a geeky, almost chemical engineer myself."

John wrapped his arms around her waist and pulled her against him. "There's not a geeky bone in your luscious little body, sweetheart. Engineer or not."

"Mmm. I like that." She slipped her hands up under his T-shirt to stroke his solid six-pack of abdominal muscles. She loved the way his hard body rippled under her touch. She'd never been with a man who was more physically fit than John. Or more handsome. He was the complete package as far as she was concerned. Smart too. They related well now that they knew each other better.

"And I like you, sweetheart. Way more than a little."

His almost-declaration made her stomach clench as he leaned in to place a row of kisses along her cheek and jaw, working his way toward her mouth. When he finally reached his destination, his tongue slipped into her mouth and sent her temperature soaring.

A knock on the doorframe and a loud clearing of someone's throat easily heard through the screen door broke them apart all too soon. It was the taller member of the cleanup team. The one John had said was called Buzz.

Donna felt the heat of a blush in her cheeks as she walked toward the door.

"Your pardon for interrupting, ma'am." The fake fisherman had his funny fishing hat in his hands as he smiled at her. She could definitely hear the southern drawl of Georgia in his words.

"Not at all." She tried to ignore her own discomfort at being caught smooching another team member. "You're Buzz, right?" She opened the screen door and held out her hand. "I'm Donna."

He shook her hand gently and smiled again. "Pleased to meet you, Miss Donna." Oh, yeah, this man definitely had the charm of the Old South in his blood. "I just came to tell you we're done with the pickup and decon of the area. It was a little awkward having to hide most of our protective gear but we managed."

That explained the bad fit of their clothes to her mind. She hadn't realized they were wearing multiple layers. Close up now, she could see a few of the layers under the tacky and ill-fitting fake-fisherman clothes.

"I'm curious. What do you do with the remains?"

"Send them back to the lab for study. The team leaders are still trying to figure out how to return those remains that we can identify back to their next of kin. Mighty big mess if you ask me."

"Yeah, I guess I can see that." Donna jumped only a little when John came up beside her and put his left arm around her waist in a clear statement. Obviously he didn't care who knew they were together. She liked that. It made her feel warm inside.

"Thanks for coming out so quickly, Buzz." John held out his right hand to Buzz for a friendly shake.

"Happy to help, John. Most of the tracks come from the direction of the estate as far as we can tell. We did our best not to disturb anything so you can track back a ways. Mighty quiet in this camp. No people about to mess up the tracks and the nearest cabins are a ways back from yours. It's a good setup for this kind of operation, I'm thinking."

"We lucked out for sure," John agreed. "Luckily the darts don't make much noise at all or we'd have had the entire neighborhood down here earlier today. There's no one in the nearest cabins. I asked the landlord to put us out on the edge away from everyone else."

"Good thinking."

They talked a few minutes more and then Buzz took his leave. He and Willie left in a cloud of gravel dust as they rolled down the road out of the fishing camp. They took the remains with them and left the scene pristine and decontaminated.

John left to take a look at the tracks while Donna tidied up the cabin a bit. She also fixed a snack for them both, which they shared when John came back in.

"The sandwiches are good," John commented as they shared their snack at the small kitchen table, "but I'd like to take you out to dinner tonight for a change of pace. What do you think?"

"You mean like a date?" She held her breath waiting for his answer.

He moved closer to her. "Exactly like a date." His tone grew more intimate. "There's nothing in the operation manual that says we have to eat every meal in the cabin. If Sykes asks, we'll tell him we went scouting the area. Murray told me when we checked in that there's a nice restaurant with a scenic overlook a few miles up the road. I'd like to take you there."

Tingles went down her spine. "Okay, but I don't have anything too dressy with me."

"You're gorgeous in whatever you wear, Donna, but don't worry. Murray said the place is casual, with a five-star view, and down-home Southern cooking."

"I've never had really authentic Southern food."

"Then you're in for a treat."

Oh, yeah. She knew she was. Just being with John—on a real date—would be a treat.

The restaurant was lovely, perched on the side of a cliff overlooking a vast stretch of the lake far below. It took some maneuvering to get to the place and the sloped drive and parking lot was paved only with gravel, but the view alone was worth every difficulty to get there. The food was good, wholesome, Southern cooking and Donna enjoyed trying new dishes she hadn't even heard of before.

"The view here is amazing." Donna sighed as she gazed out the window. They'd been seated by the window only after John had slipped a twenty to the hostess. He'd done it so smoothly, Donna hadn't even realized what had happened until after the fact. It gave her a little thrill to know he'd gone out of his way to make this dinner special.

"I agree. The lake . . . and the company." He raised his glass in her direction with a sexy wink. Oh, yeah. Her limbs were tingling, her blood singing with his nearness as he watched her over the rim of his wineglass. "It is a little odd though." He placed his glass back on the table, giving her a lopsided grin.

"How so?"

"I've never been on a date on a mission before," he admitted.

She laughed with him. "I guess this is pretty strange for you. This is only my first mission— probably my last as well—so I'm no expert."

"Oh, I think you have a bright future ahead of you, if you decide to go into covert work."

"You've got to be kidding," she scoffed good-naturedly.

"No, you've got a bead on looking the part. You don't have to act innocent. You're the real deal. Believe it or not, that's a big help. The owner of the fishing camp only had to glance at you and he gave me whatever I wanted. He bought my crazy-in-love-newlywed story hook, line, and sinker."

Another little thrill went through her at hearing the L-word coming from his lips. But she didn't dare think he might feel as strongly about her as she did about him. She didn't know when it had happened, but being here with him, in this mo-ment out of time, was like a dream she'd never known she'd wanted to come true. He was magic.

His every word, his every smile went straight to her heart.

She was on the verge of saying something all too revealing when a showy brunette swished down the crowded aisle toward their table. She must've been sitting in the private room off to one side. They could see the doors from where they sat, but hadn't been able to see inside. Donna looked up at the woman and her breath caught.

It was Dr. Bemkey. Donna recognized her from the photos in her file. She was much more intimidating in person, of course. Her perfect coiffure, manicured fingernails, and expertly applied make-up created a larger-than-life sort of presence that was backed up by the poise in every step. Designer clothes hung off her perfectly proportioned frame, and her ears, fingers, wrists, and neck dripped with gold and diamonds. All in all, she made a hell of a picture.

"Close your mouth, darling. You'll catch flies." Dr. Elizabeth Bemkey stopped before their table and addressed Donna directly before turning her attention to John. "I've seen you down by my beach," she said without blinking. "Please be sure to stay on the public side, lovey. You could get hurt and I wouldn't want to lose any more pets."

Did she mean . . . ? Donna shot a quick look at John, but he had all his attention focused on the woman standing so calmly at the side of their table.

"I'm really very put out with you for interfering with my playthings." She tapped John on the shoulder as if she were some belle at an old-fashioned ball. Her smile was brittle and her eyes didn't look altogether sane. Donna felt a chill creep down her spine. "You'd better watch yourselves or you might end up becoming one of my toys." Her gaze turned ice cold.

She turned and walked out of the restaurant without even waiting for a response. Donna turned to John only after Dr. Bemkey was gone.

"What the hell was that?"

John's lips thinned as he frowned. "That was trouble with a capital *T*."

"She knows who we are?"

"At the very least she knows what we are and what we've been doing. She may not know our names, but she knows what we're doing down here."

"I think she threatened us." Donna was shocked. "She seemed mad as a hatter too."

"Yeah." John sat back in his chair and twirled his wineglass. "She's crazy like a fox. And she needs to be run to ground."

"What?" Donna was afraid she understood what he meant all too well, but she needed confirmation.

"She doesn't seem stable and she issued a death threat. She doesn't know we're immune. But if she's running around threatening people, she's even more dangerous than I'd anticipated. In this kind of state, she could be capable of anything. We need to take her down now. As soon as possible." His gaze was hard as he looked out over the lake without really seeing it. He seemed focused on something much different and much deadlier.

They'd been on dessert when Dr. Bemkey had come over, so there was nothing keeping them at the restaurant. They paid the check and left the restaurant in short order. John had a faraway look on his face as he no doubt made plans that didn't include Donna. Or, if they did include her, only in a peripheral way. Donna was worried. She didn't like the idea of him operating out there all alone.

Originally, they'd thought they would watch, wait, and gather intel, taking out zombies along the way until they were ready to strike at Dr. Bemkey's lair—with help from the main team. Now, it looked like John planned to move up the timetable and forgo the promised help from the rest of the combatable operatives on the team. Donna didn't know for sure, but she thought she knew John well enough by now to know the way he thought.

He drove them back down the cliff toward the cabin on the lakeshore without speaking much. Most likely, he was already planning the call he'd make when they got back to the cabin.

"Yes, sir. She came right up to our table, bold as brass, and issued a death threat." John was on the phone with Matt Sykes, pacing from window to window in the main room of the cabin. They'd returned only moments before and John had immediately phoned in his report to the commander. "No, sir. I don't know how she knew who we were. She claimed to have seen us on the beach. It's possible she observed Donna that first night when her so-called *pet* chased Donna from the lakeshore. I'm not sure how she could've seen me unless there are some really well-hidden cameras there that I couldn't spot."

Donna listened to John's end of the conversation but she could figure out what was going on easily enough. John looked tense, like a coiled spring waiting to strike. She'd seen him like this before, when they were under attack. This was his moment. His element. This was what he'd been born to do.

"Yes, sir. I'm going out there tonight to take another look around," he said into the phone. She didn't like the sound of that at all. "No, sir. I won't take action unless it seems feasible and secure." There was a pause. "I understand. Thank you, sir."

He disconnected the call and stowed his phone in his pocket. Then he turned to her. "He still can't spare anyone to help."

Donna's heart sank. "I heard you say you were going out to do reconnaissance?"

"Yeah. Just a sneak and peek. I won't go in unless I think it's safe enough to do so." He armed himself from the box of ammunition the cleanup crew had restocked before they left.

"What if there are more zombies?" She hated the note of fear in her voice.

"I think we took out the bulk of them last night. Chances are she doesn't have that many of the creatures roaming around out here or there'd be a lot more missing people. Even way out here, if large numbers of people had gone missing, someone would have noticed by now." He prepared as he spoke, strapping on his utility belt and other gear. "Near as I can figure, she made the first few and then they went out and made the others. That takes time. I think we put quite a dent into her supply of *playthings* last night." He emphasized the word the crazy doctor had used to describe those she had killed.

"I can't believe she called them that." Donna

was still shocked and a little disgusted with the woman's attitude.

"She's bonkers, babe. Which is why she needs to be taken down. The sooner the better. If she'd shown any sign of being more rational, I'd feel better. As it is, people in this kind of state are too unpredictable. We need to stop her."

"I can see that, but it won't stop me from worrying about you."

John stopped in front of her. "Don't worry, sweetheart. This is what I do." He held out his arms and she walked into them, grateful for his reassurance.

She wanted to cling to him but knew she had to let him go. "Just be careful out there, John."

"It's only a little recon. Depending on what I find, I'll either go in and take her down or come back here. No harm, no foul."

Everything looked quiet to John's trained eyes. Not too quiet. Just a normal foggy, creepy night on the lake. The ambiance was right out of a classic horror movie, but it didn't bother John. A little fog never hurt anyone. It was what might be hiding in the fog that could be the real problem. But his sixth sense told him nothing at the moment. Nothing stirred in the fog that shouldn't be there. The place was clear.

He'd crossed onto the estate's grounds twenty minutes before and had circled the big place twice. Nothing appeared out of place. If his third circuit of the grounds turned up nothing again, he'd go in closer. If he could take down his mark tonight, he would. That woman had to be stopped. The sooner the better.

He moved closer. He could see in the windows. There was no activity on the first floor even though there were lights on in almost every room. Security lights, most likely, on timers. The first floor didn't look lived in. The only place he could discern traffic was near the stairs. Footprints marred the lush pile of the carpet there, but nowhere else.

There was a balcony running along the back of the house that faced the water. If he could get up there, he could get a good look inside the second story. John looked for a likely tree and found one that wasn't ideal, but would do for his purposes.

A few minutes later, John was peeking into the upstairs windows. Bingo.

The doctor was moving between what looked like her bedroom and a dressing room, changing from the elegant dress she'd worn to the restaurant into something more casual. She tossed the dress over a chair and finished buttoning an expensive white shirt over equally pricey khaki pants. Both had little men riding polo ponies embroidered discreetly on them. The woman had a lot of money and didn't mind throwing it around. Her house was testament to that.

He looked around. The sun was almost completely gone now and the fog on the water had thickened even more. There was a chill in the air, but John didn't let the sinister atmosphere disturb him. The fog would cover his activities.

He had the perfect opportunity. Dr. Bemkey was alone in the house as far as he could tell, with no zombies around to defend her. He was going in.

He turned back to the window, but the light had gone out. The doctor was gone. She'd headed downstairs. Rather than take the risk of making a racket by going through the upper floor and stalking the woman down the stairs, he retreated to the tree so he could approach from the ground.

John dropped to the ground and thought about the most likely entrance he'd scoped out before. There were a set of glass double doors in the center of the back side of the house. John had used a tree at the end of the balcony closest to the woods.

"John!"

Donna's shout froze him in his tracks. He whipped around to find her running toward him from the tree line. What in the world was she doing? John went to her, surprised to see she had her pistol in one hand. Immediately, he looked around. The fog had moved in closer to the house. It obliterated almost everything, but he could see . . . movement. In the fog. Shit. The zombies had snuck up on him after all. He pulled his weapon and met Donna in the swirling mist.

"I saw them come up from the water." She spoke in an urgent whisper.

"Honey, you were supposed to wait at the cabin." John took only a moment to roll his eyes at her so she'd know he was only kidding. "Not that I'm complaining." He kept his voice low as they edged back toward the trees.

"I was watching the sunset over the lake when I saw something strange. John, they're actually hiding *in* the lake!"

"Son of a bitch." He shook his head. "That's a new one."

"They don't need to breathe," she went on in a

whisper. "They can stay in the water all day while the sun is out and only come out of the water at night."

"I don't think they've seen us." They'd reached the tree line safely. John tucked Donna next to him under the cover of some thick branches as he watched the proceedings.

A cluster of dripping zombies paraded past them toward the house. A light clicked on in the upstairs room and the French doors opened to reveal Dr. Bemkey standing like some Eva Perón–wannabe on the balcony, ready to address her people.

"See that old guy at the front of the pack?" John whispered in Donna's ear. So far neither the creatures nor their creator had detected them. He wanted to keep it that way.

Donna nodded. Her eyes were glued to the action on the back lawn of the estate, but she was attuned to John's every word.

"Judging by the file photos I've seen, I'd say that's Dr. Bemkey's ex-husband. File said he left her for his secretary. I'd say the blond bimbo in the bikini is probably her."

"The others all look like fishermen. Mr. Bemkey isn't too damaged, but the rest all have bad bite marks. Dr. Bemkey probably made her ex her first victim and he made the others."

"I believe you're right." John was counting heads, trying to assess troop strength.

"Look at that big one. He looks like the fishing guide that advertises on those billboards."

"Bubba's Bass Tours." John remembered seeing that billboard as they drove here. Sure enough, the big guy from the sign looked a lot like the zombie that stood head and shoulders above the rest. Tall as well as wide, this guy was imposing. The creatures stopped beneath the balcony, all looking up at the woman above them. "Here we go. Evita's about to address the peons."

Donna stifled a laugh but John could tell she was nervous. Her body trembled in the chilly mist as she pressed against his side. She wasn't snuggling too close, but she seemed to need the bodily contact. He could understand that. This was a situation unlike any he'd ever been in before.

"My creations." Dr. Bemkey's voice floated down to them from the balcony. "Our time has come. Men have come to destroy you, but I want you to destroy them instead."

"Oh, shit." John felt his stomach drop as he reflexively checked his ammo supply.

"Your mistress wants you to go to the fishing camp. I want you to kill. Kill them all!"

The zombies began to stomp their feet and make those inhuman sounds. A few began to chant the word "kill."

"This can't be good." Donna looked from the zombies to John and back again. They were getting riled up into a frenzy.

"I counted twenty-three of them. I think we can take them, if we're smart about it."

"That sounds like an awful lot, John. Are you sure?" Donna's eyes were wide and fearful as she looked up at him in the misty darkness.

"The fog can work to our advantage. You just can't let too many of them track you at once."

"Now, my lovelies," Dr. Bemkey shouted from her balcony, "go now! Kill them all! Make me an army."

"Our time just ran out." John dragged her close for a quick kiss. "No matter what happens, I want you to know . . . I love you, Donna. It's crazy and it's sudden, but I love you more than any woman I've ever known."

"John . . ." Her reaction was a mixture of shock and what looked like joy, but it was dark and misty. And they had bigger fish to fry at the moment. He shouldn't have said anything, but he couldn't help himself.

"Go, sweetheart." He turned her around and pointed her toward the cabin. "Get all the ammo we've got left and meet me on the porch. I'll be right behind you. I just want to divert some of these guys first."

"Why?" she asked even as she took a step away, toward the cabin.

"Divide and conquer. We've got to get them into smaller groups so we can pick them off and they don't overwhelm us. I'll start that now while you get the ammo. We're going to need every last dart."

"Be careful." She gave him a pained look even as she sprang away through the trees toward the cabin.

John watched her go for only a moment before she was swallowed up by the swirling mist. John turned back to find the zombies heading slowly toward the tree line. All but one. It looked like Evita had held one back from the class: her ex-husband.

"Go jump in the lake," she ordered him and John wasn't all that surprised when he turned around and walked right back into the lake. Fine. That left twenty-two creatures for him and Donna to deal with. They'd handle Mr. Bemkey later.

CHAPTER SEVEN

John came in hot, creatures on his trail as he hit the porch running. Donna was waiting there for him, bless her heart, with every dart and weapon in their small arsenal. She handed him a fresh clip before she said a word and he slammed it into his empty dart rifle.

"I'll reload this empty for you." She grabbed the empty clip he'd just taken from the weapon. Her small fingers deftly reloaded the clip with its deadly cargo and handed it back to him.

"You've got the pistols?"

"Yeah." She turned to show him her hip where one of the pistols rested in its holster. She handed the other to him.

"You keep it." He tried to hand it back.

"You fire faster and more accurately than I do. You need it more," she argued. "I'm good with the one I have and I packed plenty of ammunition in my bag."

He saw she had a canvas bag slung across her

chest. It was the one that had been loaded with their pistol rounds.

"Open the bag. Let me see how much you have in there."

She turned the other way and lifted the flap on the rectangular bag. It was half full. She'd divvied up the pistol ammo to his satisfaction. She had about three quarters of their supply and he had the rest.

"Good. I want you to start down by the lake. Beware of anything coming from the water. There shouldn't be any left in there except Mr. Bemkey, but you never know. Start at the shoreline and work your way inward. Don't let anything get past you. We need to keep the zombies away from the other cabins. The line we don't want them to cross is from the lake to our cabin. I'll watch the woods on this side, you take the area from the lake to about halfway to here. We'll meet in the middle and overlap."

"All right." She looked scared but willing to do her part. Damn, he loved her courage and spirit as much as he loved her.

"Drop tags as you go if you can, but don't let it slow you down. We can always go back later to drop the transmitters."

She nodded, handing him the last clip and watching him stow it in a pouch on his utility belt. They were armed as well as they could be. He looked at her, wanting to say something meaningful but he saw her eyes widen as she peered over his shoulder.

He spun.

Damn. The zombies had found them.

"Be careful. Head for the water. I've got these guys." He gave her a quick kiss and vaulted off the porch. He hit the ground running, already firing darts at the zombies coming toward him.

They spent the next few hours zigzagging through the woods between the cabin and the lake, shooting zombies left and right. Some went down easy, some were more canny. Most were wearing fishing gear of one kind or another and John surmised that most of the victims had been fishermen, attacked while out for a day of leisure.

John met up with Donna every fifteen minutes or so as their paths intersected in the woods. The bulk of the creatures had come through the woods farther away from the waterline, as he'd hoped. So far, they were doing well. None had gotten through their defensive line. John still worried for Donna's safety when she was out of his sight, but there was no help for it. They had a job to do and, so far, Donna was holding up well.

He was so proud of her. She'd stolen his heart with her smile and her personality. Her courage under fire impressed the hell out of him and only made him love her more.

The girl in the bikini had no doubt once been beautiful. Her silicone-enhanced breasts were now a thing of the past. The bikini was lopsided with prominent chunks of her flesh missing. She'd been chomped on by the zombies and the result wasn't pretty. Not at all.

Donna watched her disintegrate with a feeling of compassion. The girl—even if she had been a home-wrecking bimbo in life—hadn't deserved to die that way. Nobody deserved to die like that.

As she fell into a pile of goo at Donna's feet, something silver glinted in the grass, catching her eye. She bent down to take a closer look, using a stick to push the tattered remains of the bikini aside.

"What's this?"

John crouched to look over her shoulder.

"A tracker. And it's not one of ours." Donna looked up to catch his expression. His lips had thinned into a grim line. "That had to have been implanted beneath the skin. I've seen something like it before."

She didn't ask where. As a CIA operative, John had lots of secrets she would never be privy to. She knew better than to pry. If he said it was a tracking device, it damned well was a tracking device.

"You think Dr. Bemkey implanted it?" Donna stood, dropping the stick next to the remains. It would have to be collected and burned along with the rest of the surrounding debris that might now be contaminated.

"That would be my guess. This girl was her ex's mistress. Bemkey's crazy enough to want to keep tabs on her."

"So Dr. Bemkey probably knows she's gone, right?"

"Right." He checked his ammo and she did the same. She was down to a measly six darts. They would have to be enough. "We'd better get over to the mansion. With this one, our count is twenty-one. If my numbers are right, we've got two more to hunt down, plus their creator."

"I don't have enough ammo for two more. I've only got six darts left." But she was game. She walked fast, beside John as they crossed through the trees heading for the mansion's backyard.

"I've got eight. We need to make every shot count." He slowed as they reached the tree line.

The fog had dissipated. They could clearly see the lakeshore, though a fine mist still swirled above the water's surface. Dr. Bemkey paced on the sand, screaming. Her tone alternated from glee to anger and back again in violent swings of emotion.

"You stupid bastard! Your bimbo is gone. Do you hear me? Gone! And good riddance. She ruined my life and I took away hers. And you can't do a damned thing about it, you bastard."

"Oh, no." Donna saw something come out of the trees. "She doesn't see him."

It was Bubba. The tall wide mountain of a man who had towered over all the other creatures. He was heading right for the doctor and he looked hungry.

John was already running down the long expanse of lawn toward the lake. The doctor was still ranting, shaking her fist at the water and screaming. John fired as he ran, plugging the giant zombie with three darts in quick succession. Donna followed behind, saving her darts until she had a better shot. She couldn't fire on the run and hit anything the way John could.

John was still ten yards away when Bubba grabbed the doctor in his meaty fists. The woman screamed even more shrilly as Bubba sank his bloodstained teeth into her shoulder.

"Damn." John slowed to a stop and fired two more shots into the behemoth zombie. That made five. It had only taken four darts to stop the other creatures, but Donna agreed with John's unspoken reasoning. This guy was huge. If weight and height had anything to do with dosage—and it usually did—he'd need more than the usual four darts to take him down.

"John!" Donna saw Mr. Bemkey rising from the lake. He just walked straight out of the water and headed for Bubba and his struggling ex-wife.

"I see him." John fired another shot into Bubba. "Use your darts on the husband, Donna. I'm concentrating on Bubba for the moment. Four shots, Donna. The ex is normal size and we might need more for the big guy, the doc, and any stragglers who might show up."

Donna went to work, taking her shots carefully, making every one count. She shot at the ex-husband as he bit into his ex-wife's flesh, infecting her with the deadly contagion she'd invented. She'd killed him with it. It was a sort of poetic justice that he was doing the same to her.

But John and Donna had wanted to take her alive. They hadn't planned to kill her. The likelihood that she would survive this was small. They had the doomsday shot that had saved one person to date, but it wasn't perfected. It likely wouldn't work on the doctor. Still, they'd try. As soon as the coast was clear.

Donna paused to fire her last shot, taking aim and firing. Her darts were spaced out evenly over the ex-husband's body. If all went well, he should be disintegrating any minute now. All she had to do was wait. And withstand the screeching from the doctor as the two zombies continued to munch on her flesh.

"This big guy isn't going quietly," John muttered. "How many darts do you have left? Two?"

"Yeah. Two. That's it."

"I've got two. So between us we have enough to take down one more. Let's hope there aren't any more zombies down in that lake who decide to come up for a stroll right now."

Donna was too keyed up to smile, but she appreciated his attempt at humor. They'd been through hell that night and it was almost over. They'd taken out a lot of dangerous creatures that night. Now all they had to do was wait out these last two and deal with the doctor.

"Finally." Donna heard the satisfaction in John's voice as he watched the struggling threesome on the beach. The big man named Bubba slithered to the ground, disintegrating before their eyes. The ex-husband followed suit a moment later. The doctor hit the sand with a splat as John and Donna ran over to her.

She was bleeding from multiple bites. Her eyes fluttered open as Donna reached her side.

"Is he dead? Is the cheating bastard really gone?"

"Yes, Dr. Bemkey. He's gone." Donna tried to break the news gently.

A cackling laugh was the doctor's response. Her eyes flared wildly, showing the whites around her dilated pupils and shocky irises. "Good riddance to bad rubbish, I say. My only regret is that the bastard managed to take me with him."

"Maybe not." John had been working steadily,

removing things from his utility belt as he prepared the Hail Mary dose that just might save the woman's life if she was one of the lucky ones.

"Don't be silly, boy. The contagion kills. It kills everyone."

"It didn't kill me," Donna said softly, dragging the woman's attention back to her. "I was attacked and I didn't die. I'm naturally immune."

"No such thing." The doctor looked scandalized and very upset that her killing cocktail wasn't one-hundred-percent efficient.

"I'm afraid you're wrong."

"And this could save you, Doctor. Brace yourself." John aimed the long needle for the doctor's heart. He paused only a moment to perfect his aim, then pushed it inward and depressed the plunger. The doctor screamed as the needle went into her flesh.

"You stupid son of a bitch!" Dr. Bemkey raged. "That hurt."

"It might save you, it might not." John removed the needle and sat back on his haunches. "Frankly, the chances are slim, but we had to try. Do you have any final messages? Maybe to your business partners? Now's your time to come clean. You may never get another chance to drag them down with you."

"Why would I want to do that?" The doctor seemed to lose strength before their eyes. "Henry is my lover as well as my business partner. I wouldn't hurt him for the world."

"Henry? Henry who?" John prodded.

"Nice try." Dr. Bemkey turned her head as she began to fade. "Henry's identity will go with me to my grave. But I'll give you one tidbit before I go.

Zalayat. Berthold Zalayat. The evil bastard cheated me and called me crazy. Take him down and I'll have my revenge."

"Where do we find him?" John pushed, but the woman was gone. Her eyes closed and her breathing stopped. She was dead. "Damn." John put away the special serum and took a deep breath before moving on. "We'll take her inside and keep an eye on her. If she rises, we'll use the last of our darts. This has been one hell of a night."

The gray light of dawn gave way to the pink and gold of true sunlight as they sat there, looking at each other. Donna greeted the sun with enthusiasm. If the sun was out, the zombies—if any still existed—would be in hiding.

John stood and lifted the doctor's body into his arms. He strode to the mansion at a fast clip and Donna did her best to keep up. She preceded him to the double glass doors and found them open. Dr. Bemkey must have come out this way and left the door open behind her. Convenient. Donna threw the doors open wide ahead of John and his gruesome burden.

She went ahead of him into the house. He placed Dr. Bemkey down on a chaise longue near the back door. He then stalked through the lower floor of the two-story mansion, checking each room while she followed.

"The place looks okay. I'll watch over her and call the cavalry. We have to go out there and drop markers for the cleanup team."

"I'll do the two at the beach. I marked all my other targets along the way."

"Good girl. So did I. So it's just those last two, and

her. . . ." He looked over at the body by the door. "Run down to the beach and mark them. I'll watch you from here while I make the call. We can't leave her unattended."

Donna ran outside and dropped the markers quickly, walking back to the house at a slower pace, enjoying a quiet moment in the early morning sun. By the time she got back to the mansion, John had hung up the phone.

"We're staying here for the day. I called the cleanup team. They'll be here in about an hour. I also reported to the commander. He wants us to search this place, but we need sleep too. I saw a guest room down the hall, or you can sack out on the couch until the cleanup guys get here."

Donna didn't want to leave him in the lurch, but now that the excitement was over, the adrenaline rush that had kept her going was leaving her drained. "I'll lie down on the couch for a few minutes. I'm not used to these all-nighters anymore." She smiled at him, weariness sapping her energy. "But if you need me, just let me know. I don't want to leave you shorthanded."

John caught her hand as she passed him on her way to the couch. He reeled her in and placed a lingering kiss on her lips.

"You're perfect, Donna." He smiled at her as he let her go. "Get some rest while you can. We're going to have a busy day."

He wasn't kidding. Donna napped for only about forty-five minutes before the cleanup crew arrived in the house. They took Dr. Bemkey's body away. She hadn't risen . . . yet. But they had the equipment to deal with her if and when she did.

They also replenished John's supply of toxic darts. He split the wealth with Donna when he saw that she'd awakened.

"The guys will be working out there for the next few hours," John told her, sitting on the edge of the couch. He stroked her cheek with the fingers of one hand. "There's a nice guest room at the end of the hall. Why don't you go in there and get some real rest? I'll join you in a bit. We can sleep while Buzz keeps an eye out. We're both wiped out after last night."

"Are you sure?" It sounded heavenly, but could they really afford the time away from the mission?

"Yeah." He stood and ushered her to her feet. "Let's get you to bed."

"Oh, I like the sound of that." She couldn't resist teasing him as they walked down the sumptuously carpeted hallway.

"Vixen." His voice growled in her ear as he bent to nibble playfully on her earlobe. "Sleep first. Then work. Then fun and games. If you're good."

CHAPTER EIGHT

Donna woke to warmth. John knelt over her, his big body cocooning her in his heat, his masculine strength. She loved the sensation. As much as she loved him.

He'd told her he loved her, if that speedy declaration could be believed. She'd have to hear it again to be sure. She knew people said things sometimes in extreme circumstances that wouldn't necessarily hold true later. She prayed that wasn't the case here. She loved John with all her heart and wanted his love in return. It would be a dream come true if he really had meant what he'd said.

"Stop faking. I know you're awake." His voice growled near her ear before he placed a sharp nip on her earlobe that made her yelp and laugh at the same time.

"How can you be so sure?" She kept her eyes closed, rubbing her cheek against his. He'd shaved recently. His skin was smooth against hers.

"I'm a highly trained CIA operative. It's my business to know these kinds of things." His mouth drifted down over hers as he crawled over her on the bed, bracketing her with his knees on either side of her thighs and his forearms beside her head.

Their kiss was filled with languorous wonder. It was a slow exploration of a kind they had never shared before. There had always been a hurried quality to their encounters—even the slow times. There was always a sense that they were on the job and couldn't spend too much time away from the mission.

That was gone now. John's kiss drugged her, dragging her under with him where he was her anchor, her safety line, and the very air she breathed. She trusted his passion to guide her own.

"I thought we were going to save the fun and games for later." She smiled playfully at him when he let her up for air.

"I decided it couldn't wait. Buzz is keeping watch outside while we rest. We'll sleep . . . eventually." His wicked grin rocked her world. "But loving you couldn't wait."

Her breath caught at his words and the look in his beautiful eyes. He paused.

"What? You didn't believe me before?" His smile cajoled but there were serious depths to his words. "I love you, Donna."

She was stunned by the sincerity in his expression, the way he put himself out there on the ledge. She'd never had a man be so open with her. Never.

"Hey, babe, tell me I'm not alone here." Doubt crept over his features and she rushed to reassure him.

"You're not alone." She felt her cheeks flush

with excitement. "I love you too, John. I just thought—"

"What? What did you think?" He moved closer again, nuzzling the tip of her nose with his.

"I thought maybe, now that things have calmed down . . ."

"That I'd take back what I told you in the woods?" He pulled back, a chastising look on his face. "Oh, baby. You'll learn I never say anything I don't mean. And I've never said the L-word to any woman before."

"That sounds serious." She was basking in the moment. He had the most delicious way of speaking and the way he looked at her melted her heart.

"Very serious." He moved in for a quick kiss that ended too soon. "Like, rest of our lives serious." He kissed her again and drew back with obvious reluctance. "Damn, I was going to wait for the right time, but I can't wait. Donna, I know I'm no prize, but I can't see living without you. I need you in my life, uncertain as it is. I figure you've already seen me at my worst and you know what I do for a living. There are no secrets between us and I've never had that with anyone before. You see me as I am and yet you still seem to like me." He chuckled at his own words as tears filled her eyes. "Will you marry me?"

"Yes!" She could only manage the single word as emotion overtook her. It didn't matter though, as his lips covered hers, his body sheltering her in his warmth.

Their clothes disappeared as their temperature rose. The loving was slow and sensuous, with none of the urgency that had marked their previous times together. They were in tune physically, mentally, and emotionally. She felt it in his kiss and in his touch.

John licked his way down her body and back up, pausing at all the interesting points in between. He paid special attention to her breasts, drawing on her nipples with wet, warm suction that made her arch off the bed in pleasure.

She wanted to touch him but he wouldn't let her. He took both her wrists and placed them against the headboard with an admonishing look.

"Keep them there, Donna. I mean it."

"Or what?" she dared to challenge him.

"Bad girls get punished, baby." He winked at her.

"Sounds like it might be fun to be bad."

He pretended to consider. "It could be at that, but let's save that for another time. This is special. It's the first time I'm making love to my fiancée."

"Fiancée." She marveled at the word. "I really love the sound of that."

"Mmm." He nuzzled her neck. "Me too. As much as I love you." He looked deeply into her eyes. "I love the way you stand up to me and with me. I never expected to feel this way about anyone, Donna."

Her stomach clenched at the honesty in his eyes.

"I never expected this, John, but I hoped. Even when I shouldn't have, I hoped you'd want me. I've never met anyone like you before. From the beginning, we've fit together."

His gaze turned wicked. "Oh, yeah. We fit together perfectly." He nipped her earlobe. "Let me remind you."

Her excitement was already spiking with need. Having John naked in her bed and against her body did that to her. He turned her on like no man before. She lay under him, willing to do whatever he wanted, wanting to bask in this first time—as he'd called it—being with the man she loved, knowing he loved her in return.

Just knowing they'd admitted such intimate feelings made the whole experience all that much more special. She felt alive in a way she had only ever experienced with John as he brought her senses to a peak with hot strokes of his tongue over her most sensitive places.

When he joined his body to hers, she moaned with pleasure, welcoming him.

"You feel so good, Donna," he gasped near her ear as he lowered his body over hers, blanketing her in his warmth and strength.

"So do you." Her voice was breathless as her fever rose. Then he began to move and she lost the ability to speak at all.

Long, slow strokes interspersed with hard jolts made her sigh in delight. He kept her guessing and kept her arousal on the knife's edge between passion and ecstasy. She felt his body gathering for the coming explosion and joined him, riding the tide of pleasure along with him.

When the wave broke over them, it swept them up in unison, awash in bliss. He held her through the tremors of her completion, giving and taking with equal measure as they shared the most perfect moment ever.

A long time later, they let each other go by slow degrees. John looked into her eyes, a wide grin on his face and love in his gaze. She basked in that look, knowing it was just for her. And she let her own feelings show as she gazed back.

"I love you so much, John." Her hand rose to stroke his rough cheek. He turned his head and dropped a kiss in her palm.

He rolled away and tucked her close, spooning with her from behind.

"Let's get some sleep. Buzz will wake us before the cleanup team leaves."

She drifted off as John settled the soft comforter around them, too tired and sated to stay awake any longer.

In the late afternoon, John left the bed. He let Donna sleep while he did a thorough search of the mansion. The cleanup guys were still hard at work. He'd wake Donna up before they left, but he didn't have the heart to rouse her yet. She was tuckered out from the night they'd spent in the woods chasing zombies. Hopefully, there wouldn't be too many more nights like that in their future.

The fact that they had a shared future still amazed him. He'd never felt such love in his heart for a woman, never admired one or cared for one so deeply. That she felt the same about him in return still made him grin like a fool. There was no doubt they'd signed on for a tough mission chasing zombies and bad guys who wanted to zombify the world, but they'd face whatever came together.

He'd never had that before. Sure, he'd worked with team members and comrades in arms that were like brothers, but he'd never been part of a couple like this before. He worried about her working in the field, but he'd worry more if he weren't able to be there with her, watching her back. She'd already proven she could handle herself well. With his tutelage, she'd have every advantage to come out alive from the situations in which they'd no doubt find themselves in the future.

She taught him things too. She'd sharpened his appreciation for scientific method and protocols. She was one of the most intelligent and quick-witted women he'd ever been with and he was still a little amazed that she'd fallen in love with him. He wasn't questioning it. He wouldn't point out that he was probably getting away with something. If she was willing to be his, he'd take her on any terms. He loved her that much.

His only worry was how the rest of the team would react to their return to base as a couple. Would she want to hide their relationship? Would she be embarrassed by him? He wasn't sure and it was driving him a little crazy.

They'd talked about their feelings, but they hadn't talked about how those feelings and this new relationship would work day to day, working together with the rest of the team. Maybe he was borrowing trouble but Donna was such a special woman, he didn't want to hide his love for her. He was prepared to take the teasing—maybe even a reprimand or two from some of the more stodgy higher-ups—but was she?

He didn't want their relationship to make her uncomfortable. He knew how some of the guys would react with teasing and even lewd remarks. He'd clobber anyone who said anything disrespectful around Donna, but the possibility was there. He didn't know the rest of the team that well yet. They seemed like good guys but he wasn't one hundred percent sure of them all yet. Time would tell.

He only hoped Donna was willing to give him the time. In the back of his mind he still worried that she'd jumped headlong into this relationship too fast. He worried that circumstances had thrown them together and somehow she'd wake up and realize she'd made a mistake in thinking she loved him.

He planned to tie her to him and convince her that was where she really wanted to be before anything like that could happen. She was the best thing that had ever happened to him and he wasn't about to let her go.

John was thinking about all this as he searched the big house from top to bottom. Nearing the end of his search, he finally found what he was looking for. A secret room was built cleverly into the house, hidden in the architecture so well, he'd almost missed it.

Inside, he found the doctor's secret lab, along with all her notes and files, a computer, and a laptop.

"John?" Donna's voice came to him faintly from another part of the house.

"I'm in the west wing," he shouted back.

Before long, he heard her footsteps drawing closer.

"In here, Donna."

A few more footsteps drew closer and then her head peeked into the hidden room.

"What is this place and how in the world did you find it?"

"It's a hidden laboratory. Every self-respecting

mad scientist has one. Didn't you know?" He grinned at her as she advanced into the room.

"What did you find?"

"Paydirt. There's a complete list of all the rogue science team members and their foreign contacts. Dr. Bemkey may have been insane toward the end, but she was meticulous. Her lab is spotless and all her notes on the experiments she was conducting are neat and tidy. I already forwarded all the electronic files to the team at Fort Bragg. We can leave the paper documents for the techs to decontaminate and package up for shipment as soon as they've dealt with the zombie remains."

"Wow. This is really good." She paged through one of the notebooks on the table. "I bet the docs back at base will learn a lot from this."

"No doubt," John agreed, moving close to her and swooping in for a quick kiss. "Damn, I needed that."

"Mmm. Me too." Her fingers stroked over his chest in a way that made him want to forget all about the work they had yet to do.

He cuddled her for a while but he knew he had to get back on track with the mission so they could wrap things up and head home to base. What kind of reception they'd get once the commander realized they'd become a couple, John wasn't sure. There wasn't really a chain-of-command issue. They both worked on the same team but for different branches. Donna wasn't CIA, so fraternizing wouldn't really be an issue unless Commander Sykes wanted to make it into one. Judging by the way he'd seemed to accept Sarah and Xavier's engagement, John didn't expect too much trouble from that direction.

The possible complications could come from higher up or from the other team members. The other guys would tease the hell out of John for hooking up with his first female partner. First, last, and only, as far as John was concerned. Donna was it for him. The other guys would just have to deal with it.

"The cleanup team is finishing up," Donna said, her head tucked under his chin. "They brought some stuff we could make for dinner if you're interested."

At the mention of food, his stomach rumbled. She laughed.

"I guess we should eat. Once it gets dark, we'll have to do some patrolling to make sure we got them all last night."

"I hope we don't find any more of them." She shuddered and pulled away. He let her go but followed her out the door of the hidden room.

"I honestly don't think we will." John took her hand as they went through the house, just wanting to touch her. "But we need to be absolutely certain before we call this done."

They ended up in the kitchen where a few MREs were waiting for them on the center island, courtesy of the cleanup team. Donna dug into the packages with gusto, reading the directions. John was well familiar with the Meals Ready to Eat and didn't have to waste time figuring out which packets held what and how to prepare them. He tore in and started handing stuff to her that he thought she'd like.

They played with their food like kids, throwing morsels into each other's mouths and clowning around with lots of laughter and love. John had never had so much fun with a couple of MREs. It was Donna that made all the difference.

"Do we really have to go out there?" Donna's gaze was caught by the setting sun out the window.

"You don't." John covered her hand on the table, drawing her attention. "But I'm going out to do the check. You can stay in here. It's safe. The creatures weren't able to get in here while the doc lived here."

"Yet they still got her." Donna shivered at the memory and John took her hand in both of his, drawing closer.

"Only because she went outside to nag her husband. Let that be a lesson for the future."

She burst out laughing as he'd hoped she would and the disturbing memory left her eyes.

"I'd never nag you, John. Maybe just . . . forcefully remind you of things now and again."

He pulled her in for a quick hug. "I think I can live with that."

John patrolled the woods around the house and the fishing camp most of the night. Thankfully, all was quiet. Donna had volunteered to come out with him, despite her obvious reluctance. She was a trouper. He admired the hell out of her courage and willingness to do the hard jobs.

He'd left her inside, cataloging some of the scientific evidence they'd found in the hidden room. The last time he'd cruised into the mansion to check on her, she'd been on the phone with some of the other team members, relaying newly discovered information.

He'd checked in with the team leader earlier

and received new orders. If he found no evidence of further zombie activity in the area tonight, they were to hightail it back to North Carolina. The team there was still in trouble and needed help. John was more than willing to enter the fight back on base, now that he could fully join the combat team. It had been hard for him to sit on the sidelines in a support role. He'd done it in order to be involved in the mission in which his little sister was so heavily involved. Meeting Donna had been a fortunate twist of fate.

Who knew he'd find his soul mate on a top-secret mission? John still couldn't quite believe it. For sure his sister, Sarah, was going to be surprised. John smiled as he thought of his little sister. The smile widened as he finished his last circuit before dawn with nary a sign of a zombie. The place was clear. They'd gotten all the creatures the night before, thank goodness.

Donna was waiting for him with open arms. He stepped into her embrace and swept her into a hug that made her squeal as he swung her around. He dipped his head and gave her a smacking kiss.

"Now that's something to come home to." He loved the way she smiled at him with that soft look in her eyes just for him.

"But we're not *home.*" She rolled her eyes around at the mansion that was serving as their base for the moment.

"Anywhere you are is home to me, Donna."

"That is the sweetest thing anyone's ever said to me."

She actually teared up. Damn. He hadn't meant to make her cry. John dipped his head and kissed away the tears as gently as he could, which only seemed to make it worse. Double damn.

"Don't mind me." She tried to downplay her emotional response and he let her.

"You're beautiful, Donna." He set her a little away from him. He couldn't let her go completely, but he walked by her side as they entered the mansion. "So what have you been up to while I was out chasing shadows?"

"I found a lot of great information and sent it back to the docs at the base. I was on the phone with them most of the night, in fact."

"Do you think you got it all? Or is there more to discover here?"

"There's probably a lot more good information to discover, but it's beyond my technical skill. I think I hit the most important stuff for now, but the lab contents have got to be boxed up and sent back to the science team."

"Good. Buzz is going to do that while we head back to Fort Bragg tomorrow." He paused as she turned to face him inside the giant kitchen of the posh house.

"You got new orders?"

He nodded. "We both did. I spoke to Commander Sykes a couple of hours ago. They've still got big problems on base and need all hands on deck. We're heading back to North Carolina. You okay with that?"

"Yeah, I guess. So you didn't find anything in the woods?"

"Not a trace. I think it's safe to say that we got them all." He hooked his thumbs into his utility belt as he leaned back against the kitchen counter.

"Thank goodness."

"We have to drive to Knoxville this morning and we'll catch a flight from there. You ready to face the rest of the team as a couple?" He laid his worries on the line. He wouldn't hide their new relationship. He wanted her to acknowledge his claim to all and sundry.

"Sure, why not?"

Her easy acceptance floored him. In a flash, he realized he'd made a mountain out of a molehill. She'd never know how uneasy he'd been. No, that would remain his little secret.

"Yeah, why not?"

He laughed at himself and hugged her close. Damn, his woman was perfect.

They packed up and headed for Knoxville a couple of hours later and were back at Fort Bragg that night. John was proud of his new fiancée when they reported to Commander Sykes's office for a full debrief. She took the bull by the horns, so to speak, surprising both men.

"Commander," she spoke forcefully as he motioned for them to take the chairs in front of his desk, "John and I are engaged. Is that a problem?"

Sykes sat back in his chair and just looked at them for a long minute while John's tension mounted. Then a slow grin stole over the commander's face.

"I can't say that I ever intended to run a team quite like this before. Seems like Noah's Ark around here lately with everyone pairing off, two by two. But I have no objection. In fact, I'm very happy for you. Congratulations to you both." Sykes leaned forward to shake both their hands, his smile genuine and friendly.

"Thank you, sir," John replied, a little stymied by the man's easy acceptance.

As usual, Donna was more open with her reaction. She gave Sykes a quick hug and accepted a friendly kiss on her cheek.

"Thanks, Matt. And thanks for pairing us up to begin with. I guess, in a way, we owe our happiness to you."

Sykes held up his hands, palms outward. "Oh, I can't take credit for this. This is all on you two. And if the brass gets on my case, you can be sure that's exactly what I'll tell them."

They all laughed. John knew in his heart that Matt Sykes wouldn't hang them out to dry. No, the commander was definitely on their side and he'd go to bat for them if necessary. He was that kind of guy.

John didn't know how he'd gotten so lucky. Sure, being picked for a team that had to fight zombies in total secrecy wasn't really the greatest stroke of luck, but it turned out to be a blessing in disguise. Not only had he found a mission that got his blood pumping, but he'd found a woman who would complete his world now and for as long as they were blessed to be together. If he had anything to say about it, he'd keep her forever.

Donna turned to him and took his hand. It was an inappropriate move in a military office, but he said nothing. When she looked at him with those beautiful eyes full of love, he'd give her anything. His heart, his soul, his life. And most especially, his love.

Epilogue

"Bemkey, the crazy bitch, offed Wallace. He was our main contact at Praxis Air."

"I told you she was going to be trouble," the man complained.

"It couldn't be helped. She was part of the original team. She knew too much. She had to be let in. I never planned to leave her around for long though. She was a good scientist, but personally she was a liability."

"Was?" The man sounded curious.

"She's dead. One of the zombies must've got her or there would've been more to bury. I got the news through our source in the mailroom a half hour ago."

"Can't say I'm sorry. In fact, I'm glad we don't have to worry about her anymore. She was a loose cannon."

"I agree. But we'll have to cultivate our other contact at the airline. We need them."

"Not to worry. I've got some leverage against one of the owners. Praxis Air won't be a problem."

"You're sure?"

"Positive. Leave it to me."

Redeeming the Wizard

JENNIFER
LYON

Chapter One

"What's taking so long, Mira? If the wizard shows up . . ."

"He won't." Mira Tate kept her eyes on the road while answering her cousin on the Bluetooth. In seventeen years, the Wizard of Raven Mist had never attended the Remington Day Celebration. The entire town turned out, bringing gifts, drinking wine and celebrating the day the wizard had banished the demon who killed two of their citizens—Mira's parents.

"He might," Lacey insisted. "Besides, the party has started, the winery is brimming with townsfolk and Gram needs to give the toast."

Mira turned down the private lane to the lakeside cabin and forced her jaw to unclench. "Lacey, you're the one who forgot to pick up Gram."

"I had an exorcism that took longer than I expected. It was for a couple moving into a new house. There were two spirits there who didn't want to move or share."

"You could have called." Mira parked the car in front of the lake house.

"I sent Gram, Mom and Damon a psychic message. I couldn't send the message to you, you're magic-blind."

She valiantly fought the urge to bang her head against the steering wheel. She loved her family, but they lived in a different world than Mira. A world of magic, while Mira lived in a little place she liked to call reality. "Your mom is on a private island doing readings for minor royalty, so she's out of range. Your brother"—is an idiot. She sucked in a breath, trying to be fair. Damon was the strongest psychic in the family, but—"needs to scry to get the message. If he's busy or distracted"—by his latest bimbo—"he won't pick up the message in time."

"But Gram usually gets my messages," Lacey pointed out.

Twenty-four years old and she still hadn't learned. Quit trying to reason with magicals. They were used to being special and getting away with crap like this, while the magic-blinds cleaned up after them. "Lacey, just take care of the party until Gram and I get back." She turned off the car, killed the lights and was cast into darkness.

Total darkness.

A chill went down her spine. If Gram was here, why weren't there any lights on in the cabin? Oh God, what if she'd fallen? Or had a heart attack? Or— "Stop it." She flipped on her dome light and got a flashlight out of the glove box. Then she grabbed her keys and cell phone and got out of the car.

Her heart rate skyrocketed and bitter fear coated her tongue. Gram was all Mira had. Her parents had been killed when she was seven. Gram raised her, loved her. Gram never cared that Mira was magic-blind.

She made her way up the stairs. The door was unlocked. If Gram was in there that wasn't unusual, which increased her fear that the older woman was hurt. She didn't want to take the time to call for help, not when Gram could be lying on the floor with a broken hip or something. Easing open the door, all she saw were shadows. She flipped the wall light switch revealing the living room and kitchen. Empty. She saw the suitcase sitting by the couch. "Gram?"

No sound came except the hum of the refrigerator. Mira checked around the corner in the kitchen: no Gram. She checked the two bedrooms and the bathroom, but there was no sign of her.

She walked back out to the main room, willing herself to think. Gram couldn't just vanish. She'd come to the cabin to meditate and consult with the spirits. Gram was a soul harmonizer and folks paid her a lot of money to find their soul mates. She didn't drive though, so . . .

A lump on the floor by the suitcase caught her eye.

Mira walked over to it and bent down, ignoring her too tight skirt. It was a palm-sized, misshapen lump of purple plastic with black scorch marks. "Gram's cell phone!" It looked like it had been hit by lightning or—

A wizard.

Her cell rang. She jumped, her heart slamming

against her ribs. She glanced at the display. It was her other cousin, so she hit the button and answered, "Damon, Gram's—"

"Been kidnapped! I just scryed a message from her that said, 'Kidnapped, get the wizard.' Then nothing, all contact was cut off. Mira, Gram's in trouble! We need the town wizard. You have to get him to find Gram."

A wizard kidnapped Gram? Mira's fear turned to anger so fierce that it throbbed a violent red in her head. Why in the hell would a wizard kidnap her seventy-six-year-old grandmother for?

"Mira?" Worry threaded into Damon's voice. "Remington's a recluse, won't even talk to citizens. What if he won't see you? Or refuses?"

She walked out the door, locked it and started down the stairs to her car. "He'll do it." She'd make damned sure of it. Gage Remington owed her.

That wizard had gotten her parents killed.

Gage looked at the BlackBerry screen, noting where the two troll-demons were skulking in the forest behind his house. These giants from the first ring of hell were butt-ugly, vicious fighters. Every year on the anniversary of Gage's sending back the higher-ranking demon that killed two of his citizens, the seal on the portal weakened.

Troll-demons slithered out.

While the town was celebrating with drink, food and gifts, Gage tracked and killed the trolls. If they escaped into town, people would die. The more human blood they collected, the more powerful their demon master in the upper rings of hell became.

If they could kill Gage and harvest the blood from his master wizard triskellion over his solar plexus, their demon boss would rise to the ninth level of hell and become a demon lord.

Not a fucking chance. Shoving the BlackBerry into the pocket of his pants, Gage moved with the silence acquired from decades of training and nearly two centuries of being a master wizard. His shirt had been torn off in his battles with the trolls he'd already killed tonight. The half-moon filtered through the tree branches and wind filled the air with the troll-stench just ahead. He caught sight of the two he was searching for and frowned. They were running toward his house. Why were they going that way instead of deeper into the forest where they had a chance of losing him, or doubling back and killing him? He lifted his sword and prepared to move.

"Oh shit!" Rhys yelled.

Gage stopped and jerked his BlackBerry from his jeans. "What?" he asked the ghost on his screen. Rhys Warwick had been the wizard who trained Gage into a master wizard. He'd been dead and quiet for a decade before Gage had fried his powers and then summoned his old mentor from his death-sleep. Unfortunately, Gage didn't have enough power to send Rhys back to his rest.

"There's a woman at your front gate and the troll-demons smell her." The screen changed to show him the image. His wrought-iron fence was eight feet high and stretched across the front of his house. The woman was stabbing the buzzer at his intercom.

"I silenced it," Rhys said. The ghost wore a karate gi stamped with the master wizard triskellion symbol, a black belt and a steely-blue-eyed gaze.

"Gage Remington!" a woman's voice hollered loud enough to shake the trees.

She must have realized the buzzer wasn't working. "Troll balls," he snarled and shoved the Black-Berry into his pocket. Then Gage launched into preternatural speed and caught up to the two trolls. Using the element of surprise, he killed them quickly.

"I know you're in there, Remington!" the woman yelled, rattling the iron bars.

Gage wiped the sweat pouring into his eyes and whipped around to race toward the gate.

A scream pierced the night.

Gage broke through the edges of the forest. Ignoring his gothic monstrosity of a house on the left, he ran full bore for the gate. He saw the problem immediately—another troll had reached through the gate and had grabbed the woman's neck. Two other trolls were climbing over the fence.

Gage reached the fence in time to see the woman shove her fist through the bars.

The troll holding her bellowed and fell back, releasing her.

Stunned, Gage looked down to see that she'd stabbed the creature in his bulging eyes with her keys. The thing was rolling on the ground, trying to jerk them out.

Brutal and resourceful—he admired that. He jerked his sword up and beheaded the creature. Then he turned to the two crawling over the fence. He reached out his hand and grabbed the iron bar to send enough power to the motor to open the gate and get between the trolls and the woman. Instead, his triskellion—the three spirals within a spiral—shorted out and sent a bolt of pure electricity into the bars.

The trolls touching it shrieked in agony and went up in flames. The bars turned molten red, then gray and finally fell to the ground in a long row of chunky ash. It smelled like burning iron, hair and rotten, greasy meat.

Gage sighed, so damned tired of his fucked-up power. He ignored the burn on his hand and glared at his unwanted guest. She was a plain-looking woman wearing a black skirt, an ugly blouse and high heels. Although he did notice her hair. It was a deep mahogany color that gleamed over her shoulders. Her face was pale and tight, her brown eyes huge. "You need to get out of here," he growled, while trying not to breathe in the lingering stench.

Her eyes widened and she yelled, "Behind you!"

Gage gripped his sword with both hands, ignoring the hot flash of pain in his burned palm and swung around, beheading the troll just as it leapt toward him with its teeth bared.

"You are summoning demons."

The accusation hit him in the back and boiled his blood with outrage. He had spent the last seventeen years doing everything within his severely limited power to protect the town. Gage turned and narrowed his gaze. "Pay attention, woman, I am not summoning demons, I'm killing them. Besides, these barely qualify as demons; they are merely trolls." Real demons would be a more serious problem with his fried magic. "But they won't hesitate to kill you and consume all your blood. Run along while you still can."

She shivered, wrapping her arms around her waist. "How did they get here?"

Gage didn't have time for this. "Get out of here. Now." He made it a command.

"Demons don't just appear." She sucked in a breath, her chest rising with clear outrage. "You've opened a portal!"

He didn't need this shit. "Lady, I'm about ready to open a portal and toss you into hell. Get the hell out of here before I do it." He had to get her away from the danger. The portal should reseal any minute now, but until he was sure no trolls were on this side, she was at risk.

Her eyes widened until he could see the ring of white around her irises. Hot color flooded her face. She dropped her arms and took a step toward him. "Don't you dare threaten me, wizard!"

Swear to the Realm, could the gods have found a more irritating woman to drop on him tonight? He took a step closer to her and looked down at all five feet, eight inches of her and refused to notice the way her breasts filled out that ugly top. "Leave."

She tilted her head back. "Can't. My car keys are in that . . . mess." She gestured to where he'd killed the troll she'd maimed with her keys.

Gage felt his left eye begin to twitch. He walked over to the troll rotting into dust and snatched up the keys. Shaking off the remaining troll filth, he held them out to her. "Go."

She ignored the keys. "Not until I get what I came here for."

He knew he was going to regret asking this, but this woman was sticking like glue and he had to find a way to peel her off. "And that would be?"

"I want to hire you."

He had to do another sweep of the forest for remaining trolls, have Rhys check with his spectral eyes and make sure the portal was sealed. And this woman wanted to hire him? Because he looked, what, bored? "Too late, already have a job killing the trolls." A spider-crawling sensation went up his spine. He jerked around, trying to see what set off the feeling.

"You have to find my grandmother!" the woman yelled at his back.

He didn't see anything in the direction of his house. "I don't do missing persons." He barely paid attention to her. Instead he shifted his gaze to study the shadows cast by the branches waving in the breeze. He couldn't pick out any trolls.

"She's been kidnapped!"

"Call the police. Call a psychic. Call Ghostbusters. Just get the hell off my property." The spider-crawling sensation wouldn't ease, but he couldn't see the threat.

"A wizard kidnapped her."

Gage spun around, holding his sword carefully. "A wizard? Are you sure?"

She nodded. "Gram sent a psychic message to my cousin. Plus, I found this." She held up a lump of . . . something. "It was Gram's phone. It looks like it's been hit by lightning. It was in the house where she went missing and there's no storm tonight, so it couldn't be lightning. That only leaves a wizard."

Fuck a troll, his night just got worse.

Another wizard kidnapping someone out of his town was a direct challenge to his authority. For seventeen years, Gage had managed to keep his fried powers a secret by living as a recluse and scaring away anyone who came near his house. He forced those who needed to contact him to use the Internet, and he had a staff of paid liaisons to keep an eye on the town. But now he needed more information. "What's your name?"

"Mira Tate."

That last name was like claws digging into his gut. "One of the Tates who own the Enchanted Winery?"

"Yes, my grandmother is Calia Tate." Her eyes went hard. "And you're going to help me find her."

"Give me the phone and I'll see what I can find out." He held out his hand.

She snatched her fist away. "No. I'll pay you but I'm working with you. I'm not going to let you get my grandmother killed the way you did my parents. We work together."

The shock punched him. She was the *daughter* of the couple that the demon killed. He refused to let the guilt surface. Emotions got in the way. Moving quickly, he caught hold of her hand, took the phone and replaced it with her keys and stepped back before she registered what happened.

She looked down at the keys, then back up at him. "You can't—"

"Just did." He forced his voice into flat disinterest, but his fingers were tingling. Was it from touching her? No, it had to be the phone. He most definitely felt a wizard's power, so Mira was correct. The phone was destroyed, but maybe Rhys could get some information out of it. "You can't bully a wizard. Go home. I'll let you know if—"

"How about blackmail?"

He jerked his gaze up.

She lifted her chin. "You work with me to find Gram or I'll tell the whole town you're opening a portal and summoning demons. You'll be fired as town wizard."

It took an entire three seconds to get control of the white-hot fury racing through him. The little mortal had no idea of the consequences of her actions. Without him there to guard that portal until he could fix his fried magic and permanently reseal it, the town would be slaughtered. Forcing the anger back, he considered his options when he saw the large figure come at them from the left.

Mira screamed just as the hulking creature grabbed her up and ran.

Chapter Two

Blind terror blasted adrenaline through Mira. She hit the massive arm clamped around her waist and holding her like a rolled-up rug. Her head and legs hung down and she saw the ground flying by at a sickening rate. Her feet, fists and keys had zero effect. The thing's skin was leathery and covered in coarse hair. It had to be seven feet tall, three hundred pounds and man-shaped with a serious case of ugly.

Jesus, it stunk like skunk and sewage.

Horror seized her, squeezing her chest and forcing the air from her lungs, until her throat burned with terror. She knew it would kill her, ripping her apart and feasting on her blood just like the demon that had killed her parents. She'd had this nightmare over and over after their deaths.

The thing kept running, bouncing her mercilessly, and from the look of the thickening carpet of leaves, they were heading into the forest.

Oh God, oh God . . .

She heard a whistling sound. Felt a breeze.

Then she was suddenly released and slammed into the ground, leaves and dirt billowing up around her. She sucked in a breath and felt a spray of hot wet drops splatter over her. Shoving herself to her hands and knees, she saw the troll-thing toppling over, its head gone. Blood poured out the gaping neck. Its thick, hairy body was already caving in and decomposing at an accelerated pace.

She screamed and tried to crawl away.

"Stop it!" the wizard snapped at her. "Get up. Hurry, damn it, you have troll blood on you." He grabbed her hand, jerked her to her feet and started running.

Mira stumbled. Her legs felt like noodles. Her pumps were gone, having fallen off when the troll had her, and she was stumbling on rocks and twigs in her bare feet.

Gage wrapped his arm around her waist, lifted her and ran. This time, at least, she was vertical, held against his body. She tried to open her mouth, tried to figure out what was happening, but the pure speed and strength of the wizard stunned her.

He ran up the steps to his porch, into the house and up the stairs, carrying her and the sword, and still leaping up three steps at a time. He blew down a hallway, into a bedroom and finally came to a stop in a huge bathroom. That was when she became aware of the pinpricks of pain stabbing her skin—on her face, her arms, her legs.

Gage set her on her bare feet. "Strip now!" He put his bloody sword on the counter and pulled a

BlackBerry out of his jeans and studied the screen while walking to the brown marble shower and turning on the jets.

"Are there any more of those . . . things?" Her voice echoed in the bathroom. She raised her hands and saw tiny red drops and started to shake. She could still smell that skunk-and-sewage stink. Still feel the terror. She'd been sure she was going to be torn apart, ripped to shreds like her nightmares. She watched as the spots on her trembling hands burned. Deeper. Burrowing into her.

"No. Portal's closed and a scan shows all clear."

Ignoring the sounds of Gage moving around, she watched as the little spots spread. "It's burning," she mused.

Gage moved back into her line of vision. "No time." He grabbed her hand and dragged her into the shower. Warm water hit her from three sides, drenching her in seconds. Gage shoved her hands in front of a spray that was at waist level.

The shock cleared, washing away in the water. Mira opened her eyes and said, "You're naked." Her body went tight and the prickly burns didn't seem to matter anymore. The man was sculpted! His dark hair was wet, lying against his skull and touching his shoulders. His face was lean and hard, his silvery-blue eyes had a ring of dark gray. She dropped her gaze to his naked torso. Through the blood and cuts scattered on him, she saw hardcore, lean muscle that roped up his chest, bulged at his shoulders, then ran down his arms. But the most astonishing thing of all were the markings. They started as a triskellion just below his heart and between his ribs. It consisted of three spirals within a spiral done in pure black lines that seemed to actually move. From the outer spiral prongs snaked out into flowing, henna-colored markings up over his shoulders, rolling down his arms, wrapping around his torso and disappearing lower.

She followed those lines and heat burst into her face and chest. The ribbons of color went down his tight stomach, some rolled over his lean hips, and others went down into his pubic hair.

Even his penis had lines, which grew and swelled as his dick rose under her gaze.

"You need to get these clothes off." He reached for her blouse, undoing the buttons at an astonishing speed.

Mira jerked her head up and grabbed his hands.

His silvery-blue gaze rose to hers. "We have to get all the troll blood off. It's poisonous." He undid the last button.

"But you were covered in it." Her voice came out a whisper.

"I'm magic-born so it doesn't affect me as much, and I've built up an immunity." He pulled the shirt apart, his stare dropping to the wet bra covering her breasts. Then he pushed the shirt off and tossed it away.

Then her bra.

The warm water cascaded over her bare shoulders and hit her lower back. Gage blocked her front from the water, but his gaze felt more powerful than the water jets.

Her nipples puckered, the skin over her breasts felt tight and sensitive. "You don't have to stare!"

He flicked his gaze up to her face. "Like you

stared? My cock liked it." He reached behind her
and dragged down the zipper of her skirt. Then
he crouched, pulling her skirt and panties down.
He had her step out of them and tossed them
away.

Mira stood there naked, vulnerable and unable
to believe she was in a shower with the Wizard of
Raven Mist. The wizard she blamed for her par-
ents' murder. Yet he'd saved her life tonight.
Twice. She had to pull herself together. "Get out,
I'll do this." She reached for his bottle of soap.

He rose. "Oh no," he said in a low voice that
throbbed with a promise. "We work together. Isn't
that what you said?" He picked up a bottle of
shampoo, poured out a dollop and began to work
it into her hair.

His long fingers stroked her scalp and made her
shiver. "To find my grandmother!" He had her off
balance. He was ruthless, dangerous, but she hadn't
expected . . . this.

He pushed her back into the spray and rinsed
her hair. Then he turned her so that her back was
to his chest. Pouring soap from another bottle, he
lathered up his big hands and ran them over her
arms. Then her chest. He leaned forward and said
against her ear, "These were the terms of your
blackmail scheme. Together." He ran his soapy
hands over her breasts, circling them, sliding beneath the heavy globes.

"To find my grandmother," she repeated, grit-
ting her teeth against the prickles of pleasure.

"Yes, and what do I get in return?" He stroked
his palms over her nipples.

A slice of heat ignited and raced down to her

groin. "Money!" She blurted it out, wondering why she was letting him touch her.

"I have more money than you can ever conceive. No, I believe"—he trailed his hands down her belly—"I want something more than that."

Dear God, she was surrounded by this huge, powerful man, and it was confusing the hell out of her. "What?"

He slid one hand down her stomach. "Spread your legs." He pressed a foot between hers, forcing her to widen her stance. He slid his hand between her thighs, his long fingers stroking intimately against her sensitive flesh.

Mira grabbed his arm, feeling the heat penetrate her fingers where she touched his odd markings. What were they? *Focus!* "What do you want from me to find my grandmother?"

He moved just enough to feather the pad of his finger gently over her clit. Back and forth. And again. Mira's stomach tightened to a knot of need. She dug her fingers into his arm and fought to keep from moving, from pressing herself onto that finger touching her, tormenting her.

Gage pressed his hot mouth close to her ear. "What are you willing to give me?"

She couldn't stop herself from blurting out the truth. "Anything." She'd do anything to save the woman who'd loved and raised her. Anything.

And now the wizard knew it too.

Gage walked into his workroom, still tense with unspent lust. Dragging his ass out of that shower, away from Mira Tate and her hot little body, had taken a tremendous force of will. He dropped his sword and Calia Tate's melted cell phone on the desk and stared at the sleeping computer monitor. "Rhys, I need a status update. Now."

Nothing. The monitor stayed dark.

His temper sizzled. Slapping his hands down on the desk, he snapped, "Get your spectral ass over here! I know you hear me! Show up now or I'm sending a hot Latin lover into Phoebe's dreams." Phoebe had been the love of Rhys's life when he'd been alive. Rhys had chosen death-sleep to wait for Phoebe to join him in death, rather than moving to the next plane without her. Since Gage had woken Rhys, he now pined for Phoebe and met up with her in her dreams when she slept.

"What?" Rhys appeared on the screen wearing a chocolate-brown silk robe, his eyes furious. "I told you the portal was sealed and I didn't detect any more troll-demons." When he didn't get an answer fast enough, he went on. "Well? Come on, spit it out, boy! Phoebe has insomnia and might wake up any moment." Lightning flashed in hot, bright streaks around the image of Rhys on the screen.

"Can't help it. We have a problem." He explained about Mira and her kidnapped grandmother. Rhys had heard some of it through the BlackBerry, but Gage filled in the holes. "I can't rely on my power to find this wizard. I need you to see if you can find anything in Calia's burnt phone. And search through cyberspace for any sign of them." Rhys said it was easier to move through cyberspace as a ghost, that it drained less of his ghostly energy. "Find out as much as you can."

Thunder cracked through his computer speakers. "Phoebe's asleep! I spent the whole day and night helping you with the portal and trolls. Now you expect me to leave her and run around town, doing what? Just guessing where the wizard might be?"

He didn't flinch. "Yes." Holding out the phone, he said, "There might be a clue in here."

Red flames exploded on the screen. "Why should I?"

He knew why, but Gage told him anyway. "Because I'm the only one who can send you back. When Phoebe dies, do you want to be stuck here? That could happen if this wizard kills me."

The flames stopped and Rhys shifted his image from wearing a robe to wearing tailored slacks and a crisp white shirt, his hair freshly combed. "What are you going to be doing?"

"Keeping Mira distracted."

Rhys looked skeptical. "How? She's not stupid if she blackmailed you."

"Not a coward either. She stabbed a troll who was trying to choke her in the eye with her keys." He'd been pretty damned impressed with that. However, now that he knew who she was, he remembered an important detail. "She's magic-blind. Her parents sought me out all those years ago for a private consultation about their daughter who was one hundred percent magic-blind. Completely frigid. She'll never know if I'm doing real magic or faking it. I'll convince her we're following the trail while you're finding Calia and the wizard."

"And if I do find the wizard? Then what? You're

fried and we haven't found the way to ground your powers."

Gage didn't need to be reminded. Seventeen years ago he'd had taken on an apprentice, Jillian. She'd been smart, powerful, beautiful and completely untrained.

He should have told her no. He had been just over two hundred years old and extremely powerful, almost completely full up with power. It was too dangerous a time for him to take on an apprentice.

But he had. Jillian seduced him and Gage had let her. Without his knowledge, she had stolen enough of his power to raise a demon.

Her plan had been to have the demon kill Gage and steal all his power. Instead, she'd lost control of it, and it killed the couple who'd been there waiting to see Gage.

Gage had discovered what she was doing, but he'd been too late to save Mira's parents. He'd banished the demon back to hell and killed Jillian.

But before she'd died, Gage took his power back from her. He had known what would happen, but he'd had no choice. She'd bargained with a demon and would go into hell when she died. Gage had to take his power back so the demon didn't get it. And when he did, his triskellion and the mantling that held all his power overloaded and short-circuited.

In short, he had fried. No wizard that Gage knew of had ever recovered from becoming fried.

That was why he'd raised Rhys. His old mentor had stuck by him for the last seventeen years, helping him keep the portal closed, and finding any trolls that got through all while looking for a cure.

Rehashing all this didn't help. Running a hand through his damp hair, he said, "I'll find a way to deal with the wizard. We've always found a way to keep the town safe."

"I'll see what I can find out," Rhys said.

"Check in on my BlackBerry."

Rhys nodded, then disappeared in a huge explosion that filled his screen, then faded away like fireworks.

"Show-off," Gage said. But his mentor was right. He needed to find a way to ground his power and fast.

CHAPTER THREE

Mira dressed in a pair of sweats rolled up at the hem and a white T-shirt the wizard had left for her in the bathroom. He'd said her clothes had to be burned.

Once dressed, she found Gage in a large room the size of a three-car garage that was half chemistry lab and half office. One wall had a built-in desk with five flat panels mounted over it. Four of them flashed images of the grounds around the house. The adjacent wall had a bookcase filled with tomes. The rest of the room had shelves containing jars holding colorful herbs, strange liquids and various items. There was also a stainless-steel industrial refrigerator.

There were two six-foot-long, black granite tables at the far end of the room. Gage stood at one of them with his head bent, his naked shoulders bunching and releasing as he moved.

"I need clothes," she announced.

"You're fine." He didn't even look up.

"Fine? I don't have shoes, this shirt is white and you can see right through it."

He jerked his head up. His gaze hit her face and slid down. Slow. Searching. Seeking.

Her skin broke out in goose bumps, her heart stuttered and her hands grew damp. She'd never felt a gaze like that before. It hit her, sank deep into her skin to light her nerves on fire. She almost felt more exposed than when she'd been naked in the shower with him. "Stop it! Can you manifest clothes magically or can we run by my apartment? I can't walk around without underwear."

"Later, busy here." He dropped his head.

She walked toward him to see what he was doing.

"Don't step in the circle."

She looked down. Sure enough, there was a circle drawn on the tiled floor. What she'd seen of the rest of the house, it was all wooden floors, but this room had a light gray tile.

Her eyes were riveted on the circle, and her stomach turned over. Circles were for dangerous magic—like summoning demons. Staring at the black outline of the circle, she asked, "Is this where my parents were killed?"

"No."

She looked up to see him open a bottle of water and pour it into an iron pot sitting over one of those chemist burners. His coldness rubbed at her skin. Her parents were nothing to him.

She was nothing to him. He'd touched her in the shower, making her feel vulnerable and desirable. But when he'd gotten the admission he wanted from her, he'd shifted from hot and sexy enough to melt her resistance to cool and efficient. She stalked around the circle to stand across the table from him. "Where exactly were my parents murdered?"

He lifted his eyes. "Not here." Then he picked up the mess that had been Gram's cell phone, and using just his hands, broke off a pea-sized chunk. Then he dropped it in the mortar.

"Where?" It was somehow vitally important that she know.

"It was another building. I had a separate lab and office on the property. It's gone now." He picked up a magnet and ran it over a grater, letting the pieces fall into the mortar's bowl.

"Gone?"

His jaw clenched, but his hands were smooth and steady as he scraped the shavings from the grater and set it aside. "I destroyed it. Completely."

That made her feel a little bit better, but her stomach churned with worry for Gram. "What are you doing?"

"Making a potion to find the wizard. I'm using the cell phone as the link since he used his power to destroy it." He picked up the pestle and began grinding the plastic from the phone and the magnet shavings.

She tried to keep her gaze on what he was doing, not his chest and arms and stomach covered in those amazing markings. "What's the magnet for?"

"It creates a magnetic effect between the potion and the wizard." Setting down the pestle, he lifted the bowl and used his fingers to sweep the ground-up components into the simmering water.

He had long fingers and strong hands. Heat rose in her chest and face at the memory of his hands touching her in the shower. She'd had a couple boyfriends, but the way Gage had touched her seemed more intimate than her previous sex partners.

Probably because he was a wizard, and she'd heard that before her parents' murder, he'd been quite the partier. Women had flocked to him, and all but begged him to have sex with them.

And she'd been no different, had she?

A flash of silver caught her attention. She shook off her thoughts and watched as Gage took the cap off a silver blade, pricked his finger and then squeezed a drop of blood into the mixture.

The brew sizzled loudly like frying bacon and white fog billowed up into a fast-expanding cloud.

He dripped in a second drop of blood.

The intense fog retracted, pulling all the white smoke back into the potion.

Then the potion sat there, gurgling softly, looking a little bit like a murky-brown whiskey. Gage grasped the handle and poured the stuff into a tall beaker. The mixture bubbled and spit.

"What's it doing? It's not going to explode is it?"

Gage picked it up, swirling the liquid in the glass with an intense look of concentration on his face. "The hissing and popping is from the hot liquid hitting the cooling beaker. It brings it down to room temperature in seconds."

She was intensely curious, and trying to keep her mind off Gage and his naked chest. "Are you going to drink it? With the plastic and magnet pieces in it?"

He raised an eyebrow. "It's not going to work by staring at it." Then he drank it.

"Condescending bastard." She turned and walked around the table to a shelf filled with several crystal balls of different sizes, all on stands. They all looked the same to her—murky. It had always been that way. All her life she'd been on the outside, unable to see, feel or sometimes even hear magic like her family did. They all looked at her exactly the way Gage did. Her own parents had been so disappointed they'd made an appointment to consult Gage about trying to fix her. Except for Gram. Gram loved her the way she was. Tears burned behind her eyes. Blinking them away, she said, "How long will this potion take? We have to find her."

"Depends on how powerful this wizard is. If he's created a strong cloak around them, it will take time to break through it."

"What do you mean you don't know how long?" She turned, but he had his back to her as he cleaned up the table. "You're supposed to be a master wizard, one of the most powerful in the world." Her mind began churning with rapid thoughts. She'd heard stories of his power, of his ability to flash-jump from one place to another, summon and banish demons, call lightning, manifest items out of thin air . . . but he didn't know how long it would take to find one old woman and a wizard?

He didn't answer, just ignored her.

She narrowed her eyes on his powerful back. "You didn't use magic to banish the trolls." He'd used a sword, although he'd been faster than any mortal she'd even seen. Wizards were magic-born and not mortal. Magic-sensitives were mortals born with varying abilities to feel, touch and sometimes manipulate magic, but they were still mortal. And of course, magic-blinds like Mira were mortal and the bottom of the food chain, considered by magic-borns and magic-sensitives to be the worker bees of the world, "Why is that, wizard? Why didn't you just blast those trolls back to hell?"

He turned from the sink and strode toward her with a powerful, ageless grace that silenced the sound of his boots on the floor. He was in front of her before she took her next breath. "You're questioning me?"

How many times had some magic-sensitive given her this exact same attitude? "Damn right I am. It's my grandmother's life at stake and I'll do everything within my power to get her back."

He raised an eyebrow. "Your power? And what power would that be?"

Maybe she didn't have magic, but she was smart, determined and resourceful. Ignoring the way he towered over her, she said, "I have the power to destroy you and your cushy little job as the town wizard. I know you have a portal on the grounds here somewhere. I've seen those ugly-ass trolls." She took a breath and added, "If I need more, I'll find it. Who knows what secrets you're hiding here?"

His face transformed as he rolled out a slow smile and he lifted his hands to rest them on the shelf behind her, trapping her between his powerful arms with those beautiful markings. "You've seen all of me, my little blackmailer. I have no secrets from you. You've seen just how far my power goes."

His scent surrounded her, soap and amber

mixed with a wild electric tang that she could almost taste on the back of her tongue. "How far your power goes?"

"My mantling, Mira. The lines that flow out from my triskellion. They are the power I've built since being branded a master wizard."

She looked down at the symbol, the three spirals within the spiral. "The circle that never ends," she said, watching as the spirals seemed to turn like a lazy fan. "It's a brand? Like a cow is branded?" Master wizards and their traditions were secretive and mysterious.

"Branded by our mentors. If we are true and have acquired the level of control required, the red-hot brand won't hurt. From then on, our power grows and spreads in the mantling."

She looked at the henna-colored ribbons trailing out from the triskellion. One curled up over the muscles in his chest, over the contours of his shoulder and wound around the muscles in his arm until it finally vanished just past his wrist. "You're covered in that . . . mantling . . . everywhere." She remembered the way his penis looked as it had engorged. A hot need pulsed deep inside her, making her shift with a restless ache. She wanted to touch him, trace those lines. . . . She had to get herself under control. "How long did it take to get this much power?"

"Nearly two centuries."

She jerked her head up. "Two . . . how old are you?" She could feel the heat from his arms stretching past her face, and almost hear a faint hum. As if his mantling whispered.

"Two hundred and nineteen."

"Years?" She gaped at him. She'd known wizards

weren't mortal but . . . "You look thirty-something! How can you be this . . . *hot* . . . and so old?"

His eyes crinkled at the edges. "Good to know you think I'm hot. I was branded at thirty-six, and all the power running through me slows aging."

Unable to resist, she looked at his triskellion, at the pure black lines that swirled into those three separate spirals, then flowed into the outer spiral, then branched off into the mantling. The beauty and symmetry spellbound her, drew her. Yet, as she stared, she noticed that the turning spirals didn't quite rotate in the same rhythm. Something was off and disturbing the balance of one spiral feeding into the next. She lifted her hand and laid it over the triskellion.

Gage sucked in a breath and didn't move.

His skin was hot, but it was the vibration of those lines that told her his magic was *alive*. It felt like velvet ribbons sliding up around her fingers, circling her hand, cradling her wrist and starting to trail up her arm. It was incredibly sensual and almost unbearably intimate.

It was as if she were touching more than the man, actually touching the very magic that defined him.

She knew then that Gage Remington was everything she was not.

She jerked her hand back.

Yet velvety power still caressed the sensitized skin of her fingers, hand and forearm. The touch kept swirling and seeking, making her shiver and need something she couldn't define. A longing welled up in the deepest part of her chest. "No," she said, shaking her hand at the wrist, trying to disconnect, to separate back into herself.

The sensation began to slow and she looked down at her hand.

Curling up around her wrist and arm was a single henna-colored ribbon, just like Gage had all over his torso.

She gasped, then locked her gaze on the wizard and demanded, "What did you do?"

Chapter Four

Gage was frozen in place with his hands braced on either side of her.

Mira's touch had sucked the breath from him. Then the air returned, laced with an energy he had not felt since that day one hundred and eighty-three years ago when he'd knelt naked in the moonlight in the Realm and Rhys lifted the iron brand from the flames, turned and pressed it over his solar plexus.

There had been no pain, but he'd felt the energy fire into his body, root in his blood and begin to grow.

That was precisely what he felt when Mira touched his triskellion. As he watched now, the mantling on her wrist and arm faded and vanished.

She stared up at him with huge eyes, her face flushed and her full lips parted. Her hair cascaded down, coming to rest over the tops of her breasts. She had asked him what he'd done to cause her hand to mantle like that, but he didn't know. All he knew was he wanted to do it again.

And again.

Taking his hand from the shelf, he lifted a lock of hair resting against her breast, feeling the heavy silk and said, "What? I didn't do anything."

She looked down at her clear hand, then back up. "You didn't see that?"

He loved the feel of her smooth hair. "See what?"

"I . . ." She dropped her hand. "Nothing. Just a shadow." The gold color of wonder in her eyes turned hard. "You must be doing something. Bespelling me, or something. Knock it off and move."

"What?" He wasn't lying now. He was truly surprised.

She pulled her hair from his hand. "In the shower, here, this isn't me. You're doing something with your magic. I'm even seeing things." She leaned back into the shelf and crossed her arms over her chest, obviously trying to put distance between them. "Let's get something straight, wizard. I don't trust you, I don't even like you. I just want to find my grandmother."

Ouch. She was suspicious. He had to stay focused on his priorities—finding the wizard who had kidnapped Calia and figuring out how to ground his power. His magic had seemed to react to Mira. He needed to find out if that was real or just some kind of fluke. His body sure as hell was reacting to her. Lust coiled low in his gut and swelled his cock. He leaned closer, crowding her, and said, "You felt it, my frigid little mortal. You felt the sexual charge between us. You want to hate me, fine, but don't lie to me. Or yourself."

She sucked in a breath and refused to meet his eyes. "I don't fall into instant lust. You did something, maybe bespelled me with your wizard gaze. Probably the same thing you do to all women when you want to get laid."

She was really starting to piss him off. He never used magic to get sex; hell, he hadn't had to. Women vied for his attention, for the chance to have sex with a wizard. "Close your eyes."

She pulled her eyebrows together. "Why?"

"You accused me of using magic to make you want me. I'm going to prove I didn't." He leaned his head to her ear, inhaling the scent of his shampoo on her. "Close your eyes, Mira. Then you won't be able to see my eyes when I kiss you."

He felt her slight shiver. Then she jerked her head to the side, away from him. "I'm not—"

Pulling his head back, he watched the flush that warmed her cheeks and made her eyes sparkle. She licked her lips and he fought back a groan. Instead, he said, "Unless you're willing to concede that you're turned on by me."

She closed her eyes, her shoulders tensed and her jaw went rigid.

Gage cupped her chin and stroked his thumb over her lips. They were smooth, slightly damp and warm from her tongue. His balls tightened and his dick hardened. Her feminine scent of warm vanilla mixing with his soap and his shampoo from the shower was arousing as hell. Using his fingers, he stroked along the sensitive line of her jaw to her ear and down the curve of her neck.

Then he leaned down and brushed his mouth over hers.

Nice. But not earth shattering. So why had he seen mantling on her skin before it faded? Maybe it was just another side effect of his fried magic? He meant to find out and slid his hand up into her silky hair, tilted her head and took the kiss deeper.

Then Mira laid her hand on his shoulder, sighed in his mouth and touched her tongue to his.

A shock of pure, white-hot pleasure exploded, slamming into his chest and heating up his mantling. Gage forgot about his magic, forgot about everything. His focus, all his need, narrowed down to the hot woman in front of him. His skin burned for her touch, his tongue longed for her taste, and his cock throbbed to fill her. He shifted, wrapped his arms around her waist and pulled her off her feet.

She gasped once.

He filled her mouth, tasting and exploring as he slid his hand over her hip. There was no panty line beneath the cotton of the sweats. He moved his hand beneath her thigh, urging her leg higher.

She wrapped her thighs around his hips and kissed him back. She pressed her core right against the erection trapped in his jeans. The explosive lust raged and burned until it felt like they were caught up by a tornado and spun . . .

Oh fuck. Ripping his mouth from Mira's, Gage realized they *were* spinning in a flash-jump. Being thrown through space at a speed that could not be seen or measured. Only master wizards were able to flash-jump and Gage hadn't been able to do it for nearly two decades with his fried powers.

No time! Prepare! He tightened his arm around Mira's waist and cupped her head to press her face into the curve of his neck to protect her.

His feet hit the ground and he automatically bent his knees and caught his balance. In seconds, he regained his equilibrium. For an instant, fierce joy broke through him. Gods above, he'd missed the freedom and power of a flash-jump.

Then reality intruded with the question: Just where the hell had he taken them? And how?

Mira's insides felt like they had been through the spin cycle, then thrown into a blender. If Gage hadn't held her head against his neck, she thought it would have broken apart from the internal pressure. Finally, her world righted and she became excruciatingly aware of the wizard.

His rock-hard arms around her, his warm chest, the velvety feel of his mantling and his erection pressing so intimately against her that even a deep breath caused a ripple of pleasure. She had her legs wrapped around him!

Lifting her head, she looked around. "We're not in Kansas anymore, are we?" It was dark, no lights from any kind of home or business. There was only the thin light of the moon and the dominating roar of a waterfall, along with a spray of dampness.

"Looks like Raven Mist Falls," he said, his chest rumbling with the words.

Hades alive! They were miles and miles away from Gage's house. That had been some crazy ride. "What happened? I mean we were kissing, then . . ." She realized she was still wrapped around him like a blanket. Kissing the wizard created in her a raw, wild hunger to taste, touch and be filled by him. Even now, she ached with need. At the same time his arms made her feel safe, secure, like she belonged.

Her brains had obviously been scrambled after being thrown from his house to this place.

Embarrassed at herself, at the way Gage had managed to bring out her inner slut, she forced herself to drop her legs to the ground. Damn, she didn't even have shoes on. Quickly, she retied the loose sweats and said, "You can let go of me."

"Better not." He kept his arm around her waist and pulled her close to his side. "The potion flash-jumped us. Could happen again."

"Why are we here?" She looked around. She'd heard about the falls. They were out in the Cleveland National Forest and required several miles of hiking to reach. They were standing on a shelf of rock between the cliffs and the churning pool where the falls spilled into it. From there, the water then cascaded into a second waterfall to another pool far below them. It was like being on a twelve-by-twelve island. "Is my grandmother here?" Hope welled in her chest. *Please let her be okay.*

She saw him search the small ledge with his gaze. His dark hair shimmered in the moonlight, his face was expressionless and his eyes distant, as if he were thinking. "I don't feel any energy from another wizard. They aren't here."

She shivered as the spray from the falls dampened her shirt and disappointment chilled her heart. "You said the potion did this, so where is she?" What the hell was going on? Why were they on this rock trapped between a cliff and a churning pool of water?

Gage's jaw clenched, and his fingers pressed into her waist. Then he turned, his light blue eyes slightly narrowed as he said, "The potion is magnetized, pulling me to the wizard who kidnapped her, but it takes time. We're not all the way there yet."

The great Wizard Remington didn't like her questioning him. Like she gave a shit about his feelings.

He turned away from her and held out his hand. She heard a pop, then sparks exploded from his fingertips.

Mira *felt* her hair frizz. Lifting her hand, she touched the staticky strands poufing out like a bad perm. What the hell? She glared at Gage. "You frizzed my hair!" I mean seriously, she had one good feature. *One.* Being attacked by trolls she could handle, but frizzing her hair?

Gage's right hand began to glow like a lightbulb, illuminating his hard face pulled tight. His lips were edged in white fury. He stared at his hand, ignoring her.

"At least fix my hair," she griped. She'd been a good sport about the clothes, but she had her limits.

"Do you want to get off this rock or not?" he snapped, then lifted his glowing hand to get a better view of their position.

She forgot her outrage when the light hit the water cascading down the side of the cliff and splashing into the pool. Her breath caught and she whispered, "Beautiful. The moonlight makes the water look silver, almost ethereal."

"You've never been here?"

She shook her head, her hair moving in a frizzy clump. "No time." She had meant to hike out here, but there was always something that needed to be done. Her cousins, Gram or aunt always needed something—the oil changed in their car, catering arranged for a dinner party. She just hadn't taken the time.

Her gaze caught on something close to the edge of the rock by the pool. "What's that? Right there on the ground before the pool?"

Gage lowered his hand to illuminate the rock at the edge of the pool. "Just a pebble."

It had a green coloring and seemed oddly familiar. She shrugged out from beneath his arm and walked across the damp rock, feeling the spray of the falls get heavier as she got closer. She bent down and scooped up the small stone. There was enough light from Gage's hand and the moon to see the multi-green gemstone. Her heart sped up. "It's my grandmother's!" In spite of standing on the cold rock with the waterfall dampening her shirt, she felt a flash of warm excitement. "It's moss agate. One of the many gemstones Gram has in her bracelet that she uses when she consults with the spirits." Tearing her gaze from the stone, she looked up at him. "She says that moss agate is the wizard's gemstone. It's a sign . . . I guess, that a wizard has her."

Gage frowned. "She was here. So we're following her."

That odd feeling tightened her stomach. "Why

don't you know what's happening? You're supposed to be the great master wizard. Haven't you
used a tracking potion before?" Her situation hit
home. She was trapped on a rock. What if he just
left her? She didn't have shoes, didn't have a cell
phone and there didn't appear to be any way to
climb down. She was at his mercy. The sense of
safety, of belonging she had felt in his arms was replaced by cold fear and loneliness. She clutched
the piece of agate and wrapped her arms around
her waist and shivered.

He closed the step between them and glared
down at her. "I told you, the wizard has their where-
abouts cloaked. My potion is breaking through.
But if you think you can do better on your own,
with no magic, and no ability to even feel magic . . ."
He shrugged.

She felt his glare, his implication about how she
was frigid. Useless. Hell, she knew the truth She'd
known the truth since the day of her parents' funeral. Mira closed her eyes against the memory.
Gram holding her hand as they walked up to stand
with the family around the caskets. Her mother's
family, Nana, Papa and Uncle Ray, they'd glared
down at her. Papa had told her that she'd killed
her parents. She was a curse, a frigid that had
shamed her parents into going to the wizard to
beg him to fix her. If they hadn't been there that
day to see the wizard, they wouldn't have been in
the path of the demon.

She yanked herself from that painful memory
and faced the truth—she couldn't find her grandmother on her own. She needed the wizard.
Squeezing the gemstone in her fingers, she reminded herself that her grandmother loved her

just as she was. "You made your point. What do we do now?"

He stood still, watching her. "We wait for the potion to find the wizard again."

She nodded and turned, walking away from the falls to where the cliff jutted straight up. It was dry and somewhat sheltered from the wind. She sat down and tugged the too-long sweats down over her freezing feet. Then she pulled her knees up and wrapped her arms around them for warmth.

Gage sat down next to her, stretched his long legs out, then reached over and lifted her up.

Surprised, she yelped as he dropped her on his lap. "Hey!"

He cupped the back of her head and looked down into her eyes. "I am not taking a chance of leaving you here."

His intense gaze took her breath away. "Oh, if you flash-jump."

"I need to have a tight grip on you. I won't leave you here alone, Mira."

His words traveled through her and hit her heart where the fear of being left lived. "I'm used to being alone." Oh damn, she hadn't meant to say that. But when she looked up at his sky-blue eyes outlined in sooty dark lashes, she just felt . . . connected. She struggled to recover with jokes. "My cousins once left me at a Burger King when I was in the restroom. Another time, my aunt left me on a yacht where she'd been giving an astrological reading." At the time, she'd been terrified. But now it was a funny family story.

He kept staring at her. "After that kiss, you'd be hard to forget. I won't leave you here. Lay against me. I can generate enough heat to keep you warm."

She looked at his chest, seeing his intricate triskellion and mantling. Now she knew what the markings meant—that he was an incredibly powerful wizard who had lived a very long time.

"Keep staring at me like that, and I'm going to find a whole other way to keep you warm," he said in a low voice filled with promise.

She hated the idea that she was reacting to him like every other female. Jerking her gaze up, she said, "You're not in bad shape for an old guy." Two hundred and nineteen. She couldn't even imagine. "What's it like to live so long?"

With his hand on the back of her head, he pulled her against his chest, and the heat of Gage began to quickly seep into her. Just when she thought he wouldn't answer her question, he said, "It starts off feeling pretty damned good. Then people you care about start dying, and you begin to . . . disconnect. To learn to live separate from those around you." He took a deep breath. "It's one of the reasons we train out emotion as much as possible while apprentices. Not only do emotions impair judgment and cause mistakes, but they make you too fucking vulnerable."

Shock seared her deep in her blood. The unvarnished truth of his words hit her. Flattening her hand over his chest, covering as much of his skin as she could reach, she said, "I didn't think about that. So you lost all your family? Parents? Siblings?"

"No siblings. Once my magic-sensitive parents realized I was magic-born, they poured everything into me."

His voice had gone flat, unemotional. Magic-borns were rare. Magic actually originated within them. So they showed early, doing little things like moving the toy they wanted.

"They must have been proud of you. Loved you," she said, thinking that if she'd been magic-born, her parents wouldn't have been killed by a demon.

Nothing. Gage was silent.

"Gage?"

He shifted his gaze to her face. "They died angry and bitter. Always wanting more, sure that more houses, boats, servants, jewels would fill the hole inside them. But it never did." His gaze was barren, empty. "If that's love, I'll stick to sex."

Sex was how he connected. It made her chest hurt to realize it. "Rumor says that before you became a recluse, you used to have your pick of women."

"True."

"Tell me you lied to them, led them on. That you used them and threw them away." She needed to think of him the way she always had—cold, uncaring, too powerful and too arrogant.

"Why would I have done that? I didn't have to lie to get women to sleep with me, Mira. Still don't. They'll come to the house and give me what I want. I give them whatever they want, except a relationship."

She closed her eyes and knew it was the truth. His voice was just too baffled for it to be a lie. Her own raw honesty slipped out: "It's easier to hate you."

He stroked her frizzy hair and said softly, "But you don't hate me, do you?"

She wanted to. All these years, she'd eased her own guilt about her parents by fixating on the wizard and blaming him. "Not as much as yesterday."

CHAPTER FIVE

Mira woke with a jolt. Snapping open her eyes, she found herself looking at a massive bicep covered in flowing lines.

Gage. She'd fallen asleep in his lap. But now the sun was up, and though they were tucked back in the shadows, she could see his mantling clearly. She reached out and touched one henna-colored swirling line, tracing it over the hard bulge of muscle, down to the bend of his elbow.

Heat and velvet.

Intriguing.

Reversing her direction, she traced up, traveling over the rise of his shoulder, down the outside of his pectoral and back in to his flat nipple.

That little bud tightened. She ran the tip of her finger over it and every muscle in his body contracted beneath her.

She froze with her finger pressed just above his nipple. Was he awake? He didn't say a word and his breathing was steady. He had one arm wrapped around her back, his hand resting just below her breast. His other hand was on her thigh.

She was pretty sure he had a morning hard-on pressing against her left butt cheek.

Was she going to play with fire? Before she answered her own question, she traced the line that moved through his nipple down over the outside of his ribs. Where she touched skin with no mantling, it was hot and smooth. Then she moved her finger over the mantling and it was velvety with a slight vibration or hum. She followed the line to the edge of his pants.

Then it disappeared.

She stared at that spot, thinking of him in the shower. The way the lines rolled down over his hips, his butt . . .

His cock.

She moved her finger to a separate line just above the waist of his jeans on his stomach. She traced it up, over the harshly defined ridges of his stomach and through the triskellion . . . back to swirl around his nipple. Mira let herself touch and pet the hennaed nub, feeling it tighten even more.

Gage sucked in a breath.

Playing possum, was he? A streak of wickedness, or maybe it was the new knowledge that sex was how Gage connected, urged her to lift her cheek off his chest. He didn't move. She turned her head to gaze at his chest, not looking up to his face. The top of the triskellion had more lines bursting outward. One wrapped around his right nipple. Mira stroked the left nipple with a finger, leaned forward and traced another line with her tongue right to that nipple. Then she grazed her teeth over the puckered bud.

Gage hissed and shuddered, his hips pressed up against her bottom.

Mira released the nipple and looked up. He had his head tilted back against the rock. "You're awake."

A slow smile revealed his white teeth. "And very ready." Lifting his head, he looked down at her, his light-blue eyes ringed with a deep gray.

That gaze packed a punch of pure heat. "Ready?" Why was she goading him? Playing this sexual game? But she knew why. The way he reacted to her made her feel a kind of power all her own. He made her feel attractive and sexy.

He caught the edge of the too-big shirt. "Ready for a little payback." He began tugging the shirt up. "Lift your arms, Mira," he said in a gravelly demand.

A shudder surprised her. She knew no one could see them, they were perched on a rock on the side of a cliff. Slowly, she raised her arms.

Gage pulled the shirt off. Immediately the cool air slipped around her back, stomach and breasts. Her nipples tightened, and she lowered her arms. What would he think? Mira wasn't model thin. She wasn't super pretty, or special in any way. She was just plain, magic-blind Mira.

"Exquisite," he said and dropped the shirt.

She sat sideways on his thighs, feeling his erection pressing against her left hip, and his hot gaze on her breasts. He wrapped his right arm around her shoulders and pulled her back, tugging her until she lay back over his legs, her head resting against his massive bicep.

"Let me, Mira. I have to touch you."

She looked up at his face, seeing the raw need

in the starkness of his cheekbones, the way he pressed his lips together until they were severe. He lifted his hand and used his index finger to trace imaginary lines from her collar bone over the slope of her breast to her nipple.

"Close your eyes, I want to feel what I felt."

She lifted her gaze to his. The lightest blue surrounded by a dark gray that told her that true pain lived inside him.

"I've got you," he said simply.

She believed him and closed her eyes. She felt him slide his finger over her nipple. The pad of his finger had work-roughened ridges and teased her nerve endings. She sucked in her breath and arched into his touch.

Gage trailed down underneath her breast, then cupped her. "Big enough to fill my hand."

Sensations shot to her belly and then straight to her groin. It was like he was getting beneath her skin, touching more of her. Baring more than her breasts. Seeing more than skin and nipples. The connection was too much, too soon. "Gage . . ."

He used his arm beneath her to lift her into a kiss. His full, firm lips sliding over hers. "Felt it too. It's like you're a witch, casting a spell on me."

She opened her eyes. "I'm no witch."

Lifting an eyebrow, he used his thumb to torture her nipple. "No. You're Mira. Mira Tate."

She knew then that he saw her. As she was. And liked it. It tore through her, made her body soften, open.

Trust.

She sat up, turned and straddled him. Putting her hands on his shoulders, she felt the lines of his power practically burrow into her palms and fingers.

He closed his large hands around her rib cage and ran his thumbs under her breasts. She saw his nostrils flare as she leaned closer.

And closer.

"Don't stop. Please." He urged her forward until the tip of her breast just touched the heat of his mouth. He cupped the weight in one hand, squeezing slightly and drew the nipple in, then suckled.

A shudder ran down her back. She dug her fingers into his shoulders as pleasure burst in hot little rivers.

He pulled and suckled, then turned her to capture her other nipple.

She rubbed her hands over his hot skin, then sank her fingers into his thick hair, holding him to her. Hot need roared through her, making her skin burn, her thighs clench and that deep ache yearned to be filled. She couldn't hold still, and she cradled his head to pull him from her breast. Then she laid her mouth over his.

She licked his lips, then swirled her tongue deep into his mouth as she lowered her body until she felt the hard ridge of the erection trapped in his jeans press between her legs. Her swollen folds were so sensitized, she shuddered.

Gage groaned into her mouth, caught hold of her hips and thrust against her.

"Gage . . ." Whatever she'd been going to say, whatever raw words were trying to escape were lost when she was thrown into a whirling vortex. The rock beneath them vanished, and suddenly there was nothing. She was spinning through nothingness. Terror exploded in her mind as she squeezed her eyes shut.

Then she felt strong arms lock her to a powerful body. Mira held on to the one safe thing: Gage.

Gage landed on a large, soft bed with Mira sprawled on top of him. He had a hand on her ass covered by his sweatpants. Her big, warm breasts were crushed into his chest.

His first thought was that it was a damned inconvenient time to have flash-jumped again.

But they had landed in a soft bed. He liked that. Oh yeah, it was perfect.

"My head is trying to explode." She lifted her head—which forced her hips down right onto his cock.

He groaned at the feel of her hot core pressed against his jeans. He knew she didn't have panties on beneath that well-washed cotton. She was so hot, so incredible, he was desperate to get her completely naked.

He had seen her naked once and it hadn't been enough. It wouldn't be enough until he'd touched all of her. Tasted all of her. And until he'd been so deep inside her, she'd come apart, screaming his name while he filled her again and again.

He looked up at her shocked eyes, frizzed hair and that full mouth slightly open. She looked like a woman ready for hot sex, except that there was a tightness at the edges of her eyes and she'd paled a bit from the jump. He reached up and ran his hand over the wild frizz. "Breathe. The throb in your head will fade in a second. Flash-jumping puts tremendous force on your body."

He saw the confusion completely clear and the remaining desire drain off. Her brows snapped together. "We flash-jumped again! What if Gram is here?"

Shit. He could cheerfully electrocute anyone that got between him and this hot, sexy woman. But she pushed off him to stand up. He reluctantly let her go and sat up to look around. "Hotel room of some kind."

"Gage, I don't have a shirt."

He forgot the room and looked back at her. She had breasts big enough to fill his hands. His cock went rock hard again. But what struck him right through his solar plexus were the henna-colored ribbons marking her skin around her breasts. It was the sexiest thing he'd ever seen.

His mark on her. Where his mouth had been, his fingers.

He looked down, taking in her slightly rounded stomach and hips a man could hold while burying himself deep inside her. Dressed only in his too-big sweats, with her ridiculously wild hair and his mantling caressing her full breasts, he wanted her more.

Without looking down, she wrapped her arms around herself and shivered. "I can't let my grandmother see me like this! Or that wizard! If they are here . . ."

The lines faded away as she spoke. His brain finally snapped into action. Sitting up, he picked up the shirt that he'd pulled off her. He'd dropped it down on his lap, and it had been scrunched between them. Standing up, he handed it to her. "I don't think they are here." He'd have felt the wizard's energy instantly.

Mira yanked on the wrinkled shirt. "I'll look around." She moved past him to walk between the bed and the dresser with the large flat screen mounted over it and disappeared through a door. She came back out, her mouth flat, her brown eyes wide. "Gram's not here, but I found this."

He crossed the room and looked down at her outstretched palm. She had two gemstones now, the moss agate from last night and a bloodred ruby. He looked up to her eyes. "From her bracelet?"

She nodded and frowned in concentration. "Ruby is the most powerful of the gemstones. Gram said the ruby is my stone." She lifted her stare from her palm to him. "I don't know what she's telling me. I get the first stone. That told me a wizard took her. But this?"

Gage got it. Her Gram was smart. "A powerful wizard, as powerful as the ruby." And that was a big problem. Now that he had his mind off Mira's body, it was clear to him that he was dealing with another master wizard. Only a master wizard had the ability to flash-jump, and this wizard had to be flash-jumping. How else would he have gotten Mira's grandmother to that ledge they'd spent the night on?

"Oh." Mira's shoulders lowered. "Will he hurt her?"

Her question hovered, and her deep worry punched him in the gut. Gage clenched his fists to keep from reaching out to her and drawing her to him. He actually wanted to comfort her.

Unproductive and useless. He had to get his priorities straight. Find the wizard, save Calia and reestablish his authority in town. Then fix his powers so he could seal the portal on his property forever.

Mira's shoulders shot back up to her ears and

her chin rose as she announced, "I won't let him hurt her! We have to find her!"

He refused to get caught up in her emotional swings. She'd distracted him last night when he'd been more concerned about her comfort and safety than anything else. He'd only made one attempt to summon his BlackBerry to check in with Rhys. That had ended badly, with his hand frying and glowing like a flashlight, and frizzing out Mira's hair. He told her, "The potion is working, breaking through the cloak the wizard is using. The wizard who has Calia isn't going to hurt her. He wants something from her."

She closed her fist around the two stones. "So we'll jump again?"

He suspected they would. They seemed to be following the wizard. Which meant his power must be healing to do even that much, but it wasn't completely healed or the potion would have taken Gage right to the wizard. But he needed Mira to believe he knew what he was doing. "Yes, but we should have some time."

She turned and went to the telephone on the bedside table where she picked up the directory and read it. "We're at Raven Mist Resort." She looked up. "If you flash-jump without me, call me here and tell me where you are."

He wondered at the look in her eyes—so hard assed and bossy—until he remembered what she'd said last night. Her family forgot her places, just left her behind.

Her parents had left her too. It hadn't been their fault, but she'd just been a little girl. The core of his magic sizzled in his triskellion, the spirals turning out of sync and emitting a couple sparks.

Mira's gaze dropped to his chest. Color washed into her face. "What . . . ?"

Like he knew? And shit, he saw her gaze warming with desire, causing a strange zinging reaction in his mantling. He'd been desired thousands of times, and it had always been his cock that reacted, not his magic. Abruptly, he said, "I'm going to take a shower." He went into the large bathroom with the separate shower and Jacuzzi tub. After shutting and locking the door, he held out his hand and concentrated on his BlackBerry, just as he'd done the night before.

Sparks shot off his palm like a Fourth of July sparkler, followed by the stench of burnt plastic. Then a hard black lump appeared in his hand. "Damn it," he hissed at what used to be his Black-Berry. His powers half worked, summoning the BlackBerry but frying it along the way. Furious, he dumped it in the waste can, then turned on the shower. Stripping, he got under the hot spray and washed faster than any mortal. Then leaving the shower running to cover his sounds, he got out. Grabbing a towel, he quickly dried off and knotted it around his waist. He went to the steamed-up mirror and placed his right hand over his triskellion. Because Rhys trained him, then branded him, they had a strong connection. It was how Gage had raised his spirit from the death-sleep. Gage concentrated and called out, "Rhys, find me."

A point appeared in the steam on the mirror, then fanned out and Rhys materialized. "Why am I in a mirror? Do you know how hard it is to project my form in a mirror? I work best in cyberspace! And I hate this suit!"

He was wearing the black suit with the blue tie

he had been buried in. "I'll release you from the mirror as soon as we're done." As long as he kept his hand on the triskellion, he held Rhys's spirit in the mirror. "What have you found?"

Rhys's blue eyes grew brighter and the mirror shook with a rumble. "It's Sinclair St. James."

"Sin?" He was as old as Gage and damn near as powerful. They'd been friends for a century until Gage fried and cut off all contact. "Why the hell would Sin kidnap an old woman?" He tried to reason it out.

"Calia's phone was destroyed and it took every skill I have to get an old voice mail from Sin offering to hire her at any price." Rhys paced the mirror. "It can't be a coincidence that Sin had contacted her, then she's kidnapped by a wizard. It has to be him."

"Troll balls," Gage snarled, keeping his voice lower than the sound of the water running. "Does he know I'm fried?"

Rhys shrugged. "He probably suspects."

Not good. Sin was an old master wizard and, even at his best, it would be a battle for Gage to defeat him. He had to be smart, had to find out as much as he could. "Where is he?"

The fog surrounding Rhys turned red. "I don't know. I can't find a cyber-link to him. No cell phone, no computer, not even GPS in a car. The wizard has unplugged. He does not want to be found."

Real worry snaked up Gage's spine and clenched his jaw. "What the hell is doing?" Then quickly, Gage summed up his experience with flash-jumping and finding the two gemstones.

Rhys's face was grim. "Then we know he's not fried if he's flash-jumping. At least not yet, but he could be close." He blew out a breath that melted away more steam. "You have to ground your power, Gage. Now. If Sin is on edge, he's extremely dangerous."

He had to find and then stop or kill Sin. Ignoring the pang in his gut at the loss of yet another person in his life, he dealt in the facts. "The potion is working. I'm flash-jumping . . . but I'm behind Sin. He has a cloaking spell around the two of them."

Rhys dropped his gaze over Gage's chest. "If you're flash-jumping, then your powers are healing. What's grounding them?"

"Mira. I think." Without revealing too much, he told about his markings on her.

Rhys looked as surprised as Gage, then turned his head to the right, looking at something Gage couldn't see. "Your magic fried when you pulled the power Jillian stole back to you before killing her. It was too much, like too much electricity and it had nowhere to go. You short-circuited."

"My mantling on Mira, you think she might be able to absorb the excess power?" She was magic-blind, completely frigid. Was that possible?

Still staring off at something only he could see, Rhys said, "Sexual energy could be a conductor. And Mira the vessel that grounds you."

"Vessel?" He glared at his mentor. "Do not ever refer to her that way. Ever." She was not an object.

Rhys snapped his head around. "Bad choice of words. If this woman can ground your powers, she's damned amazing. She's unique. Special."

He nodded once.

"But you have to find out. I am surmising you have not had full sexual intercourse. Don't growl, boy. I am not asking for details. Your town is in serious danger. You have a possible rogue wizard on the loose and you still need to seal that portal on your grounds." Rhys bored his stare into Gage and added, "If Mira can ground your power with sexual intercourse, and she is willing, then do it. Or people are going to die."

There was a reason Rhys had been his mentor. He had been an excellent master wizard, and he'd never abused his power. He'd also treated Gage more like a son than his father had. His old man had wanted sexual details. Wanted Gage to provide him with women for sex. It had disgusted him. Rhys, on the other hand, never said much about his sexual encounters. Gage had seen numerous women in and out of Rhys's life. And he'd seen them call Rhys later when they needed help.

Rhys had been there without question.

Rhys had taught Gage more about being a man and a wizard than his parents had.

"All right," Gage said. "I'll do it."

"Are you going to tell her about your fried power?"

"Can't." Part of him wanted to. Like he'd told her about his parents, about what it was like to live so long and lose so many. But Mira had blackmailed him to get his help. He couldn't trust her with the knowledge of his fried power. If she revealed it, and the town fired him, who would protect the town from the troll-demons or any number of other threats?

CHAPTER SIX

Mira spent hours organizing. This was what she was good at—making things happen. She arranged for food, clothes and cell phones. She did what work she could from the hotel room. Gage seemed to be running his own empire too. She was spread out on the bed while he used the table. She hung up from another round of coaching her cousins through everyday tasks, and then having to call three customers to fix problems. Now she picked up her coffee cup and watched Gage.

He had his phone cradled against his shoulder and was working on one of the two laptops she'd managed to procure for them. "Fifteen hundred is the total of the Remington Day gifts?"

He sounded unsatisfied. A flash of disappointment chased by a wave of anger went through her. The town honored him! Gave him what they could on top of his monthly stipend and he had the nerve to complain?

"Okay . . ." He paused scrolling through something on his computer. "Add another twenty thousand and give it all to Dr. Margaret Lewis at the children's hospital. She's doing amazing work with the cancer patients." He ended the call and put the phone down, rolled his neck, then caught her staring. "What?"

Mira closed her mouth, turned to set her coffee cup on the nightstand, then asked, "You don't keep the gifts?"

He dropped his hand from rubbing his neck. "What difference does it make?"

A hell of a lot. He used the money from the gifts to help other people. It made a difference. "The twenty thousand you added, where does it come from?"

He lowered his eyebrows. "Private donors."

His answer was too flat, too pat. He was lying. She felt it in her gut. "It's your money." How many times had he done stuff like this? It wasn't public knowledge.

He picked up his bottle of water and stretched out his long legs in front of him as if the whole subject bored him.

Curiosity burned in her chest. Who was this wizard? He was huge, warrior-like with his massive size, muscles and markings. She'd thought him hard, cold, selfish and dangerous, but was it possible he had a heart? "How many people work for you?"

He drank a long swallow, then said, "Full-time, I have a staff of twelve, and another half dozen part-time. Then there's my personal staff of three."

She lowered her mug of coffee to rest on her jean-covered leg. She'd had the store deliver a pair of jeans and another of those soft cotton shirts for him in a blue that brought out Gage's eyes. The short sleeves gave her a nice view of his masculine arms covered in mantling. "Fifteen full-time and six part-time? What do they do?"

"My personal staff is my housekeeper, business manager and secretary. Then there's the dozen or so who run my website and man the phones, the liaisons with the police, mayor's office and city council, still others cover the town looking for trouble or people who have needs. I also have people connecting with the hospitals, shelters, etcetera." He shrugged, stood up and walked to the dresser across from the end of the bed. "They do what I tell them to. With my being gone right now, they are all working harder." Gage picked up the bottle of pinot grigio chilling in the ice bucket, opened it and filled two glasses. He picked them up and walked to her.

She lifted her gaze to the man towering over the side of the bed. He smelled of soap, rich amber and that ever-present tang of electricity. The mantling lines snaked down his arm. Did she hear a hum? A whispered plea for her to touch his magic?

Or was she just horny for the wizard? Like so many other women before her? If they hadn't flash-jumped this morning . . .

She reached out and took the glass of wine. "Thanks."

"Move."

She drew her eyebrows together at his gruff order. Since nearly ripping his clothes off and having her way with him on that rock, she'd kept her distance, unable to trust her rising desire. "Why?"

"Because it's been hours since we last jumped. I want to make sure I have you."

"Oh." How could she argue with that? She shifted her work and scooted over. The bed dipped under his weight as he sat down and stretched his legs alongside hers. He dwarfed her, making her almost feel delicate. Besides the jeans, she was wearing a black T-shirt and tennis shoes. She wasn't going to be caught barefoot this time. She had the two gemstones tucked into the cup of her bra. The heat of Gage touched her thighs and brushed along her arm. She took a long drink of her wine.

She was still hot. Still . . . empty. A tiny voice in her brain said she should climb up on Gage's lap. You know . . . in case they jumped.

That voice was a big, fat, horny slut. She took a deep drink of her wine to shut it up. Nope, still there, still whispering . . .

Annoyed and embarrassed at her reaction, she frantically tried to think of something to say to quiet the voice. She blurted out, "You're practically an empire with all the people you employ." Oh real smooth, she thought dryly. But still, being the town wizard was harder than she'd imagined. She wanted to know more about him. Like why he was a recluse, why his house was like something out of a bad horror flick on the outside, and perfectly normal on the inside. She started with, "Why do you refuse to come to Remington Day? It's rude. All those people are there to honor you."

He looked down at her, his gaze threaded with something dark and dangerous. "You saw why, Mira."

More cool wine slid down her throat, then she lowered her glass. "The troll-demon things. So you do have a portal on your land."

"Obviously."

Thinking about the demon who had murdered her parents, her stomach tightened. She could still remember her father throwing her up in the air and his massive hands catching her. She could still recall the scent of apples from her mom's shampoo when she'd snuggle in bed and read to her every night. "What about now that you're not there? Will the troll-demons get out?"

"No."

"How can you be sure?"

He studied his wineglass. "It only happens once a year for about ninety minutes. The rest of the year, the portal is completely sealed. Nothing can get out."

She didn't understand. "But . . . only once a year? On Remington Day?" That was the anniversary of her parents' deaths and when he'd banished the demon that— "Oh gods above, that's the portal your apprentice opened!"

He nodded. "I sealed it, but every year on the anniversary of the demon's banishment, a weakness in the seal appears. Only troll-demons can get through. There's not enough of a break in the seal for more dangerous demons to get through."

Fear kicked up her pulse at the realization that if Gage hadn't been protecting them all these years, those hideous trolls would be crawling all over the town. It was like her nightmares when she'd awaken in hot terror, then cold shakes, terrified the demon was coming to get her, to tear her apart limb by limb. "I didn't know. . . ." she said softly. Feeling the warmth of Gage next to her drove the old terror back.

He set his glass down beside her coffee cup and

said, "No one knows. Not until you showed up and saw them."

"That's why you scare people away. You don't want anyone to get hurt." Mira was facing a truth she didn't want to face. One she had resisted, no matter how much the town bragged about their wizard. She'd misjudged him and she owed him an apology. "I'm sorry. I guess . . . it's just always been easier for me to believe you didn't care. That you're selfish and self-involved. That . . ." *Shit.* She drained the wine in her glass.

Gage caught hold of her face, turning her head to face him. "That what?"

Just kiss him, then you won't have to tell him! She was tempted, but after what he'd just told her, after all that she'd learned about him, she couldn't avoid the truth. "That if you're not at fault for my parents' death, then I am."

His hand tightened on her face. "You? But you were only a kid. What are you now? Twenty-three?"

"Twenty-four." He had her trapped in his gaze.

"So you'd have been seven years old. How the hell can you blame yourself?"

It was an effort, but she turned her gaze away to look out into the darkness outside the window. When had it gotten so late? She hadn't noticed.

"Mira? Tell me," he encouraged softly.

She twirled the stem of the wineglass in her fingers, feeling the weight and heat of him next to her. "I know why they went to see you that day. Because of me. Because I'm frigid and they were . . . ashamed. *A curse* is what my grandfather, my mother's father, called me at the funeral. But I blamed you."

* * *

Holding her face with his hand, Gage felt like he'd been kicked in the stomach. She blamed herself? Dark guilt crawled through him. She'd been a child! And yeah, her parents had been there to ask him to infuse her with magic so she'd be sensitive, a risky thing he would have refused.

But he hadn't been there.

"You were right to blame me. It was my fault." Gage heard the words coming from his mouth, seventeen years of guilt, of regret, spilling out of him.

Mira went still. He felt her jaw flex beneath his hand. Then she pushed his hand off her face, put her wineglass down on the nightstand and leaned back against the headboard. Crossing her arms over her stomach, she stared at the blank TV screen mounted over the dresser. "What happened that day?"

"Your parents had an appointment with me. I knew it. But I left anyway. I went to the Realm."

She turned to look at him. "What's that?"

"It's a plane of existence that only wizards can reach. We hold our sacred ceremonies there. It's where I was branded a master. More rarely, a mating ceremony is held there. But most wizards never mate."

She frowned at that. "Why?"

He shrugged. "Our training is rigorous and intense, all about the mind and body connection, about studying and more studying. We cannot control what we do not understand. We are trained to think with logic, never emotion. It makes us stronger, better decision-makers and better protectors. But we don't really connect and form mating bonds."

Soft gold color spread in her eyes. "That sounds . . . cold."

He shrugged. "It's what it takes to achieve a master wizard level of power. We train out emotions that can cloud judgment. With so much power, we must be solid and grounded or we are too dangerous."

"So how did this happen? How did you allow your apprentice to summon a demon?"

His gut burned at the memory. "I let emotion, lust, cloud my judgment. Jillian applied to be my apprentice. I was very attracted to her and knew I should turn her away. But after a couple centuries of women vying for sex with me, sex with a wizard, it was getting tiresome. Normally, sexual energy fuels our power. But it was just getting . . . flat."

"There are stories how women gathered around you and you'd just pick like from a buffet."

The disgust in her voice made him feel old. "I am what I am, Mira. I'm magic-born, and I worked for decades to achieve my master wizard status. It has its perks, and it's also why you blackmailed me into helping you."

She wrinkled her nose. "Yeah, yeah, you're top of the food chain. We all bow down as you walk by. Go on. Tell me how your apprentice, a woman, of course, brought you down."

Amusement tugged at his mouth. She clearly wasn't impressed with his status. Mira treated him like an equal who had to work for her approval . . . and it didn't suck. It made him want to be better, to get a smile or admiring word from her. He had an even stronger urge to take hold of her, roll her beneath him and kiss her into silence. Or moans.

She snapped her fingers in front of his face. "Hello?"

He caught her wrist. "Don't make me bite you," he teased. Holding her hand on his thigh, he told her the story. "I began to train Jillian. She had the raw talent and power, but her self-discipline was lacking. I went to her room one night to tell her she had a choice. Work harder or get out." He felt himself sliding back into the memory.

She squeezed his hand, pulling him back. "And?"

He kept it simple. "She was naked."

Mira took her hand away. "Can't pass that up."

Gage fought his need to grab her hand back. "She did work harder, for a while. She also came to my bed. A lot. It seemed mutually beneficial until I caught on to the pattern. She was stronger after we had sex. Every single time. I had to be sure." He turned and faced Mira. "So even though I had scheduled an appointment with your parents, I left and went to the Realm."

Her face was tight, her eyes uneasy. "Why?"

"I needed clarity and the Realm can provide that by allowing me to open my third eye to see what she was really doing. I saw it all, how she was using sexual energy to steal power from me." He'd been furious, but what he saw next had been a betrayal of everything Gage believed in, of all the things he'd vowed as a master wizard. "It gets worse," he warned. "I saw that Jillian was raising a demon, hoping it would help her kill me and steal more power."

Mira's face drained of color. "But the demon killed my parents."

His muscles tensed at the memory. "I flashed back to earth and my house as quickly as I could. But it was too late. Jillian couldn't control the demon, so she ran and hid. It found your parents."

Her shoulders dropped and her hands curled into fists in her lap. "And killed them."

He nodded. "I found the demon and banished it. Then I found Jillian. She'd been hiding from the monster she summoned. When I dragged her out, dragged her to that—" He remembered how she had barely looked at the two people whose lives had been brutally torn from them. Instead, she'd tried to seduce him, and begged him to not kill her. "I did what had to be done and killed her."

He had to clamp his mouth shut to keep from telling her the rest. How he'd pulled his power back from her, making sure she couldn't take it with her into hell where the demon she'd bargained with would get ahold of it. Gage had already lived a couple of hundred years and was covered in mantling. There was nowhere for all that power to go. The power hit his triskellion and mantling. His power had overloaded, then short-circuited. In short, he had fried.

And Mira might be the answer. She could be the one woman who could ground his power and free up his magic. He needed her to trust him, believe in him. Help him heal. And in return he'd rescue her grandmother. But he couldn't reveal any more weaknesses to her, couldn't let her know he was fried.

Instead, he turned toward her and touched her face. "It wasn't your fault. You were a kid."

"None of that changes why my parents went to see you."

A helpless anger filled his chest. The damn woman was turning him inside out. "Get over it, Mira. So you were born frigid. Deal with it. Quit feeling sorry for yourself."

Her eyes blazed with hot gold and she slapped his hand off her face. She got to her feet, turned to face him and jammed her hands on her hips. Her skin flushed all the way down to the top curve of her breasts in that black T-shirt. "Sorry for myself?" she snapped. "I'm glad I'm magic-blind. It forces me to be human and not treat others like they are usable and expendable! My parents wanted to change me, and my grandparents on my mother's side wanted to get rid of me. Well, you know what? Screw them. I like me the way I am."

The wave of pride in her rolled over him. Mira was self-confident and flat-out refused to allow other people's opinions to define her. She didn't fall over herself trying to impress him or manipulate him, not his Mira. No, she stood there and told him that she liked herself just the way she was. That kind of confidence in a woman was just plain sexy. He grinned at her. "I like you."

She narrowed her eyes. "Why? Magicals either want to change me or use me. The only thing you need from me is to not expose your secret about the portal."

She was sharp. And she challenged him. It was a new experience. Gage moved fast, getting to his feet to tower over her by a good eight inches. "I have a business manager, a housekeeper and all the staff I want. I don't *need* you. . . ." He trailed off on that lie. He needed her to fix his powers. He was using her. He put his hand on her shoulder and then slid his fingers to cup the back of her neck and told her one thing that was true, "I *want* you. I like your fire, your confidence. I like the way you care enough for your grandmother to demand and blackmail me into finding her." He lowered his head and tugged her closer to his mouth. "And I like the way you kiss."

CHAPTER SEVEN

He didn't *need* her.
He *wanted* her.

Mira felt a new warmth blooming around her heart. As if that secret place where she'd kept her deep wish to be desired, wanted and accepted was unfurling with soft sweeping wings. His long fingers intimately cupped around her neck drew her toward him. He watched her with those turbulent eyes with roiling blue-and-gray desire. Real desire. His full mouth was so close to hers, she could feel his breath and almost feel the tang of his rich amber taste on her tongue.

Desire shivered down her spine and spread a pool of thick yearning in her stomach.

If this was what magic felt like, then her rule of not dating magicals was meant to be broken. She went up on her toes, meeting his mouth.

He groaned, his other arm snapping around her waist and lifting her off her feet. Instinctively, she wrapped her arms around his neck, feeling the cords and muscles bulging with his incredible strength. He tilted his head, his breath hot as he sucked her lower lip into his mouth, abraded it with his teeth, then soothed with his tongue.

Her body flared to life, her nerve endings begging for his touch. She twined her legs around his hips, trying to ease the need. *More!* She ran her hands over his shoulders, the soft cotton of his T-shirt frustrating her. She moved her mouth over his jaw, kissing, licking, tasting, needing more of him. Down the strong column of his neck, shivering at the electric-salt taste of his skin, the deep male scent filling her nose and throat. *More!* She dragged her tongue along the collar of his T-shirt and tasted the velvety hot edge of his mantling.

Her tongue hummed.

"Damn, you're a wildcat," Gage groaned. He planted his hand on her butt and pressed her aching core to his hard dick straining his jeans.

A jolt of pure, untamed heat shot through her. Rubbing herself against him, with her mouth pressed to his neck, she demanded, "Not enough. More skin, more of you."

His chuckle rumbled against her breasts. Her bra was too tight. . . .

Then it was gone. All their clothes just vanished! The cool air of the hotel room blew against her back, while the heat of Gage's naked chest pressed against her nipples and his . . .

She pulled back, instinctively trusting his arms to hold her and looked down.

They were both naked and the two gemstones, the moss agate and the ruby that had been in her bra, tumbled down to rest where her legs wrapped around him. His erection jutted up, with the thin lines of mantling swirling around the almost plum-colored head. The two gemstones were nestled together, green and red, at the base of his penis where their bodies met.

It struck her as meaning something. The togetherness, the way the stones touched both of them so intimately. It sent shivers through her and those soft wings in her chest fluttered. She started to reach for the stones, and the back of her hand brushed against his cock.

It jerked and swelled impossibly bigger.

She forgot the stones and, instead, brushed the tip of him with her thumb. Then she curled her fingers around the hard length, feeling the pulse of his magic. It was moving into her, through her, touching so much of her. She slid her legs to the ground, scooping up the gemstones with her left hand.

Gage didn't stop her. He let her be free.

She pressed her mouth to his triskellion and felt the answering hum. It shivered through her, reaching into her and she stroked the symbol with her tongue.

"Mira." Gage breathed it out in a whisper as soft as the hum of his power. He cradled her head as she kept bathing the symbol with her tongue, tasting the ancient amber power. She stroked her hand down the hard ridges of his stomach and curled her fingers around the length of his swollen cock. She brushed her palm up and down, then feathered her thumb over the tip.

When she felt the bead of moisture on her thumb, she moved down his stomach and licked him.

"No more, wildcat." Gage pulled her up, then pressed her back onto the mattress. She watched the mantling on his chest and stomach; the colors were pulsing and deepening into a vibrant plum with swirls of gold. She reached out to touch—

In a move so fast she couldn't really track it, Gage gathered her wrists in his hand and stretched her arms over her head. She still had the gemstones in one fist. He looked down into her eyes, the blues and grays churning with a promise. "I'm going to make you purr for me, little wildcat." His voice was low and thick.

She opened her mouth.

He ducked down and slanted his mouth over hers, wet and demanding, kissing her with fierce possession. Violent, rolling need had her arch beneath him, pressing her breasts against his chest.

Her nipples brushed across the velvety hum of his mantling, wringing a gasp from her. It was like ... magic caressed and stroked the sensitive buds, making her pant and her stomach jump while she clenched her thighs together hard.

Gage kissed along her jaw, sliding his body down, his mouth wet on her neck, while his chest and mantling caressed her nipples. She writhed, desperate for more.

He held her wrists pinned with a gentle strength and kissed down her collar bone.

Her skin was so sensitized now that everywhere he brushed sent wild, desperate sensations through her, then pooled deep in her womb. And when his mouth closed over her nipple, she bucked upward.

Gage slid his thigh between her legs, holding her open while he licked and sucked one nipple, then the other. The heat of his thigh teased her but never quite pressed against her.

A low sound of frantic frustration slipped up her throat.

He lifted his head, those eyes latching on to her face. "Not quite a purr, kitty. I'll have to do better."

"Gage! I can't take any more!"

He released her wrists.

She barely moved her arms before he slid down her length, rubbing his magic over her belly, then dropping down to the ground on his knees. His hands took hold of her thighs and spread them apart. The cool air touched her hot, aching clitoris.

It was followed by the touch of his thumb feathering that sensitive spot.

She jerked her hips.

He cupped her bottom and lifted her up and leaned in. She couldn't move, as if his sheer power and intensity held her pinned, while her nerves screamed for release.

He licked her.

Mira slammed her hands to the bed, clenching one fist around the gemstones, and gathering the spread in the other one.

Gage groaned as if he'd just tasted his favorite dessert. The rumble shot through her. And then he was licking her again, his tongue rolling and caressing her clit. Her body wound tighter, her heart pounded, and she was close, wild, writhing when he penetrated her with a finger, then two and stroked deep. Pumping in and out. Building. Tension twisting. Need growing sharp and vital. She lifted her hips higher, spread her legs wider, giving him everything.

He growled against her, his mouth closed over her clit just as he bent his fingers inside her.

Spasms slammed into her, a white heat of pulsing pleasure ripping through her. A deep sound of pleasure rolled out from her throat and mouth. Her muscles sang with the bliss dancing across her nerve endings.

And then she was flying . . . in a spinning vortex. Panic exploded. Her purring moan turned to a scream locked in her throat as she hurtled through darkness.

Gage's powerful arm caught her and slammed her against his chest as time and space spun around them.

Her brain finally caught on. They were flash-jumping.

Decades of training kicked in and Gage landed flawlessly. His mind was still on Mira.

The taste of her. The feel. The sounds of her low cries of pleasure that resembled a purr. His need to be inside her, feel the waves of her orgasm clamp around his cock as he drove into her.

His cock throbbed against her belly. When they'd jumped, his fingers had been deep inside her, his other hand on her thigh and his mouth suckling her clit. He'd felt her bone-deep panic when they'd jumped, and managed to shift their bodies to grab her and press her against his body to protect her.

He looked around and recognized the place. "The Wizard Room." Fuck, he hadn't been here in seventeen years. The wall behind his chair was painted black, with glittering knives, swords, crystals, scepters and books floating across it. The massive black-leather chair was up on a bloodred dais. A bar stretched across the back wall, and in between were leather couches around glass tables. Track lighting ran around the room, flashing colored strobes. He knew there was a door to a bedroom in that black wall.

A strange sensation moved through his chest, where Mira was pressed up against his triskellion. He didn't want her in here, didn't want her to be touched by this place. By his memories. This had been the ultimate VIP room. Women vied, schemed, begged for an invitation to this room.

For the chance to get picked to screw the wizard.

"What is this place?"

He looked down at her face. The color of her orgasm had drained off, and she looked strained. "Raven's Claw Nightclub. You've never been here?" He saw gleaming bottles of liquor in a row beneath the massive flat screen that took up most of the wall space over the bar. The last time Gage had been here, there'd been a bulky TV mounted in the corner.

"Not in this room. I usually meet Bret in his office. We have to find some clothes! What if someone sees us?"

He didn't care about clothes. "What the hell are you meeting Bret for?" Gage knew he was the magic-sensitive that owned the club.

She snapped her head back, but couldn't get free of his arm around her waist. "I sell him wine for the club and don't take that tone with me, wizard."

He narrowed his eyes, not liking the hot stab of ugly anger roiling in his gut. Frustration added to the mix. He'd forgotten about his magic, about flash-jumping, about everything but making love to Mira. He looked down at her and his brain froze. He turned her to face him.

"What?"

His gaze tracked where his markings curled like possessive ribbons around her breasts and rolled down her belly disappearing into her hair, then reappearing on the insides of her thighs. Swear to the Realm, he'd never seen anything more breath-taking.

Her gasp caught his attention. "What is it? This is what I saw in your lab." She jerked her head up. "What have you done?"

Ignoring her, he looked down at his triskellion, watching the slow turning. The three spirals were not completely in sync, one feeding into the next in a perfect symmetry, but it was closer.

More powerful.

"Gage!"

He looked at her face. "You're grounding my—"

Voices close to the door cut him off.

Mira froze, turning, trying to cover herself with her hands.

Gage felt the heat of his magic rush through him. Using that, he quickly conjured up clothes. For himself, jeans, T-shirt, boots and jacket. For Mira, he knew just the thing.

"Oh!" Mira said in surprise.

The voices moved away. He looked down and saw the way the halter cut showed off her breasts, hugged her body and ended at mid thigh. He'd paired the dress with strappy silver sandals. She looked gorgeous. Her brown eyes sparkled, her face was flushed and her brown-and-gold hair floated around her face. How had he ever thought she was plain? She glowed. He lifted his gaze to her eyes.

"This isn't my usual style."

"It's how I see you."

Her skin warmed to that golden tone he loved. She shifted on her sandals, worry eating away at her smile. "What were you going to say? About the mantling on me?"

He'd been going to tell her the truth. He wanted to tell her the truth. Except he couldn't be sure, not yet. He hadn't been fully inside her, hadn't . . . He ran his hands through his hair. Mira wasn't his parents who had just wanted more and more from him, and she wasn't Jillian. But she was desperate to find her gram and no telling what she'd do if she found out he'd lied to her. He looked in her eyes and said, "It's temporary." Then he took a breath and changed the subject. "Do you have the gemstones?"

She frowned at him, her intelligent eyes narrowing. But she pulled her hand up and showed him the two stones. Then she said, "My gram and the wizard aren't here?"

He took the stones from her and put them in his jacket pocket. "No. Let's look around and see if we can find another gemstone."

Mira walked across the room toward the dais. He fought the urge to stop her. He didn't want her up there. Memories of all the women vying for his attention, fetching him drinks, feeding him delicacies, leaning over to show him their breasts, or bending over to reveal no panties . . . in a roomful of people. Mira would be disgusted.

She was a wildcat in bed, in private, with a man

she trusted. *Trust.* She trusted him and he was using her to restore his power.

She stopped at one of the leather couches below the dais, running her hand along the cushions.

He sighed and dragged his gaze away from her ass cupped in that dress to search the bar.

"You said this is the Wizard Room?" She walked across to another couch. "I thought you were a recluse and didn't go out?"

He kept looking around the bottles and glasses. "Not anymore. Years ago I came here. It's obviously still a VIP room."

She stood and looked at the dais. "You sat up there like king or dictator. Let me guess." She half turned to shoot a look at him. "Women begged for your attention, throwing themselves at you."

He shut the door to the fridge and turned. He didn't want to talk about this. "Jealous?"

She turned away and marched up the three steps. "Do you miss it? All that admiration, all that fawning."

He'd been working seventeen years to get it back. It's what he'd worked for from the time he'd been born. His parents, once they found out they'd had a rare magic-born, had raised him to be master of the universe. It was his due. If he'd worked hard enough . . .

And he had. He'd made it. Then he'd spent the next thirty years fulfilling their wishes. Houses, cars, boats, trips, jewels, clothes . . . it was never enough. He always owed them more. They'd nearly sucked him dry with their endless demands until they'd died. They'd both been bitter, angry shells, furious that all the stuff never fulfilled their expectations of . . . hell, he didn't know. "I thought I did. Then I met you." Now he didn't know what the hell he wanted. "Just search, Mira." It felt like the walls of this room and his memories were closing in on him. He wanted to get the hell out of here. If Mira grounded his magic, then what? Could he just walk away?

He grabbed the edge of the bar. *No. He couldn't.*

"Oh, it's here! On the chair. A rose quartz. For love, healing and power. It blends the heart and solar plexus."

Gage turned away from the bar and his dark thoughts. He strode across the room with his preternatural speed. There, sitting on the leather chair that dominated the dais, was a small pink stone with just a hint of white marbling.

Mira lifted the stone in her fingers. "Here, put it with the other two." She dropped it into his palm.

The cool feel of it seem to shoot through him, stirring his magic. Then he dropped it into his pocket. There was a soft *clink* as it hit the other two stones.

Mira stared at him. "Now what?"

He wanted her out of this room. He wanted to finish what they'd started, but not in here. Mira was special. She deserved better than being one in a string of women.

"Let's go down to the club." He took her arm and hustled her out, not looking back at his old life.

CHAPTER EIGHT

Mira walked out of the room with Gage holding her hand and was slammed with the beat of pounding music and pulsing colored lights. The air was thick with sweat, perfume and a strange desperation. There was a balcony area with a few tables and chairs that overlooked the dance floor. From this height, they had to be three floors up. Across the room, there was a second-story balcony and what looked like four doors to more VIP rooms. They took a glass elevator down to the first floor.

The doors slid open. People writhed and shimmied on the two dance floors, or lounged at the bars or private booths. The pulsing lights made it hard to see details, but she noticed that the sound of voices talking over the music began to fall off. It started closest to them and moved in a wave through the bottom floor.

All heads turned.

Mira grew hot and prickly under the stares. Then she heard the whispers.

Wizard. Remington. It's him. Who's she?

Gage's hand tightened on hers, but when she turned, his face was hard, his blue eyes unreadable.

Bret, the club's owner strode up. "Mr. Remington. Welcome to Raven's Claw. I didn't know you were here or I would have greeted you sooner."

Bret barely looked at her. She wasn't worth his attention, not now when he had the Wizard of Raven Mist gracing his club. Annoyed she said, "Hello Bret."

He glanced her way and nodded. "Mira." Then he added, "Get Mr. Remington whatever he'd like to drink. On the house, of course. Get something for yourself too."

And just like that he dismissed her as an invisible servant. The unfairness of it tasted like indigestion. "Bite me, Bret," she said in a voice that thundered over the music.

The silence rained down. Everyone in the entire club turned to look at her. At magic-blind Mira Tate. Bret's chiseled jaw dropped.

Mira wouldn't back down. She had had it. "I'm not your servant, nor am I the gofer of the great and mysterious Wizard Remington. If he wants a drink, he can walk over to the bar and get it himself." Her blood raced so fast that it sounded like the roar of the ocean in her ears. But that little rant had felt pretty damned good.

Bret's hazel gaze burned with fury. "Then you don't need to be here at all, do you?" He lifted his hand and snapped his fingers.

Two tanks in suits slipped up to him.

"This lady is leaving."

Now she'd done it. She needed Gage to find Gram! But no way was she going to—

The music stopped suddenly and Gage's voice boomed through the club, magnified either by the speakers or magic. "She's with me. No one touches her. No one." He turned his gaze to Bret. "Get Mira a glass of wine. She likes pinot grigio."

Bret backed up a step, his tanned skin turning red. "Of course." He turned to the security. "See what the fuck is wrong with the music and get it playing!" And he stormed off.

The music burst through the club again.

Mira frantically looked for a dark booth. She'd made her big stand; now she needed an exit.

Gage still had ahold of her hand and he pulled her to the center dance floor. She hadn't danced in a couple of years. Not since college when she'd occasionally go out with girlfriends. Before she knew it, Gage turned her back to his front, put his hands on her waist, then leaned down and said, "Those are some claws, wildcat. Are you going to claw my back when I'm pounding into you until we both come?"

Heat roared through her body and with it, a sense of power. A feeling of exhilaration flooded her that the man with his hands resting just above her hips wanted her, admired her, liked her just the way she was. He even stood up for her in front of all these people. Was it possible that a real relationship was building between them? She began to sway to the dance beat, letting herself go and just feeling the music.

And Gage. He kept his hands on her, turning her to face him, his gaze only on her as they danced.

When the song changed, Mira took a look around and noticed the dance floor had filled. There were a lot of couples, but there were a few knots of women moving closer and closer. They were drawn to Gage, their gazes shifting to him every half minute.

Gage's hands tightened on her waist, pulling her into his body. "I'm only looking at you. Know why I picked this shade of blue for you?"

She could almost feel the mantling on his arms and chest reaching out to her, like strokes of warm ribbon sliding over the skin where his hands held her. Looking up, she saw that his raven-dark hair flowed around his wizard-hard face. But it was his eyes that radiated aged power and raw magnetism. "Why?"

He leaned closer until they breathed the same air. "Your electric-blue panties under that drab black skirt. I saw them when I stripped you to wash off the troll blood. I knew then that you might be frigid in magic, but you're a sensual, passionate woman." He rubbed his thumbs over her waist. "And you do purr when you come, wildcat."

"Guess what color panties I have on now?" She had no idea because she hadn't seen them. He created them so he would know. She was just thankful he'd thought of panties.

He grinned at her, obviously willing to play along. "What color?"

"Wet."

He pressed her hips to his and brushed his mouth across hers, whispering, "Bad kitty."

But she didn't feel bad. She felt safe to be who she was. Drawing her head back, she laughed.

His eyes darkened. "That laugh is doing wicked things to me, kitty cat."

More warmth filled her chest. "I want to do wicked, bad things to you, wizard. With my hands, my mouth . . ." She leaned up closer to his ear. "What sound do wizards make when they come?"

A low growl rumbled in his chest. "I'll show you." He grabbed her hand and turned, heading toward the back of the club. "I know another private room."

Thrills shot through her. Mira followed, feeling slightly buzzed, even though she'd only had a glass of wine back in the hotel room. They moved unimpeded through the crowds because everyone parted, leaving a clear path. Staring at Gage's massive shoulders in that jacket, she wondered if she was becoming a pathetic magic-groupie that—

A massive flash-bang exploded, rocking the club. Gray smoke colored by the pulsing lights billowed around them. Someone grabbed her hair, jerking her back. Her head spun from the smoke and disorientation. She tried to pull free, but they had a vicious hold on her hair and forced her down to her knees.

"Remington!" The voice boomed behind her.

The smoke cleared.

Gage stood four feet in front of her, his jaw clenched and his eyes blazing. "Luther. Something on your mind?"

"You were wrong."

Gage straightened his arms behind him and slipped off his jacket. "How so? I believe I said you were a magic-born hack who would never amount to more than a party magician." He casually tossed the jacket away and frowned. "Have you surpassed that? Perhaps gotten your own show in Vegas?"

The hand tightened in her hair as Luther snapped, "I got the drop on you here, took your little piece of ass away from you in front of hundreds of witnesses."

Gage shook his head. "See, this is one of the many reasons why I refused your application as my apprentice. My laws are absolute. You hurt someone in my town, and the death penalty will be strictly enforced."

"I'm taking over this town, Remington."

Mira stared at Gage. He stood perfectly still, his T-shirt stretched across his massive chest barely showing any rise and fall. But the mantling on his arms was darkening to an angry shade of deep red. Yet his voice was barely interested as he said, "Have you achieved the status of master then?"

The hand clenched tighter in her hair. "That's archaic. A secret club made up by a bunch of old men."

"Says the magician hiding behind a woman."

The wizard shoved her hard and another flash-bang exploded.

Fuck a troll to all nine rings of hell and back. Gage was so furious, he wasn't going to need magic to kill this asshole. Pulling on centuries of physical and mental training, Gage forced himself to ignore Mira and center, allowing his senses to fully emerge, and then held out his hand for his *balisong*. The deadly butterfly knife appeared in his palm, the blade safely ensconced in one of the two handles.

There were three men coming for him. One behind, one in front and another on his left. He'd known the pissant coward wouldn't take him on alone. To kill him, they had to get close enough to stab him in his triskellion. Gage waited, allowing them to approach until he had them where he wanted them. Moving with master-level speed, he snapped his left elbow into the face of the man on his left. That one flew back several feet.

He flicked the blade out of his butterfly knife and shoved it beneath Luther's ribs and sliced up to his heart. Maybe two seconds had passed. Shoving Luther off his knife, he spun, deflected the knife in the last man's hand and cut his throat. Gage jumped back from the blood spurt.

He felt a burning slash across his back and whirled, ignoring the hot flash of pain.

It was the man whose face Gage had smashed with his elbow. That was all he realized before he heard a screech and Mira flew into the guy, slamming him to the ground.

The bastard threw her off and roared, "I'll kill you, bitch!" He dove for his knife.

Gage caught him by the neck, jerked him up and cut straight through to his heart. Yanking his knife out, he cleaned the blade and dropped the body. After closing the blade, he went to Mira. She'd been thrown to her side, and was on her knees, trying to get up. He took hold of her waist and lifted her. "What were you doing attacking him like that!" He ran his hands down her arms looking for any injury.

"That animal cut you! I saw the knife, I saw him . . ." A wild tremor wracked her.

Her words punched right through his chest to

take his breath away. She had tried to protect him.
This little magic-blind woman had tried to protect
him. Another fierce tremble rocked through her.
He recognized the signs of adrenaline overload.

"Holy hell, Remington, you killed those three in
less than thirty seconds! It was . . . I've never seen
anything like it." Bret moved up between them,
holding out Gage's coat.

Gage took the jacket and wrapped it around
Mira's bare shoulders.

Bret went on. "My security team will get rid of
the bodies. I have a first-aid kit and a bottle of
good scotch in my office."

Gage kept his gaze on Mira, watching her fight
down the shakes, willing herself to breathe. She
hadn't hesitated to attack a man to save him.
"Where's your office?"

"Behind the elevator to your VIP room. Come
on, we'll toast your . . ."

He turned his gaze. The blond man was so
hyped up with excitement he was bouncing. "Mira
and I will need your office." He slipped his arm
around her and guided her past the glass elevator
and through the door. Inside was a massive desk
with a large leather chair on the left. Straight
across was a cabinet with very expensive liquors,
and on the right was a leather couch. Gage shut
the door and locked it.

Mira slipped out of his hold. "Take off your
shirt. Let me see your back." Her voice was firm,
demanding.

He reassured her. "They have to stab deep into
my triskellion to kill me. This little scratch is nothing."

She threw his jacket on the desk, put her hands

on her hips and ordered, "Take it off and turn around."

Gage set his weapon on the desk, then wrenched off his shirt, handed it to her and turned around. He felt the gentle touches of her cleaning off the blood with his shirt.

Her fingers brushed softly below the cut. "The cut is six inches long!"

"It'll heal." He started to turn.

"Wait."

Turning his head, he watched her dig into his coat pocket. "What are you doing?"

"The gemstones, they have healing properties." She withdrew her hand from the pocket, clutching the stones. "Gram used to let me hold them when I had night terrors after my parents were killed."

Gage got a mental picture of Mira as a little girl, huddling in her bed, her little heart shattered at being left an orphan. Tortured by nightmares and the feeling that she was at fault because she'd been born magic-blind. The truth twisted inside him. He'd failed to protect a child.

A child who had grown into a strong, courageous woman. She was much like that ruby they'd found—the most powerful of all gemstones. Mira, to him, was the most powerful of all of them. Her love for her gram gave her more strength and courage than he'd ever seen.

"Gram had a chant too," she said, her breath blowing softly on his back.

He felt a small, cool stone sliding along the hot edges of the cut. The touch was so full of care. He closed his eyes and absorbed the sensation.

"Body and magic share one heart," Mira said softly, as she circled the cut.

Her words mixed with the feel of the stone. A low buzz began in his chest and spread outward, almost like a tuning fork.

She picked up another of the gemstones. "Beat now together with healing light."

The vibrations increased as she circled the cool rock around the wound. It traveled to his solar plexus, gathering and growing.

"Heal this wound with magic and love," she said in her melodious voice. She reached up with the last stone and said, "Body and magic share one heart."

Fiery magic bloomed hot and needy in his triskellion, then burst through his mantling and pooled in his groin. His balls and cock throbbed. Mira kept touching his back with her fingers and the stones, each brush firing his lust and need for her. For the very soul of this woman who touched him right to his heart.

"It's healing."

Gage whipped around, trapping her against the desk. He saw her more clearly than he'd ever seen anyone in his two-hundred-plus years. Her hair was wild and wavy around her face, her eyes gleaming with a golden light, her full mouth partly open. She was a wildcat with a heart, and so fucking beautiful it stunned him to his soul. He had to have her, to feel the very essence of Mira.

"Gage?"

He swooped down and tasted his name on her lips. He cupped the back of her head and explored her mouth.

She ran her hands over his arms and shoulders. His mantling shivered beneath her touch, sending shafts of pleasure rippling through him. He growled against her lips, reached up and untied her halter, freeing her breasts. He cupped one heavy globe in his palm, loving the weight and shape. Then he thumbed her tight nipple.

Mira arched against him. Her hands dropped down his stomach, undid his belt, unbuttoned his jeans and slid down his zipper.

His engorged cock surged out. He didn't have to look to know he was swollen bigger and harder than he'd ever been. Desperate for her, for Mira's body to slide down around him and hug him tight. She stroked her fingers along his length and circled the weeping head. He saw lights flash behind his eyes.

Dragging his mouth from hers, he said, "You want to play, wildcat?" He reached down and pushed her dress up over her hips. Then he stepped back, forcing her to release his cock.

Blue panties just covered her mound. He could see she was swollen and damp through the silk. The memory of her rich spicy taste filled his mouth. His ears rang and his cock beaded at the sight. Gage slid his finger along her satin-covered seam, feeling the heat of her through the material.

He needed more.

He needed to put his mark back on her. It had faded away and he didn't like it. His magic on her was the most erotic and fulfilling sight he'd ever seen, or ever would.

His magic poured through his finger and the panties vanished. With the dress pushed up over her hips, he saw his finger slide deep into folds of her cleft. Hot, wet, the deep pulse of need. He looked up. Her face was growing more flushed, her pupils dilating with desire. "More, Mira. Give me more."

She leaned her hips back against the desk and spread her legs.

Gage slid his finger inside her, feeling her body clamp around him. He circled her clit with his thumb and stroked her walls in and out.

Mira dropped her head back, her mouth falling open as she rode him. Harder. Faster. He couldn't take any more. He stood up, cupped her hips and lifted her to rest her butt on the edge of the desk.

She kept her hands braced on the desk, but angled her head down. "Your penis is covered in mantling."

"Watch, sweet cat, while I fill you with magic." He pressed the head against her folds.

"I feel your magic, it's filling me." She shimmied her hips, trying to draw him in. "More." It came out a purring demand.

He thrust into her. Her soft, wet channel gloved him and he shuddered with waves of hot ecstasy. The intensity robbed him of speech, only sensation. Feelings. Locking his hands on her ass, he thrust, surged and filled her.

Still not enough. More. He lifted her higher, off the desk and down onto his cock.

Mira dug her fingers into his shoulders, wrapped her legs around him and rode him with a roiling passion. He lost track of everything but the joining of their bodies and the building pleasure. The intensity ramped up. Thrusting harder, deeper, feeling her muscles tighten and ready.

Then he thrust home, so deep within Mira that everything broke free. She cried out, digging her nails into his shoulders. Searing pleasure raced down his spine and detonated. He held Mira tight, his wildcat, and let the pleasure crash over them until they were both spent.

He shifted her in his arms, leaning her back and looked. His mantling swirled around her breasts, curled down her belly, tucked between her legs and feathered down over her thighs.

The sight shifted his heart in his chest, then sent a wave of power crashing through his triskellion. For a long second, everything stopped.

His magic, his breath, even his heart.

He just stared at his magic on Mira.

Then a whipcord of power shot through him, his heart began to beat again, his breath flowed and the three spirals in his triskellion fell into perfect sync, each spiral turning and feeding the next one and so on in a perfect, endless circle.

His powers had grounded.

Gage felt the magnetic potion bind around his triskellion in a cold flash. This was what the potion should have felt like when he drank it. All his magic went on alert, seeking . . . searching . . . working.

Then he felt the click, like two sides of a magnet snapping together, when his powers locked on to the wizard and Calia Tate.

He held Mira protectively as they flash-jumped.

But this time, Gage was in control.

A master wizard once more.

CHAPTER NINE

"Where are we?" Mira's head spun and she was completely disoriented. Her ears were clogged, and she couldn't get her bearings. This was worse than the other jumps.

"Easy," Gage's voice reassured her and his face filled her vision. "The potion tore through the wizard's cloak and tried to flash-jump us to him."

Mira's ears popped and her heart skipped. "Gram's here! Where?" She lifted one hand to her heart and realized that her dress was tied around her neck, and Gage had his pants buttoned and belted. He'd somehow fixed their clothes while they jumped.

"Not here," he said softly. "We hit a ward and bounced off it. I took us to my house. We're in my bathroom."

"Ward? What?" She looked around to see a huge Jacuzzi tub, double-sink vanity, walk-in shower and toilet. She'd been here before after the troll blood got on her. Gage waved a hand at the tub, and water started filling it. Steam rose enticingly. The bathroom lights dimmed and a dozen candles flickered around the tub.

Then Gage turned his gaze on her. He brushed her hair back off her face and bare shoulder, then reached behind her neck and untied the halter straps. "Wards are protection fields a wizard creates to keep others out. It's like hitting hard rubber and why you probably feel a little more dizzy than the other jumps. But I got a quick glimpse and they are in a hotel room. Your grandmother was asleep. She's fine, I swear it. Once they are on the move, he won't be able to use wards and we'll find them."

She grabbed the straps of her dress and held them as she tried to process it. "What if we don't? What if—" What if Gage didn't really care about her? What if she'd just given her body and heart to a wizard with too much magic and no emotion? Sex was how he connected.

Not emotion.

He took hold of her face. "Mira, he's not hurting her. He's trying to get something from her. She must have him convinced she's doing it. Or maybe she is doing it."

"Gram is smart. She'll take care of herself." She had to believe that. Had to.

"Like her granddaughter." He tugged the straps from her hand and pulled the dress down and off her. As he went to work, lifting each foot to slip off her silver sandals, he said, "A bath will help relax you. We'll rest up and be ready to find them in the morning." Gage stood then, kicked off his shoes and stripped off his jeans.

Feeling strangely vulnerable, she turned and stepped into the tub and quickly sank down into the hot water. The jets pulsed and churned, easing her tight muscles.

Gage stepped in, the candles flickering golden light off his body.

Mira looked up. His legs were solid, the ribbons of richly colored mantling accentuating his hard muscles. She lifted her gaze to his hips and his penis began to thicken.

The pit of her stomach turned over.

She forced her gaze up to the intricate triskellion. The three connected spirals looked different, more in sync than before as they churned out power into the mantling. She forced her gaze higher, traveling up his chest that broadened into shoulders wide enough to fill the average doorway. Then his face, the full lips softening the hard planes. And his eyes—they could look distant and cool blue, or churning colors of emotion, or almost tender as they were now, with that hint of gray riding the blue.

"Done looking?" His voice was low.

He had done this hundreds of times. Thousands. Mira was just another woman in a string of women stretching out over centuries. He was ancient, powerful and she was . . .

Not enough. She wouldn't be enough. Hell, she'd grow old while he would just grow more powerful.

Sitting straighter to remember she had a backbone she said, "Not bad for an old guy."

He narrowed his eyes as he sat down. "Old?" He reached out, lifting her soaking wet, one hundred and too-many pounds, and pulled her over his legs and onto his lap. "Did I feel old to you when I was thrusting into you, making you purr, kitty?"

Her stomach tightened with the tiny after-shocks. She never felt that free and sexy with any man. She tried to keep it casual and shrugged. "My experience is limited, I haven't even had sex in a year or so."

His arms tightened around her and his face soft-ened in the glow of the candles. "No?"

The water bubbled around them while his arms held her anchored to him. "That must sound rather pathetic to someone like you."

His face tightened. "Mira, look down. Look at your breasts, your stomach, your thighs."

She dropped her gaze and sucked in a shocked breath. "Your mantling." She touched the line going down her stomach.

His hand covered hers. "Damn right. You're wearing my magic. You are like no other woman I've been with. You are special, to me and to my magic."

She watched as he brushed his thumb over a line low on her stomach. "It's never happened be-fore?"

"Never. But I like it. A lot. It's the sexiest thing I've ever seen. I'm hoping you like it too."

It was on the tip of her tongue to ask if it was permanent, but that was wading into territory she wasn't ready for. Right now, she just wanted to be with Gage. Tomorrow morning they were going to find and rescue Gram and then face reality. Tonight, she just wanted . . . this. "I like it," she said and laid her head against his chest, feeling a sense of warm security.

He stroked her hair. "Not having sex for a while, that doesn't sound pathetic to me. It sounds like a woman who values herself."

She could hear the steady beat of his heart, and the soft *whoosh* of his magic in his mantling and the accepting tone of his words. As if he valued her too. "Last guy I dated was named Palmer. He was a grade school teacher and wanted to write a mystery." She didn't talk about this. Ever. Even to Gram. But she wanted to tell him, wanted him to understand. "Turns out he was a low-level medium and he was using me to try and raise my parents from the dead. He wanted to write the story of the Demon Massacre in Raven Mist. He wanted to be famous."

Gage's voice hardened. "Did he raise them?"

It was a horrible thing to consider. "No. At first, I didn't realize what he was doing. . . ."

He brushed his hand along her face. "Magic-blind, so you couldn't feel him trying to channel through you. He used sex to get you to open up to him, to trust him, didn't he?"

Mira had wanted to love Palmer. Wanted someone of her own, someone who made her feel respected and important. "Yes. I didn't even realize . . . not until I went to his house for a special dinner with lots of wine. Once he thought I was drunk enough, he started trying to channel my parents."

Gage's eyes churned like the ocean. "What did you do?"

That lightened her mood. "You're sure I did something?"

"Hell, yes."

She grinned. "I set his research notes on fire and left."

He laughed. "That's my wildcat."

She wasn't his . . . was she? She didn't even know what she was doing sleeping with the wizard.

How could she trust a man who wielded so much magic? It made her feel vulnerable, exposed. She blurted out, "I won't be lied to and used."

He tensed, the mantling along his arms and shoulders seeming to twitch. Then he relaxed and said, "What would I use you for? You're the one who blackmailed me."

True. What would he use her for? He could get sex from most any woman he desired, and he was a magic-born wizard who had achieved master status. He didn't need to resort to stupid tricks. She grinned, teasing him about the blackmail. "I also don't like being told no. I usually get my way."

He shifted her so that her back rested against his chest. Then he lazily traced the lines curling around her nipples while leaning down to whisper in her ear, "How do you feel about touching?"

Hot sparks of pleasure arrowed straight down her belly. "Touching might be okay."

"And licking?" He drew his tongue over the shell of her ear. At the same time, he rolled her nipples.

She squirmed on his lap and felt his erection pressing against her lower back. "I'm not completely against licking."

He chuckled and she felt it rumble up his chest against her back. He dropped his hands to her thighs, spreading them wide in the water. "What about this, kitty?" He ran his fingers up the inside of her thighs. "I'm going to need to know how—"

His fingers slipped into her folds, gently parting her. She held her breath, waiting for his next move, his next words . . . desire and heat building. She couldn't stay still. Then he touched her, the pad of his finger sliding over her clit.

He whispered roughly—"you feel about petting. The kind of petting that makes my kitty purr."

She was caged in his powerful arms, his words and touches making her crazy with need. He circled her clit, petting, stroking until she had to grab on to his rock-solid forearms. "Gage!"

"Oh yeah, you like that." He licked the tender spot at the curve of her neck. "But what about this?"

He slid two fingers into her channel, pressing deep, and then gently bit her shoulder. He withdrew his fingers and did it again. And again.

Mira held on to his arms, riding his fingers, feeling Gage everywhere. Safe. Hot. Sexy. She closed her eyes and surrendered to it all.

She surrendered to him.

The shock of sensations raced through her and tossed her over the cliff into a blinding orgasm. Gage held her safe and kept her pleasure going, thrusting his fingers in, biting and licking her tender skin as she gave herself over to him.

Once she got her breath back and control of her limbs, she leaned her head back and looked up into his face. "There's one more question you haven't asked."

He quirked his mouth up in a self-confident grin. "I don't need to ask if you liked coming for me, kitten."

She had never imagined being called pet names, but she liked it coming from him. Using his arms as leverage, she got up, turned and straddled him. Watching his face, she said, "What about this, Gage?" She stroked his erection, gliding her fingers down to his balls and back up to the swollen head. "Don't you want to know if I like this?"

"Hell, yes," he growled out.

Spreading her thighs, she pressed him against her folds. She watched his face, saw his pupils dilating, his nose flaring. She had control of Gage, the powerful wizard. "Or this?" she asked as she took him in an inch. Then another. His eyes closed and he groaned as she lowered herself another inch and clenched her muscles around him.

His muscles bulged like he was straining for control. Opening his eyes, he demanded, "Do you like it, Mira?"

His gaze was stark, real, so full of such raw passion that she forgot her game and captured his face with her hands. "Yes." Then she kissed him, tasted him, stroking his tongue with hers while she took Gage all the way into her body.

And her heart.

Gage worked fast, while Rhys paced on the screen and said, "Sinclair St. James is as old as you, probably as powerful."

"Yes." His lab was cold, but even though he was wearing just a pair of sweatpants it didn't bother him. He stood at the granite table, adding ingredients to an iron pot simmering over a flame. "Sin's ward was simple, basically a rubber web. I'm going to dissolve it with bicarbonate and vinegar." He had started with a spring-water base, then added a cup of vinegar and a couple of Alka-Seltzer tablets.

The whole mess furiously bubbled.

"You hit his ward. He will have recognized you," Rhys said.

"And he'll be expecting me, yes." Gage picked up the mortar where he'd pulverized the gemstones with magnet shavings. They'd left the gemstones in the office at the nightclub when they had jumped, but he'd flashed back and retrieved them. He dumped the pulverized stones and magnet into the potion, then used a long-handled spoon to stir it together. Since the gemstones came from Calia's bracelet, the potion would take him directly to her. He was sure Sin would be there too.

"You think you can kill Sin?"

Gage set down the spoon, picked up the knife and looked at his mentor. Rhys had taught him to do the right thing regardless of his own feelings on the matter. "I have to. I can't let emotions cloud my judgment. He's challenged me by kidnapping a sensitive right out of my town." He cut his finger and allowed a single drop of blood to fall into the potion to activate it.

A violent cloud of vapor billowed up.

Gage put in a second drop of blood and the cloud reversed itself and went back into the potion.

It was done.

"What about Mira?" Rhys said.

He used magic to lift the potion and pour it into the cooling beaker. "She's asleep. And since she's magic-blind, she won't feel or sense what I'm doing. I don't want her there."

"You think Sin knows you are fried? Or were fried, I should say. Nothing wrong with your magic now."

"Mira doesn't know that I've been lying to her from the start. I was able to trick her or distract her when she got suspicious of my lack of magic or mistakes. I don't want her to find out." He'd done what he had to but it felt like he'd betrayed her. Used her.

"It worked. She grounded you, freeing your power. You're not short-circuiting anymore from the overload. Your triskellion is moving in perfect rhythm."

"But for how long? What happens if Mira leaves?" His chest tightened, making it hard to draw a breath. Mira was his wildcat with a fierce and honest heart. He didn't want to lose her, and his magic needed her.

"You could fry again. We don't have any track record to go by," Rhys answered. "But what are you going to do? Lie to her forever? What makes you think she'll want to stay with you?"

He didn't know, damn it. He'd never had to try to convince a woman to stay with him. "I'll get her grandmother back and then I'll . . . seduce her or something." No emotion, he reminded himself and looked at Rhys on the screen. "I don't need any distractions while I'm dealing with Sin. He's dangerous as hell. And I can't have him telling Mira I was fried, and that I used her to ground my powers and heal." That was the logical way to handle this. Now that he had his full powers back, he needed to clean up his town and make sure his authority was firmly entrenched. People's lives depended on him, people like Mira.

A gasp caught him by surprise.

Gage whirled around and saw Mira standing in the doorway to the hall. His black T-shirt hung down to her knees, her hair was long and sexy and her eyes . . .

Oh fuck, her eyes. The pain. Gage walked toward her. "Mira."

She brushed passed him, picked up the potion, put it to her mouth and drank it.

He was too dumbfounded to react for several seconds. Then he leapt across the space and jerked it out of her hand, but she'd drained almost all of it.

She lifted her furious gaze to his and burped. Then she scrunched up her nose. "Ugh, what the hell was in that?"

Gage slammed the cooling beaker down and grabbed her shoulders. "Little late now to be asking that! What the hell were you thinking! That could be dangerous!"

Narrowing her eyes, she yelled back, "You were going to leave me, you bastard! You used me! Lied to me!" She burped and frowned. "Jesus, that tastes bad. Is that vinegar?"

It took every ounce of his self-control not to shake her. "I needed that potion. It had the gemstones that will flash me to Calia to rescue her."

She lifted her eyebrows. "Now we'll go together. After all, I know your secret. You're a burned-out, washed-up, has-been creep."

He saw himself in her eyes and Gage hated it. "Mira, I couldn't tell you. I couldn't risk anyone finding out. The only way to protect the town was to keep everyone believing I was at full power. I did my job. I kept the town safe."

"Except for my grandmother. For days we've been bouncing around while you screwed me back to full . . . uh-oh." Her eyes widened to reveal a ring of white.

"Mira?" Was she going to throw up?

She jerked out of his hold and said, "You're fired. I'll find Gram myself. Stay away from me and my family." Then she vanished.

Gage stared at the empty spot. It took his brain a second to process it. His blood had activated the potion. Mira had jumped to her grandmother. Without him.

Impossible.

Chapter Ten

Mira hit the ground like a sack of potatoes. Nausea roiled in her gut, her head pounded and her fingers and toes tingled. She forced herself to a sitting position.

"Nice of you to drop in," a deep voice said.

She looked up a pair of long legs in black pants to slim hips, a narrow waist and a huge chest covered by a black T-shirt. Lifting her gaze to his face, she saw deep hazel eyes, a scar along one temple and sandy-brown hair. She shifted her gaze to see the thick lines of mantling curling around his heavily muscled arm. "You must be Sinclair." She'd heard his name while eavesdropping on Gage.

He studied her. "How did you get here without Remington?"

Mira flinched at Gage's name, at the memory . . . it was too brutal to think about. "I drank his potion before he could drink it and leave without me." Leave her behind. Because she'd served her purpose and he was done with her. He'd been lying to her and using her from the start. Her throat tightened and hot agony twisted her heart.

"Impossible. You can't flash-jump unless he sends you with his power. Are you supposed to distract me?" His gaze traveled down her form to her bare feet.

Mira didn't like it. "I just want my grandmother." She looked around and realized they were in the mausoleum of the Eternal Wings Cemetery. The marble was cold on her feet and one long wall was lined with crypts. Overhead, the thin moonlight barely passed through the stained-glass skylight. She looked back at him. "What are you doing in the mausoleum?"

He sighed. "Calia has not been cooperative. I figured it out when she told me we had to go to Remington's VIP room in the club. I saw her leave the gemstone . . . and I knew she wasn't talking to the spirits about me, but about Remington."

That jerked her attention back. "What? No, why—"

Dryly, he answered, "A fried town wizard is next to useless."

"Gram *knew*?" Mira sputtered. She fisted the material of the oversized T-shirt, trying to make sense of it. Everything she'd believed was just . . . wrong.

"After you and Remington tried to flash-jump into the room we were in, I'd had enough of being jerked around. I sprayed Calia with truth potion and she answered my questions. She has known that Remington was fried for the last seventeen years. I played right into her hands by kidnapping her and giving her the way to bring you and Remington together." The edge of his left eye twitched.

"I was played by an old woman." He rubbed the twitch. "I brought her here where there should be plenty of spirits for her to consult."

Jeeze, morbid much? She dragged her gaze away from him. "Where is she?" She'd already looked over the rectangular reflecting pool flanked by angel statues and stone benches. It was a quiet spot for meditation or prayer in the middle of the room. This time, her gaze caught on the too-still figure sitting on a bench, wrapped in a blanket. The figure didn't move, didn't blink, and it took her a second to realize it wasn't another statue. "Gram?" she called out and took a step.

"I froze her when you dropped in."

Mira turned to the wizard and felt the last thread of her ability to cope, of her sanity, just plain snap. "Froze her? You froze a seventy-six-year-old woman?" Her voice rose and bounced off the marble in an enraged screech. Mira didn't care. She shook with an adrenaline surge. *This bastard froze her grandmother.* She launched herself at him, hit his chest and knocked him back into the rows of crypts.

A bouquet of roses rained down soft petals and drops of cold water.

The wizard moved lightning quick, trapping her wrists in one hand before she could slug him stupid. Mira didn't care. She lunged for his neck to bite him. She'd rip out his artery. . . .

She heard a sizzle behind her, felt the wave of pure power race down her spine. Before she could draw a breath or form a thought, large hands wrapped around her waist and yanked her away from the wizard. She recognized the feel of Gage's hands, the scent of his power. He shoved her behind him.

Mira stared at Gage's powerful back covered in the ribbons of mantling. He still wore the sweatpants she'd seen him in earlier. Relief mixed with sick despair. She wanted to believe he'd come for her, but she knew he came to deal with the wizard and re-establish his authority. But with her grandmother frozen, Mira needed him. She looked around to see that Sinclair had gotten to his feet. He was roughly the same height as Gage and held a wicked-looking knife in his hand.

Gage held out his hand and his butterfly knife appeared, open and ready for battle. He demanded, "Why Sin? Why kidnap a matchmaker?"

The other wizard shrugged. "She's the best and I only use the best. I tried to hire her for any rate she wished to name. She kept refusing."

"For what?" Gage asked. "Never known you to have trouble finding women."

Sinclair's jaw twitched and his eyes shadowed. "I need more. A couple hundred years of grazing through endless women is losing its appeal. I need more and Calia Tate is going to find the woman that can relieve this biting edge of fiery lust in me so I can think and work again!"

"You kidnapped my grandmother to get you a woman for sex? You don't need a matchmaker, you need a pimp."

"Mira, stay out of this," Gage said.

Stay out of it? "Are all you wizards like this? Oh sure, maybe you're devastatingly sexy, but you people need keepers! Kidnapping old women, big-ass secrets . . ."

"Not now, Mira. I have a situation to deal with here."

His cold dismissive tone was like fingernails on a chalkboard. "Well then, when, Gage?" She didn't know when she'd become this emotional, crazy woman. But she just *hurt* so damned much. "When were you going to tell me you were just using me to find this crazy-ass wizard?"

"Hey, I resent that," Sin said conversationally.

"Shut up," Mira snapped. Jerking her gaze back to Gage, she said, "Or that you were using me to fix your broken powers?"

Gage's jaw bulged, the tendons in his neck swelled and his mantling writhed with angry colors. "It wasn't like that."

"Oh right, because I'm the witless magic-blind that you can lie to and trick." The words she'd heard him say in his house. She knew this was idiotic, that Sinclair could probably kill them all. But the throbbing, raw, bloody ache drove her on. "You're right, you know. I am stupid. I believed every lie you told me. I believed you didn't need me but that you wanted me. Remember you said that in the hotel room? I believed you, I believed every fucking word." She shook with the force of the choking humiliation and betrayal. Following the deep instinct to run to the one thing she had—her grandmother, Mira started to turn. . . .

A blur flew at them and stopped her.

Gage's arm shoved her back and he attacked. The two wizards slammed into each other. They moved faster than she could see. Sparks flew, flames ignited, then died, smoke billowed, and when it ended, Sin was flat on his back. Gage straddled him with his knife tip against Sinclair's solar plexus where he had been branded with the triskellion. "I can't let you live," Gage said. "You kidnapped a woman out of the town under my protection. I have no choice."

Sin's eyes burned with green. "You kill me and granny dies with me. I have her frozen with my powers. She's tied to me and will die with me."

Mira cried out, "No!" Hot fear and grief choked her.

Gage pulled the tip of his knife back.

Sin's massive shape shimmered, then vanished.

Gage rose to his feet. He had a multitude of cuts and burns all over him from the fight with the wizard. But as she watched, the marks were already healing.

And he was stalking her. Step by step. His feet made zero sound on the marble. His sweatpants didn't so much as whisper. The knife he'd clutched in his hand vanished.

Her mouth went dry. "You let him go."

His eyes were locked on her, one hundred percent of his attention lasered in on her as if nothing else mattered. Only her. "Yes."

Mira knew Gage had made a choice, and he had chosen to protect her grandmother over his position as town wizard. This was the man she knew, the man she'd trusted and made love with, but he'd still lied to her. Still used her. How did she really know which was the real Gage? She glanced over to see her grandmother waking and stretching.

Gage grabbed hold of her arms and dragged her to him, so close she could see blue fire burning in his eyes. "Now's the time."

"What?" She tilted her head back, her heart slamming against her ribs.

He lowered his head another inch. "I lied to you about my powers, but never about the way it felt to kiss you, or touch you and or slide deep into your body. When I touch you, I forget who I am, I forget about every goddamned thing but you. Trolls could invade the town and I wouldn't have noticed. Or cared. But if anything came between you and me? I'd kill it." His fingers twitched on her arms, then he pulled her closer. His mouth came down on hers, hot and possessive. Wet. With nothing between them. Finally he pulled back.

Mira sucked in a breath.

"You're not the stupid one, Mira. Not you. You were honest and real and courageous. You were, you are, my ferocious, beautiful wildcat. I'm the one who fucked up and didn't trust you when I should have. The only question here is, will you ever be able to forgive me?"

Her mind was reeling. His magic was reaching through his fingers, touching her, stroking her, trying to seduce her. "How? How do I feel your magic?"

His smile was slow, sensual. "My magic flows in you now. It's how I got here so fast. I jumped right to you. I didn't know how this whole grounding thing would work until you jumped without me. Once you drank the potion, and you wanted it badly enough, my magic reached out and gave you what you wanted. To get away from me, and to get to your grandmother."

"I did that?"

Gage's face softened. "It's never been done before, ever. But you did it. Give us a chance, Mira. I'll do anything to prove I'm worthy of you."

She looked into his eyes. "Anything?" Did he mean it or would he just keep using her and she wouldn't even know?

"Anything."

There was only one way to see if he meant it. "Even three months of dating and no sex?"

CHAPTER ELEVEN

Two months later

Two months and no sex. The little wildcat was enjoying torturing him.

But she was worth it. Gage was surprised how easy it was to spend time with her. Get to know her and her wacky family. After spending more time with Calia, he knew where Mira got her strength and smart mouth. He'd gotten very fond of the soul harmonizer.

Gage had learned Mira's favorite color, ruby red. How she loved romantic comedies and she'd cry without shame. She'd told him stories about her cousins and aunt. Gage had told her about his mentor, Rhys. How he'd been more than a mentor, more like a father and a friend. And how Gage had raised him from the death-sleep after he'd fried, and the way Rhys had stuck by him, helping him protect the town while looking for answers.

Mira offered to go with Gage to send Rhys back to his rest until his beloved Phoebe joined him.

But that had been something Gage needed to do alone. He'd said good-bye, then flash-jumped home, tired and sad. Mira had been there. She'd walked into his arms and stayed there throughout the night. No sex, just . . .

Love.

God, he loved her. And now he felt her growing restlessness, the ache that kept her awake nights. She'd gone past torturing him; now she was just torturing herself and that he couldn't endure.

Mira stared at the numbers on the computer. It was late, past six. She had been putting out proverbial fires at the winery all day, and now she was trying to catch up on paperwork.

She wasn't sleeping. She was restless, tired, needy. The mantling from Gage had faded to mere shadows. She hated that and wanted those lines back. But she had challenged Gage to three months of no sex. Three months of dating and getting to know each other.

Stupid pride. Truthfully, she was ready to get on her knees and beg him. Or something much more interesting, as long as she was—

"Mira."

She pulled her head out of Gage's pants and said, "What, Gram?" Calia had recovered from her ordeal. She swore she had known Sinclair wasn't going to hurt her. And that she'd used the opportunity to bring her and Gage together because the spirits had told her for years the two of them were a match. That was why they'd found the moss agate for Gage, ruby for Mira and, finally, rose quartz to bring lovers together.

Gram broke into her thoughts with, "You have a client in the Tuscany room."

That got her attention. She shifted screens on the computer to her calendar. Had she forgotten? "There's nothing on my schedule."

"Oops, maybe I forgot to tell you. But the client is waiting."

She sat back in her chair and rubbed the tension tightening the back of her neck. "What are you up to?"

"Nothing. I'm old, I forget stuff." Calia blinked her big blue eyes in her delicately lined face. She weighed about one hundred and ten pounds soaking wet.

But each and every one of those pounds was filled with stubborn, crafty deviousness. "Gram, I'm too tired . . ."

"Too chicken? A coward? Afraid to take a chance on love?" Calia stormed into her office, slapped her hands down on Mira's desk and shook off any pretense of silly old woman. "You deserve the chance to be happy, to be loved and treasured. I loved my son, your father, but the truth is, he was a fool to not see how special you are exactly as you are. But you have a man who loves you for the strong, courageous woman you are. Don't let him get away, Mira. Don't be the same kind of fool as your father."

She went taut with excitement. "Gage? He's here?" They didn't have a date planned. For two months, he'd been letting her call the shots. Giving her all the power in their relationship.

"In the Tuscany room. Go, Mira. Take a chance."

She stood up so fast her roller chair hit the wall

behind her. Then she hugged Gram. "I love you." She hurried out of the office and down the hallway, her heels tapping in tandem with her nerves. The Tuscany room was a big room they rented out for parties and events. Why would Gage be in there? Finally she reached the big oak door and stopped.

Gage stood outside the door. He wore jeans, boots and a leather bomber jacket over a T-shirt. His dark hair fell over his face and his eyes tracked over every inch of her.

It made her tingle and yearn and need. "Gage."

He reached out, moving so fast she was spun and pressed up against the door, his hands flat against the wood before she finished saying his name. He dragged in a breath. His eyes burned. "How long did you think I'd let you hurt with need, Mira? How long?"

Shock ripped through her system. "You can . . . how?"

"We share magic, and damn it, I love you. The first seven weeks you were learning to trust me. And you liked torturing me. But since that night you came to me, since the night you held me in your arms when I"—he visibly shuddered—"when I said good-bye to Rhys, since then, you've been ready. You've ached and you haven't come to me."

She couldn't stand it. She reached out, slipping her hand into the jacket to touch his chest through his T-shirt. "I was scared. You are a master wizard. You will live on while I grow old and . . . what if I'm not enough?" That was always her fear.

Gage wrapped his hand around hers. "You are everything. All you have to do is trust me. Trust us." He didn't move, but held himself suspended, as if her answer mattered more than his next breath.

Mira took the leap. "I trust you. Us."

He brushed his mouth over hers. "Let's go in." He turned her, reached past her and opened the door, then ushered her in.

Her breath left her chest. She heard the door close, realizing that they passed over some barrier she couldn't see. Their clothes had vanished. She was too focused on the room to worry about clothes. On the left, waterfalls cascaded down over jewel-colored rocks. On the right, a huge fireplace crackled, and in the center sat a massive four-poster bed covered in a thick white comforter. Overhead, the full moon shone and icy stars twinkled. The air was crisp and scented with the tang of magic.

"Where are we?" She walked to the edge of the bed and realized she was walking over a carpet of soft grass.

He stood in front of her, backlit by the fireplace. "The Realm. Where all sacred ceremonies are held." He moved in front of her. His skin gleamed in the firelight, the mantling flowing out from his triskellion in winding ruby rivers with streaks of hot yellow. She visually followed the trail down to his huge erection. She reached out to touch him, stroke him.

He caught her wrist and pulled her into his arms. Holding her tight against him, he slanted his mouth over hers, ravishing her. Slipping his hand into her hair, he thrust his tongue against hers, demanding she open, demanding she give him everything she had.

Gage was taking control.

Magic crackled around them. Her body grew hot and desperate. Need built between her legs. She tried to climb up him, tried to get the hard length of him where she needed it, where the ache was turning to an unbearable fire.

He wrapped his arm around her waist and lifted her.

Mira bit and sucked at his lower lip as she rubbed herself on his erection, trying to take him deep inside her. But he kept shifting his hips, preventing her. She clawed at his shoulders in frustration, in need.

He broke the kiss. "Mira, look at me."

She forced her eyes open, responding to the hum of pure magic and the timbre of love in his voice. She saw the flush of hot desire riding his cheekbones, and his eyes churning with more than lust.

She saw love there and she saw purpose. Her body tightened and throbbed, but she focused. Trusting him to hold her, she cupped his face with her hands. "You brought me to the Realm for more than sex, more than love." It dawned on her that Gage was giving her something he'd given no one else. She didn't need to ask that, she knew it. And she simply trusted him.

"Yes." He turned his head to softly kiss her palm. Then he returned his gaze to hers. "Mira, I love you beyond myself, beyond my magic and beyond time. Magic is a circle, binding and with no end." Holding her with one arm, he held out his other hand and a small, silver knife appeared.

She looked at the silver blade, then watched as he eased her back and cut an inch-long gash in the center of his triskellion.

She winced, hating to see him hurt, even such a small pain. "Gage . . ." She watched as the line of blood welled.

He waited without words.

A choice. She knew it in her soul, and she took one hand from his face and touched her fingers to his blood.

A tremor went through him. The knife vanished and he took hold of her wrist and pressed the two fingers with his blood to the inside swell of her left breast directly over her heart. "Vowed in blood, our bond is sealed and unbreakable."

Her breath caught, and the skin over her breast tingled. She felt his touch brand her skin, not with pain but with love. Then it sank deep into her blood and took root. The sensations traveled through her, touching each cell and growing. What had been a need to share sex with him became more, morphing into a need to be one with him. She stared into his eyes. "Now."

He thrust his cock into her, driving deep and true, and said, "We are one."

Magic and love exploded, fire raced across her skin, pleasure burned, and through it all, Gage held her safe as he thrust into her, driving her higher and higher. "Say it, Mira."

She knew instinctively. Leaning her head back, she stared into his churning eyes. "I love you." She barely got the breath to finish it. "We are one."

They both shattered in a love-filled bliss.

When Mira could breathe again, she realized she was lying on the bed, cradled in Gage's arms. At some point, while she had still been in the throes of the tremendous orgasm, he'd gotten them on the bed.

"It was that or we collapsed to the floor." He leaned over and kissed her mouth.

She caught hold of his face. "You heard me? I didn't say that out loud."

He smiled. *We are joined, now and for eternity. I heard you. And you, little cat, can hear me.* "Look, Mira." He stroked his thumb over the top of her left breast.

She looked down. There, where he'd touched his blood to her, was now a small mark exactly like his triskellion. Every time he touched the spot, a fission of pleasure raced through her. She lifted her gaze to him.

"You wear my mark. You have access to my magic any time now. This mark binds us. You'll live as long as I do. And if I die first, then I will wait for you. Like Rhys is waiting for his Phoebe."

"You gave me magic," Mira said, her heart filling with joy. "And love."